NO HOPE

I stepped close, put the gun against the zombie's forehead and pulled the trigger. At the same time, I turned my face away, closed my eyes and kept my mouth shut tight, pursing my lips together so that no blood would splatter into my mouth. The pistol jumped in my grip. There was an explosion. Over the zombie's stench, I smelled burned hair and gun smoke.

The zombie went limp, slumped and then slid to the asphalt like a sack of cement. Alan collapsed to his knees. He tried to scream again, but the sound was garbled. He sounded like a wild animal. His eyes rolled up at me, wide and horrified. Sweat and blood covered what was left of his face. He tried to speak, but I could barely understand him.

"Shloo eeee…"

I backed away from him. Alan was dead. Even if I managed to stop the bleeding and somehow patch up his face, he'd been bitten. Hamelin's Revenge was already coursing through his veins. He'd died the moment the zombie broke the skin.

I heard the sound of tinkling glass from a nearby alley. The zombies were on the move, attracted by the gunshot.

"Laarr," Alan slurred. "Shloo eeee."

Lamar, shoot me….

Other *Leisure* books by Brian Keene:

GHOUL
THE CONQUEROR WORMS
CITY OF THE DEAD
THE RISING

MORE PRAISE FOR BRIAN KEENE!

CITY OF THE DEAD

"...A never-ending chase down a long funneling tunnel... stretching the reader's nerves banjo tight and then gleefully plucking each nerve with an off-key razorblade....There aren't stars enough in the rating system to hang over this one-two punch."

—*Cemetery Dance*

"[*City of the Dead*] will force even the most sluggish readers to become speed demons in the quest to reach the resolution. The pacing is relentless, the action fast and furious."

—Horror Reader

"Brian Keene's name should be up there with King, Koontz and Barker. He's without a doubt one of the best horror writers ever."

—*The Horror Review*

THE RISING

"*The Rising,* is a postapocalyptic narrative that revels in its blunt and visceral descriptions of the undead."

—*The New York Times Book Review*

"[*The Rising* is] the most brilliant and scariest book ever written. Brian Keene is the next Stephen King."

—*The Horror Review*

"*The Rising* is more terrifying than anything currently on the shelf or screen."

—*Rue Morgue*

"Hoping for a good night's sleep? Stay away from *The Rising*. It'll keep you awake, then fill your dreams with lurching, hungry corpses wanting to eat you."

—Richard Laymon, author of *The Midnight Tour*

"Quite simply, the first great horror novel of the new millennium!"

—Dark Fluidity

BRIAN KEENE

DEAD SEA

LEISURE BOOKS NEW YORK CITY

For the Peace Dogs From Hell:
Lee D. Miller, Dan Blumenthal, Greg Ward, Andy
McFarland, Lou Buige, George Vogel, J.P. Woods,
Brian J. O'Brien, and Jay Sharpes.
'No Norfallos...F.T.N!'

A LEISURE BOOK®

August 2007

Published by

Dorchester Publishing Co., Inc.
200 Madison Avenue
New York, NY 10016

ISBN-10: 0-8439-5860-X
ISBN-13: 978-0-8439-5860-7

The name "Leisure Books" and the stylized "L" with design are trademarks of Dorchester Publishing Co., Inc.

Printed in the United States of America.

Visit us on the web at www.dorchesterpub.com.

ACKNOWLEDGMENTS

Thanks to Cassandra and Sam; Don, Brianna, Brooke, Tim, Julianne, and everyone else at Leisure; Richard Christy and everyone else at the Howard Stern Show; Geoff Cooper; J. F. Gonzalez; Bob Ford of Whutta Design Agency; Shane Boucher, John Killer, and Christopher Rowley at Drop of Water Productions; David J. Schow; Mike and Greg at KNB EFX; *Rue Morgue*; *Fangoria*; John Burks and Drew Williams for their technical assistance; Mark Sylva, Tod Clark, and Kelli Dunlap for their hard work; and, as always, the F.U.K.U. and the message board maniacs at briankeene.com.

AUTHOR'S NOTE

Although Baltimore, Virginia Beach, and the Atlantic Ocean are all real places, I have taken certain fictional liberties with them. If you live there, don't look for your favorite waterfront bar or a safe harbor. The tide is rising and you won't like what it brings....

*"The summer is over, the harvest is in,
and we are not saved..."*

—Jeremiah, 8:20

CHAPTER ONE

I didn't shoot the bitch until she started eating Alan's face. Before this whole thing began, I'd never shot anyone in my life. Not once. I never held a gun until a few weeks before Hamelin's Revenge started. Hell, I never even referred to women as bitches. But that's what she was. And I had the pistol in my hand.

And I shot her.

Cue "Hey Joe" by Jimi Hendrix.

This thing . . . this plague; it changed people. Not just the dead ones, either. It changed everyone. Changed me. I'm a different person now. Listen . . . you never know what you'll do until you find yourself in an impossible situation, so don't ever say never. Survival instinct is a real motherfucker, and when your back is against the wall, everything changes. *Everything.* I know. It did for me. It all changed for me.

My name is Lamar Reed and this is the way the world ended.

It started with the rats. They swarmed out of the sewers about a month ago. Well, maybe *swarmed* isn't the right word. Swarm indicates speed, and the rats were anything but fast. The first attack took place in New York City during the evening rush hour. Imagine it. Sidewalks bustling with activity, crowds of people rushing to catch subways and trains and buses, streets choked with gridlock, taxi-cabs weaving in and out of traffic, horns blaring, manhole covers clanging as trucks drive over them. And then, in the middle of all this chaos, the rats slowly crawled out of a sewer grate on Thirty-first Street and attacked people—climbed up legs, raked at stomachs with their sharp little claws, sank their yellowed incisors into cheeks and thighs and necks; anywhere they could find a soft morsel. The rats fed.

And the rats were dead. I should mention that. Wasn't weird enough that rats attacked commuters en masse. They were *dead* rats—guts hanging out, limbs and tails falling off, and big, ulcerated wounds on their sides, infested with maggots. Rotting meat on the run.

Oh, we didn't know it at first. I remember watching it on the news that evening. Sitting on my couch in East Baltimore, eating bologna straight from the package and ignoring the stack of overdue bills. Watching the news, wondering when the cable would get shut off for nonpayment. Wondering where the hell my unemployment check was. The mail lady hadn't brought it yet, and things were tight. I'd come up with some cash a few weeks before, but it all went to my mortgage. Like sticking one finger in the dam while three dozen more leaks sprang up.

The news caught my attention because of the fucked-up factor. Rats attacking pedestrians? Crazy shit. But when the first reports started trickling in that they were dead rats—not dead as in some frantic stockbroker flung one to the ground and stomped it—but dead as in the living dead? That shit was off the hook. People scoffed, the media pundits argued, and the authorities refused comment. The cable news channels carried live footage. MSNBC called it a riot. CNN speculated about a possible terrorist attack. I don't know what Fox News called it because nobody I know watched Fox News. One thing that appeared clear was that nobody knew what the fuck was going on. New York's hospitals filled up with wounded pedestrians. Most of them suffered from bites, and others had been injured in the chaos that followed—trampled on as people fled. A few suffered heart attacks brought on by the stress. The people who'd been bitten got real sick. Then died. Then came back. Just like the rats.

They were dead, but they still came back.

The media called it Hamelin's Revenge. They came up with the name almost immediately. Hamelin's Revenge: the return of the rats the Pied Piper was hired to get rid of. But in that old story, when the mayor refused to pay, Hamelin—the Pied Piper—came up with another plan. That's how they spun it, anyway. Seems nobody bothered to tell the media that Hamelin was the name of the town, not the Piper himself. But that didn't matter. In their version, Hamelin's Revenge was when the Piper decided to get even. He took all the kids away and returned the rats to the village. Now the fairy tale had come true. The rats returned all right. And hell followed with them. Just like the Bible verse or the song. Hell.

By midnight, New York City's hospitals became slaughterhouses. Like I said, the infected died, and then came back. And they came back hungry, man. Zombies. The White House press secretary actually used the word during a news conference. Until then, the media were calling the attackers cannibals. But after the government confirmed it, zombie was the buzzword. They attacked the living just like the rats had done. They bit and clawed and fed, gorging themselves on the flesh of the living. The victims who managed to escape got sick with Hamelin's Revenge a few hours later, just like their attackers had. Then they died and came back. And the ones that got ripped to pieces, the ones who ended up (for the most part) inside the zombie's bellies? What was left of them came back, too. They didn't need arms or legs or internal organs. As long as there was a brain left attached, something to control the motor function and impulses, the remains came back. A CNN anchor actually walked away from the news desk after they showed footage of an armless corpse wandering the streets, trailing intestines behind it like a dog leash. You could hear her sobbing off camera, and some producer or technician begging her to go back on the air. She never did.

The chaos spread throughout the five boroughs. By dawn, the National Guard locked down New York City and quarantined everything. Blockaded the bridges and tunnels and left folks to die. A few soldiers even fired on civilians as they were trying to escape. Gunned them down in the dawn's early light. It was for the good of the country, the media assured us. New York was a biohazard area. Nobody could get in or out. But Hamelin's Revenge managed to escape. Hamelin's Revenge said "Fuck you" to the barricades and armed guardsmen and quarantine signs. The disease raced like a California brushfire. Cases popped up in Newark, Delaware; then Trenton, New Jersey; and then on to Philadelphia. By the next evening, it had arrived here in Baltimore. Martial law was declared nationwide and the army was mobilized. That was like pouring perfume on a pig. The troops were good at killing zombies, but they couldn't shoot a disease. All it took was one bite from an infected mouth. And you could get it even if you weren't bitten. One drop of blood sprayed from a bullet's exit wound. Pus from an open sore splattering on you as a zombie attacked. Inhale it or ingest it; get it on your lips or in your eye and that was it. Say good-bye. You got sick. You died. You returned. Folks that died from heart attacks or cancer or stabbings or car wrecks—they stayed dead. But anyone who came into direct contact with the zombies—anyone who managed to get infected—joined the ranks of the living dead.

And those ranks swelled quickly. First the rats. Then people. The disease jumped to dogs and cats in the second week. Other animals, too. They said on television that a cow attacked an Amish farmer in Lancaster, Pennsylvania. It sounds kind of funny until you think about it for too long. Then it just becomes a mind-fuck. Zombie cattle . . . this time the hamburger eats you—starring Lou Diamond Phillips and Mr. T. Sounded like a really bad Sci-Fi Channel movie.

Elsewhere, a pack of dead coyotes ripped a mother and her baby to shreds in the Hollywood hills. Gruesome shit. A herd of zombie goats devoured ranch hands in Montana. An undead bear caused chaos on the Ohio turnpike. At least the disease didn't spread to the birds. If it had, well . . . for years we'd worried about the avian flu. The idea of birds spreading Hamelin's Revenge was terrifying, because birds are everywhere. No matter where you go, there are birds. Ain't anywhere you can run where a bird can't find your ass. The birds didn't catch it, at least that we'd seen, but many other animals did. Not all of them, but enough. Sheep caught it, but not pigs. Horses were immune, but cattle were not. Apes—death equaled zombie. Deer—their deaths were old school.

And of course, some species that seemed immune at first later became vulnerable. Squirrels didn't seem affected at first, which was weird, since they're just rats with fluffy tails. But later, they caught it, too. With all the cross-species jumps, there was no stopping the disease. It happened very quickly. America fell. South America. Canada. Then Hamelin's Revenge made it overseas and infected Europe and Asia and the African continent. Then it traveled down to Australia. Last thing I saw before the power went out for good was grainy footage of a million zombie rats swarming over a million humans in Mumbai, India.

Suddenly, I didn't have to worry about past-due utility bills or if the cops had figured out that I was the one who robbed the Ford dealership during that test-drive. I didn't have to think about whether or not I had the balls to do it again. I had more important things to focus on, like staying alive and not getting eaten by my neighbors—or shot by some stupid motherfucker.

See, it wasn't just the zombies that we had to watch out for. If it was, and if the president and Homeland Security and the Centers for Disease Control and the rest of our government had acted quickly enough, then maybe none of this would have happened. But they didn't. Just like Pearl Harbor and 9/11 and Hurricane Katrina and all the other national disasters. When faced with an unimaginable crisis, the government failed to respond in an effective and timely manner. Maybe they couldn't. I mean, there's probably no FEMA playbook for what to do when dead folks start running around eating people. It's not the sort of thing the government plans for. It's an unimaginable scenario.

But it wasn't imagination. It was real.

In the weeks that followed there were dangers other than just the zombies. Looters and gangs of armed thugs roamed the streets. Cops and National Guardsmen who'd gone off the deep end shot the dead and living indiscriminately. America returned to the glory days of the Old West. Things like innocence and guilt didn't matter. The only law that mattered was the law of the gun. They evacuated Washington, D.C., and sent the president, his cabinet, and all the king's horses and men who worked in the House and the Senate off to secure underground bunkers in Virginia and Maryland and Pennsylvania. They were supposed to be able to run the country from there. They didn't. Things fell apart.

Our cities and towns resembled Somalia or Beirut. Well, to be honest, my neighborhood had been like that even before Hamelin's Revenge. Only difference was now the rest of the country got a taste of what it was like to live in the ghetto. Instead of drug gangs and tweaked-out freaks on crystal meth or crack, we now had vigilantes and zombies. Not much of a change, and in either case, the cops still didn't show up when you called them.

I remember a press conference with the secretary of state. He was sweating like a pig. Looked nervous. He assured the reporters that President Tyler, the vice president, and cabinet members were all fine—and that the crisis was passing. Things would soon be under control, and society would return to normal. Until then, martial law would remain in effect as a cautionary measure.

Except that nobody was calling the shots. The person in charge was the guy with the most firepower, and that changed from moment to moment.

People didn't aspire to cure the disease or stop it from spreading. They only aspired to not get eaten by a zombie. They'd always worried about their careers and homes and favorite television shows and what their most-loved Hollywood starlet had done. Now the only thing they worried about was staying alive. And the worst part was that if you'd asked people, they probably couldn't tell you why they bothered resisting. Did it matter? What was the point? The zombies outnumbered the living. Why not surrender, or eat a bullet? Like I said, survival instinct is a motherfucker. You do what you have to, even if you don't understand why.

Some people had higher aspirations, of course. When there's blood on the streets, there's money to be made. That's an eternal law in the ghetto, and the rest of the world learned it soon enough. Stocks, bonds, shit like that—worthless. Cold hard cash ruled the day, and price gouging was common. Twenty bucks for a gallon of gas or a bottle of water. And when the cash became as worthless as the paper it was printed on, the barter system took over. Your wife—your daughter—in exchange for what you needed to survive.

The madness continued. Burning the dead became the law, but there weren't enough fire pits or crematories to go around. Last bit of the news I saw, in Pennsylvania, a National Guard officer had reportedly ordered the death of civilians by firing squad. They were accused of looting. In Miami, zombies overran the airport. A popular television preacher committed suicide, believing that the

Rapture had occurred and he'd missed it. In China, a nuclear reactor went into meltdown. Chicago and Phoenix were on fire. The military finally retreated from New York City after losing control and admitting defeat.

More people died every day. Then they came back. And every day there were less of us. It was a cruel, cruel summer.

I stayed inside. Didn't have any family. My mama died years ago. Breast cancer. Our health insurance sucked. There wasn't much they could do, in any case. Found a lump during a routine exam. Three months later, she was gone. I never knew my old man. Heard he was useless. That's all I knew of him. *"Mama, tell me about my dad." "He was useless."* I had a brother, Marcus, who lived in California. Hadn't seen him in years, and when the phones went down, I had no way of contacting him. I hadn't been in a serious relationship in a long time—not since my last partner, Louis, moved to New Orleans. I had no one to worry about. So I hid. I was safe inside my home, and had no reason to leave.

The big thing I had to deal with was the passage of time. Trapped inside the house all day and all night with no television or Xbox or shit like that. I had to find things to occupy my mind, because otherwise I'd get very depressed and start thinking about walking outside, finding the nearest zombie, and letting him have a bite. The loneliness was the worst part, and that's why I was glad when I found out Alan was alive and he joined me (even if he was hopelessly straight). Alan was my neighbor. Nice enough guy. He'd worked at the plant too, and got laid off the same time as me. Alan took a gig with a temp agency. Did odd jobs like flagging traffic and loading trucks. Some days they had work for him. Some days they didn't. He barely scraped by. But he'd never once let his spirits get down. He was a funny, jovial person. After he'd moved in (because his house wasn't as secure) my loneliness vanished.

But eventually, with his added presence, supplies went quicker than I'd imagined. With the power out, the food in the fridge had spoiled and the kitchen smelled like the zombies. I still had plenty of beer, canned goods, and packaged foods. Had plenty of water, too. We pissed in empty beer bottles so the toilet water would remain untainted. I figured we could drink from the commode if necessary.

When we ran out of food, we had to venture out. That was when I participated in looting the Safeway. I know what you're thinking. Black man, late-twenties . . . of course he looted the grocery store. Well fuck you. It wasn't like that. I grew up hard. Lived in an old row house in the middle of Druid Hill Park. Place was a fucking dump. We had rags stuffed in the cracks in the walls and plastic over the windows in the wintertime to keep out the cold. My childhood pets were all cockroaches. The neighborhood was filthy—garbage on the sidewalks and dead grass and broken glass covering the vacant lots. I saw my friends get gunned down in the streets. Saw their dried blood on the sidewalks. Saw the cops and the preachers shrug in resigned consignation. They didn't care. Neither did anybody else. Only time people gave a fuck was during an election year—or if somebody white and wealthy got killed. I spent my childhood in shit. I stepped on crack vials every time I went outside to play. Drugs were all around me. So was crime. It was a way of life. But I didn't buy into that shit. I lived my life differently. Stayed in school. Worked a job. Never did drugs. Never boozed. Never robbed anybody. Like I said, until the stick-up at the dealership, I'd never held a gun in my life. And I ain't proud of that incident. But shove your stereotypes up your ass. I'm educated. No college, but I graduated high school. Not that GED shit, either. I actually went to class and got my diploma the old-fashioned way. I read a lot and watched Discovery Channel. I didn't talk like a thug. Didn't feel the need to emulate a rapper. Ground my teeth every time some well-meaning white acquaintance deferred to me at a party when the conversation turned to basketball or slave reparations or Colin Powell's run for president or hip-hop. I didn't flash the bling. I respected women. Didn't view them as hos. Didn't hang out in front of the liquor store. Thought P. Diddy was a douche bag. Vote or die? Fuck you, you stupid, conceited, fronting motherfucker. I felt the same way about Jesse Jackson and Al Sharpton, too. They were supposed to identify with what I'd been through? Please. None of them spoke for me. I didn't feel the need to respect them just because we shared the same skin color. Didn't drape myself in gold jewelry. Didn't let my pants sag around my fucking ankles. I refused to let a media-inspired culture influence how I dressed, talked, walked, thought, or behaved.

Don't talk to me about equal rights. I got it from both sides. The quiet, almost apologetic racism from white America, and the more flagrant disapproval from my own race, simply because I refused to live up to what they'd been conditioned to think an African-American should be. My peers thought there was something wrong with me simply because I refused to act like a thug.

And even on good days, when I'd faced down each and every one of the stereotypes that comes with being a black man—even then I'd be met with a whole bunch more prejudice because of my sexual orientation.

Think that it's hard being black? Try being a gay black male sometime.

Hamelin's Revenge not withstanding . . .

The biggest stereotype of all was my steady employment. People either expected me to deal drugs, live off welfare, or be a fucking limp-wrist hairdresser. I don't know why. There's nothing about me that's either gangsta or feminine. Maybe they'd watched too much *New Jack City* or *Will & Grace*. I had a good job on the assembly line at the Ford plant in White Marsh, and I kept it. Thing was, it didn't keep me. That's what led me to the Ford dealership with a gun stuffed in my waistband. And I was living with the guilt of what I'd done there up until Hamelin's Revenge came along.

I was thinking about that very thing when Alan and I looted the Safeway.

We showed up at the Safeway's parking lot in the middle of the night and found a dozen other well-armed people with the same plan. We grabbed two shopping carts and joined in before the shelves were picked clean. The cops weren't around, and neither were the zombies. The other looters ignored us, busy making due for themselves. Four of them stuck together in a group. The others appeared to be loners.

The meat department and the produce aisles smelled like an open sewer. The stench of rotting vegetation and spoiled meat hung thick in the air. I heard a droning buzz, and noticed that the butcher's display cases were covered with fat, sluggish flies. Thousands of tiny white worms burrowed through rancid steaks and hamburger and pork chops. I remember wondering as I watched them if Hamelin's Revenge could spread to insects—mosquitoes, ticks, or other bloodsuckers. I hoped not. If it could spread to them or to the birds, we were pretty much fucked.

But then again, we were pretty much fucked anyway.

The fruit and vegetables in the produce department were covered with fuzz and slime and more flies. We held our breath when we passed through the aisle, and again when we cut through the dairy products section. Exploded cardboard milk cartons were thick with green-blue mold and the stench was overwhelming. A fat man in a soiled T-shirt sat on the floor, his back against one of the coolers, and ate spoiled milk with a spoon, scooping it from the carton like cottage cheese.

"Hey," Alan said, "you're gonna get sick, dude. That shit will kill you."

The man smiled sadly. "I hope so. I ain't got the guts to shoot myself, or to let one of those things bite me."

"Suicide?" I frowned. "Why die at all?"

The man shoveled another spoonful of sludge into his mouth. It dribbled down his chin as he replied, "Don't you guys see? We only got two options. We can join them or we can feed them. Either way, we're dead."

A tear slid down his cheek. We walked away without another word.

"He's just given up," Alan said when we were out of earshot.

"Fuck that," I said. "I'm going to fight."

"You ever wonder why?"

"Why what?"

"Why we fight to survive? Why we sit in your house going stir crazy? I mean, what's the alternative? Shit ain't gonna get better. It's just gonna get worse. Why bother?"

I didn't have an answer for him.

Alan and I filled our carts with bottled water; canned vegetables, fruit, and meat; dry goods like cereal and oatmeal; batteries; aspirin; hydrogen peroxide; antibacterial cream; bandages; vitamins; cigarette lighters; matches; and other things we could use. He grabbed a few small propane cylinders for my grill, but I made him put them back. Even if we'd had fresh meat or veggies to put on the grill, the smell of cooking would attract predators—living and otherwise.

A fly landed on Alan's forearm as he reached for a box of granola bars. He gave a small, disgusted cry and slapped at it. When he took his hand away, the insect was squashed all over his arm. He let it fall to the floor, and then wiped his arm on his shirt. I wondered if he'd been thinking the same thing I had about the bugs.

"You ready, Lamar?" He shoved his cart forward.

"Yeah," I said. "Let's go home."

"Home?" He snorted. "Is that what it is these days?"

I didn't answer.

We now had enough goods in our two carts to last us a month. Maybe more if we rationed. I figured we'd hunker down and stay barricaded inside my house and wait to see what happened next. On our way to the exit, I added a case of warm beer almost as an afterthought. We passed by the cash registers. It felt weird not paying. Then we got the hell out of there. Our fellow looters weren't arguing with each other, but the whole place had an underlying mood of fear. It felt like any moment the whole store could explode.

Or the zombies could show up.

We were on our way back home when it happened. The streets were deserted, except for abandoned vehicles. Most of them were either wrecked or shot up. A few had been burned. The damp pavement shined. It had rained earlier in the day. With the power out, there were no lights to mark our way, but the moon was full and round. Its dull glow was strangely comforting. Broken glass crunched under our feet. The wheel on Alan's cart squeaked. Somewhere, a dog barked. A distant gunshot echoed off the buildings. A plane passed overhead, red and blue lights blinking in the darkness. I wondered who was on it and where they were going. The wind shifted, bringing the smell of decay. It was the end of August and summer would soon be over, but the days were still sweltering, the nights barely tolerable. The heat really compounded the stench of the dead, but that was a good thing. You could smell them coming before you saw them. We sped up our pace.

An undead cat lay twitching in the road, unable to move. Its spine had been crushed and a fresh tire tread stood out in its burst stomach. On the sidewalk, something that might have been a dead crow had congealed into a puddle of tissue. Nose wrinkling, Alan steered his shopping cart around the mess, and the squeaky wheel squealed in protest. I glanced at the worms squirming in the bird's remains and wondered again if they were alive or dead.

The quick breeze died down and the heat returned—as did the stench. We stayed aware; kept looking over our shoulders. The wheel on my shopping cart kept going crooked, making it a real pain in the ass to push. Every time I hit a stone or piece of broken glass, I had to shove extra hard. When we came across a cracked and rutted section of sidewalk, I wheeled the cart into the street. As we passed by a sewer drain, I noticed a severed head lying against the curb, right over the grating. A few flaps of flesh hung below the chin, but that was it. Water swirled past the head, trickling down into the drain. As we watched, a black tongue slithered from its mouth like a slug. The blue eyes turned up to watch us pass.

"Should we kill it?" Alan asked.

"It's already dead."

"You know what I mean."

I shrugged. "Why bother. It can't hurt anybody. It's just a head."

"Fucking creepy."

"Yeah."

"How long you figure it can survive like that?"

"Until it rots away, I guess. It doesn't have a stomach or anything. But look at it. I bet if we stuck our fingers down there, it would snap at us. Whatever this disease does, these things operate on instinct. Kind of like a shark. All a shark does is swim and eat. All these things do is walk and eat. It can't walk anymore. But it's still hungry. Bet it stays hungry until its brain dissolves."

Alan stared down at the head. "Wonder if they think."

I didn't reply, because I didn't know. Alan cocked his foot back and kicked the head like a football. It sailed off into the night. There was a wet splat as it bounced off the hood of an abandoned car.

"Field goal." Alan grinned. "I should play for the Ravens."

"Come on," I said. "Let's get this stuff home while the coast is still clear."

We'd gone two more blocks when it happened. Alan was armed with a sword. He'd picked it up during a vacation in Tijuana. It was a cheap piece of junk, but he'd sharpened the blade and practiced with it in my kitchen. Before they all rotted, he'd gotten pretty good at slicing cantaloupes in half, but he hadn't yet had the opportunity to try it on a zombie. I was carrying a pistol. I don't know what kind. As I said, I was never much of a gun aficionado. During the dealership robbery, I'd used a Ruger .22 pistol, purchased hot downtown. Bought a box of ammo to go with it. I'd thrown both into the harbor afterward. When things broke down a few weeks later, I'd wished I still had it. This new gun was a revolver. I knew that much. Didn't know anything else, except that if I pulled the trigger, I'd shoot something. I'd been calling it a pistol, and Alan had tried correcting me, saying it wasn't a pistol, but a revolver. I didn't see the difference. Didn't care, either, as long as it worked. I'd picked it up off a dead guy lying in the middle of the intersection. We'd come across him on our way to the grocery store. After some experimentation, I figured out how to get the cylinder open. There were four bullets inside.

Like Alan and his sword, I hadn't had to use them yet.

Until that zombie bitch shuffled out of the bushes . . .

Here's the thing about zombies. You can get the fuck away from them easily enough. They're usually quiet, but they're also slow and stupid. You see them coming, so it's real easy to run away. And like I said earlier, even if you don't see them, you can usually smell the fuckers. Ever smell roadkill? It's the same thing, except mobile. But that night, the breeze kept shifting. First it would blow off the Chesapeake Bay and away from us. Then it would switch, but that was no better, because the stench of decay would get so strong you couldn't tell if it was a zombie approaching you or just the city itself—a giant graveyard full of rotting corpses.

We passed by a small row house with a withered, brown hedge out front. The windows were broken. The aluminum siding was splattered with gore. The zombie must have come from behind the hedge, because that was the only spot to hide. We didn't see her, didn't smell her, until she'd latched on to Alan.

He was behind me, talking in hushed tones about getting out of the city and heading for the wilderness—the woods in Pennsylvania or southern Maryland. Maybe even down to the outskirts of Ocean City, around some of the more desolate beach areas. I was against it. Thought we should just stay inside my place. We didn't know shit about what was going on elsewhere. What if the woods were full of infected animals? I waited for Alan to reply. His shopping cart coasted past me and out into the street. At the same time, he started screaming.

I let go of my cart and whipped around. The zombie clung to Alan, scratching and biting. This close, her stench made me gag. She wrapped her swollen, rotting arms around Alan like an exuberant lover and then clambered onto his back. She held on tightly. He buckled under her weight, but managed to maintain his footing. Her feet dangled off the ground. She wore no shoes or socks and her toes were caked with filth.

Alan dropped his sword. It clanged onto the pavement. Panicked, I could only watch as he hunched over, beating at the harpy clinging to his back. The creature moaned and he shrieked. Her cracked fingernails raked at his arm and neck, ripping his skin. She leaned forward and her teeth snapped shut on his cheek. The dead woman jerked her head back and Alan's flesh stretched like soft taffy. Alan screamed again, and even in the darkness I could see the blood welling up inside his mouth. His skin stretched even farther, pulled taught, and then tore. His flapping cheek dangled from the zombie's clenched teeth. His screams turned into a gurgle. Other than her brief moan, the corpse didn't make a sound.

It was then that I remembered the gun. It had been clenched in my hand the whole time, but I'd been so fucking overwhelmed with shock and fear that I'd forgotten about it. The zombie's head was thrown back away from Alan's left shoulder. She was chewing the piece of meat while he thrashed and spun. Blood streamed down his neck, soaking his clothing. His skin looked garish and pale, and I saw his teeth and his tongue flopping around in the ragged hole. Amazingly, he didn't collapse. He kept beating at her, making gargling sounds in his throat. When he spun around again, I raised the pistol. The zombie's head darted forward for another bite.

I stepped close, put the gun against her forehead and pulled the trigger. At the same time, I turned my face away, closed my eyes and kept my mouth shut tight, pursing my lips together so that no blood would splatter into my mouth. The pistol jumped in my grip. There was an explosion. Over the zombie's stench, I smelled burned hair and gun smoke.

The zombie went limp, slumped, and then slid to the asphalt like a sack of cement. Alan collapsed to his knees. He tried to scream again, but the sound was garbled. He sounded like a wild animal. His eyes rolled up at me, wide and horrified. Sweat and blood covered what was left of his face. He tried to speak, but I could barely understand him.

"Shloo eeee. . . ."

"Oh, fuck." I backed away from him. Alan was dead. Even if I managed to stop the bleeding and somehow patch up his face, he'd been bitten. Hamelin's Revenge was already coursing through his veins. He'd died the moment she broke the skin.

I heard the sound of tinkling glass from a nearby alley. The zombies were on the move, attracted by the gunshot.

"Laarr," Alan slurred. "Shloo eeee."

Lamar, shoot me. . . .

I raised the gun. My hands trembled.

"I'm sorry, man. I am so fucking sorry."

I did as he asked. I shot him.

Like I said, things have changed. People have changed. Me included. I didn't even look away. The gunshot echoed into the night. Somewhere, another dog barked. Another rotting corpse shuffled into sight. When it saw me, it grinned and made a low moaning noise. Blinking away tears, I raised the pistol, and then lowered it again. The zombie was too far away to shoot with accuracy and I didn't want to waste bullets.

I forgot about the shopping carts and ran home. I saw more zombies but stayed out of their reach. They lurched out of alleyways and stumbled out of houses and apartment buildings. I didn't see anybody else who was still alive, but I heard a woman screaming. Couldn't tell where she was, and in truth, I didn't stick around long enough to see. When a rat skittered by me and disappeared behind a parked car, I nearly screamed. I didn't know if it was dead or alive. I wondered if I should consider myself lucky to be alive, or cursed because I wasn't dead yet. Of course, if I were dead, I'd be a zombie. I wondered if they knew—remembered— who they'd been. If there was such a thing as a soul, was it still inside them, conscious and staring out through those dead eyes, unable to act as its body was hijacked?

Then I decided that I wasn't ready to find out yet.

CHAPTER TWO

Once I was safe and sound back inside my house, I checked to make sure nothing had come in while I was gone. I renailed some thick boards over the front door. It wasn't totally secure, but it would be enough for one night, as long as I kept quiet and didn't alert anyone else to my presence inside the house. Too much pounding would allow the zombies or raiders to hone in on my location. In truth, I couldn't have continued barricading myself inside even if I'd wanted to. I was exhausted, both physically and emotionally, and started crying as I hammered twelve penny nails back into the heavy wooden planks. Delayed shock. Mental breakdown. Maybe a little bit of both. But deep down inside, I knew that I wasn't crying for Alan or anybody else. I was crying for myself. I've never been one for self-pity, but I felt it then.

I was alone again.

Deciding I'd be safe enough, I resolved to finish

the job in the morning. I felt exhausted and weak and dirty. I tried to remember the last time I'd showered, and couldn't. Washing up with a sponge and a bowl of rainwater just didn't cut it.

In the darkness, I ate a can of fruit cocktail. I didn't have much of an appetite, but I forced the fruit down anyway, even the chunks of pineapple, which I hated. Why is it that when you open a can of fruit cocktail, regardless of the brand, there's always too much pineapple and not enough cherries? Of course, I don't guess there will be any fruit cocktail for a long time. If humanity ever does get back on their feet, we'll have more important things to worry about first. As I sipped the juice from the can, I thought about all the groceries I'd left behind on the street. Sooner or later, I'd have to go out again. It was either starve or forage. Day or night—didn't matter when I went. The danger would be the same. Tonight it had been Alan. Next time it could be me. But I didn't want to think about that just then.

Naked and sweating from the late summer heat, I collapsed on top of the damp, dirty sheets. The pillowcase stank, even with the stench from outside creeping into the house. The pillowcase smelled like me—of dirt and grime, hopelessness and despair. I had no way to do laundry, and water was too precious to waste. I lay there, tossing and turning, thrashing around. I couldn't read in the darkness, and I didn't want to risk using the flashlight. There wasn't really anything to read, anyway, even if I had been willing to use a light. Just a stack of past-due bills and shut-off notices and a few out-of-date magazines for which there'd be no follow-up issues. It's amazing how the feature articles in *Time* magazine and *Newsweek*, the stories that had seemed so important, become meaningless and trivial. Distant, as if they were ancient history. I had an iPod and the battery was still good on it, but I couldn't listen to it without somebody else to stand guard. With the headphones on, I wouldn't be able to hear if someone—zombie or otherwise—tried to break in. (Alan and I had slept in shifts, even during the day; making sure one of us was always awake and on watch.) I couldn't read, couldn't listen to music, and didn't want to think. Add in the sweltering mid-August temperatures and the fear and uncertainty I felt. I was fucked. I didn't think that I'd be able to sleep, but eventually I did. Fitfully.

I don't remember dreaming. Not that night or any other night, either. I've never been able to remember my dreams. I used to get this weird sense of jealousy when I'd hear other people tell me about their dreams. Most boring shit in the world, but I was always fascinated by it anyway. Wondered if my own were the same. Even their nightmares held me spellbound. Now, all I had to do was look outside. East Baltimore was crawling with nightmares, and there were plenty of them to call my own. Stinking, rotting corpses ran amok in the streets, leaking fluids and shedding body parts. The gutters were thick with offal. Between the smell and the danger, it's a wonder I slept at all.

A scream woke me. I bolted upright, eyes snapping open, fists clutching the sheets. The sound had already faded, and I wondered if it had been real or if I'd imagined it. Maybe I was finally becoming conscious of my dreams. Out of habit, I turned to the alarm clock to see what time it was, but of course the clock wasn't working. With no watch and no other way of knowing, I decided to try going back to sleep.

Then I smelled smoke. Burning wood, melted plastic . . . maybe burned flesh, too. I glanced around. My pulse hammered in my throat. There was an orange glow coming through the bedroom window. I'd nailed boards over it, both outside and inside, and had closed the shades and the curtains, but a few rays of light crept around the edges. Another scream echoed through the night. I sat up the rest of the way and slid my bare feet onto the floor. The room was hotter now—hotter than it had been when I'd fallen asleep. I listened for another scream and instead heard a crackling sound.

Smoke. Light. Heat. Sound.

Fire . . .

I jumped out of bed and ran into the living room. One of the pieces of plywood that I'd nailed over my picture window had a small knothole in its center. Not enough for the zombies to see inside, but enough for me to see out into the yard and the street beyond. Alan and I had used it to spy on the neighborhood, making sure that the coast was clear and our defenses would hold. Still naked, I knelt in front of the peephole and looked outside. The sky was on fire, lit up with shades of orange, red, and yellow. The houses across the street were smoldering, and beyond them, the neighborhood was ablaze. I didn't live in a row home exactly, but most of the houses for blocks around were similar in size and shape—little run-down, one-bedroom boxes with tiny yards. They were grouped close together, and the flames leaped from one home to the next. The street was filled with thick clouds of smoke—and filled with those fleeing the inferno, both the living and dead.

It was terrifying and surreal. The parade of survivors came first. Some were naked or in their underwear, others wore pajamas, and a select few were dressed for survival: Kevlar vests, combat boots, camouflage, and stuff like that. All of them were trying to escape the inferno. There were probably two dozen total. I wondered where they'd all come from. I'd thought all along that Alan and I were the only people left alive in our immediate neighborhood, but obviously I'd been wrong. It was weird to think that while I'd been huddled inside my home, my neighbors had been doing the same, hiding in basements and attics, waiting for whatever happened next, fighting to stay alive one more day. I'd felt alone and miserable, and meanwhile, these people had probably been feeling the same way.

Most of them were on foot, some without shoes. They ran down the street without looking back. The survivalist types were armed with assault rifles. I wasn't sure what type, but they were the kind you saw in movies. A few of the others clutched weapons or belongings, but most of the people in the fleeing crowd were empty-handed. A black

Lexus coasted among them, car horn blaring, the driver trying to get through. A man dressed like he was going deer hunting spun around and fired three shots through the windshield. Screaming, the people around him scattered. The man calmly approached the car, opened the door, tossed the driver to the pavement, and then slid behind the wheel. Another guy raced by on a motorcycle, weaving in and out of the pedestrians.

The dead came next. They were mostly human, but there were a few animals as well. Some of the zombies were missing limbs. Others had huge, ugly wounds that wept blood and pus—injuries that should have been fatal. One shirtless corpse was missing its entire abdomen. A few strands of gristle hung down to its crotch. The gaping stomach cavity was empty—no organs, just pink meat and bones. I wondered if it still craved living flesh, and if so, what happened after it had eaten. How could it digest anything without a fucking stomach? How could they process food when they were dead? And why didn't they eat each other instead of munching on the living?

A naked dead man stepped out of the alley and passed through my yard. He was covered with dirt and blood, and his skin was a dark bluish-purple, the color of a bruise. There was something else wrong with him, too, but I couldn't tell what it was until he turned toward my house again. Then I saw what was wrong. His genitals were missing— replaced by a big, bloody hole. I recognized the dead man as one of my former neighbors. Never knew his name, never talked to him while he was living. Just the occasional head nod from over the fence. And now here he was, dickless and dead.

A few of the creatures were obviously from some of the higher-income parts of the city. I wondered what had brought them to my neighborhood. Had they come here while they were still alive, forced to flee into the ghetto, a place they would never have set foot in under normal conditions? Or had they come here after death, hunting for food? The corpse of a white yuppie wandered down the street, arms outstretched and mouth open. His distended belly was swollen with gas. Two shards of red, broken glass jutted from his forehead like horns. Despite the horror, I had to laugh. He looked like Satan in a Burberry shirt. Another dead man was dressed in the tattered vestiges of a Catholic priest. Apparently, they weren't immune either.

The creatures shuffled along behind their fleeing prey, oblivious to the spreading flames. The dead didn't give a shit about fire. Their only concern was dinner—and dinner was served. You'd think that as slow as they moved, the zombies wouldn't have been able to catch anyone. But they did. All it took was one stumble, one misstep. Get yourself backed into a corner, pause for a loved one, fall and twist your ankle, and that was it. You got eaten. I watched it happen right in front of me. One woman simply seemed to give up. She glanced over her shoulder, watched her house go up in flames, and then sat down in the middle of the street. Another man tried to pull her up, urge her on, but the woman waved him away. When he insisted, she slapped at him. He hurried away, resigned to letting her commit suicide. I didn't blame him. It never occurred to me to go to her rescue, either.

The first of the corpses fell on her, biting into her scalp with cracked yellow teeth. An undead dog was next. The monster buried its snout in her belly and pulled out something wet and purple that glistened in the moonlight. Through it all, the woman didn't scream. She looked peaceful.

I envied her.

Many times after things fell apart, I'd wanted to give up, throw in the towel, and see what happened next. I wasn't religious. Didn't believe in God. Didn't believe in an afterlife. But anything, even empty oblivion, had to be better than this. Like I said, survival instinct is a motherfucker, but why fight to stay alive when living itself had become such a horror? Alan and I had discussed it at length, even before our conversation at the grocery store, and neither one of us could come up with a very good reason. We didn't have loved ones who were counting on us. Had no faith that mankind would turn the tables and win the day. Civilization was pretty much finished, as far as we'd been concerned, yet we still fought on. The will to survive was strong, even when we didn't want it to be—until Alan got bitten, of course. And that hadn't been his choice.

Why go on? I don't know. Don't have an answer for that question. But I did go on. Every single time I faced down dead men walking, I fought to live.

A few blocks away, there were acres of abandoned houses and buildings. Before Hamelin's Revenge, they'd been rife with drug dealers and squatters and crime. Oftentimes, the older folks in the neighborhood would comment that the whole area should be burned down. All it would have taken was one match; the buildings were that deplorable. I wondered if that was what had happened. The fire was coming from that direction.

I got up from the window and ran back to the bedroom. The smoke was stronger, the fires drawing nearer. It burned my nose and throat, and I breathed in short little gasps. The flames grew louder, crackling and licking at my neighbor's homes. I heard a building collapse. Heard a child crying. A car horn blared. A gunshot rang out. And above it all, I heard the screams of the living. And even above the stench of the smoke, I could smell the dead.

There was a rapid-fire series of explosions. They were distant, by the sound, but coming closer. I slipped into my clothes and boots and grabbed my backpack. As quickly as I could, I threw in what canned food I could carry without being overburdened, as well as bottled water, matches, and other things I'd need to survive. I popped open the revolver's cylinder and dumped out the spent shells. I'd shot the zombie and Alan, and had two bullets left. I grabbed a long butcher knife from the kitchen and duct taped it to my leg so that I wouldn't cut myself. There was another explosion, louder this time. The house shook. My bookshelves rocked back and forth, spilling DVDs and compact discs to the floor. Pictures fell from the wall. Something heavy rained down on my roof.

I took the remaining water and dumped it all over myself, making sure my clothes, hair, and skin were wet. I soaked a washcloth and held it over my nose and mouth with one hand. Clutched the pistol in the other. And then stood there in the middle of my living room and wondered what the fuck to do next.

I couldn't just go out the front door. Smoke inhalation would kill me before I got the barricade tore down. Even if I did make it, the street was full of zombies. I could shoot two of them, but then what? Stab them with my knife? That wouldn't work. One of the weird things with Hamelin's Revenge was that you had to destroy the infected corpse's brain. Nothing else worked, except for maybe incinerating them. I could outrun them for a little while, but eventually I'd tire or the smoke would get the best of me.

Stay here, a voice whispered inside my head. *Just sit down and relax. Go to sleep. Quit running. It's easier. Why bother anymore? Does it really matter? Does anything really matter? Maybe Alan was right. Maybe this would be easier.*

I had to admit, the idea was tempting. Go back to bed and wait for the fire to engulf the house. With luck, I'd be dead before the flames even reached me. But I'd seen a documentary about burn victims. Last two things to burn were the heart and the brain. If the smoke didn't kill me, I'd be alive that whole time, aware as I burned to death.

That wasn't an option.

Deciding fast, I grabbed the hammer and ran back into the kitchen. There was a small window over the sink, and I'd nailed a single piece of plywood over it. Six nails stood between freedom and me. They screeched as I yanked them loose. I tore the board free and tossed it to the floor. Then I checked outside. The narrow alley behind my house was full of smoke, but otherwise deserted. I smashed the glass with the butt of the pistol and then tossed the backpack outside. Then I crawled through the window. Keeping the wet washcloth pressed to my face, I crouched down, retrieved the backpack, and crept through the darkness. I stayed bent over, trying to stay as low to the ground as possible, down where the air was better. Discarded trash crunched under my feet. The alley was full of debris: empty beer cans, used condoms, candy wrappers, and cigarette butts. A dead man lay sprawled on his back across the concrete. His skin looked like a greasy, bloated sausage casing. A red hole was in the middle of his forehead. He wasn't coming back. Holding my breath, I stepped over him.

All around me were screams and the crackling of flames. The neighborhood was a Molotov cocktail and God had just tossed the fucker. The fire came from three directions. The only way still open to flee was toward the harbor.

I ran into the night, straight into the inferno.

Straight into hell . . .

CHAPTER THREE

The dark sidewalks steamed in the heat. Even with the washcloth pressed to my face, sweat poured down my forehead and into my eyes. My lungs felt like they were burning. I tried to keep from coughing so I wouldn't give my location away. It was hard to see clearly. The air was thick with smoke and my stinging eyes watered. To make matters worse, I heard screams and gunshots everywhere, but couldn't see where they were coming from. All around me, the inferno crackled and roared.

I'd only gone about a half block when I encountered the first zombie, an old woman dressed in a soiled nightgown. I smelled her before I saw her, and figured that if her stench was stronger than the smoke, she must be close indeed. I had time to hide behind a green garbage Dumpster before she lumbered out of the haze. Her wig was missing. Her bald scalp looked like a peeling onion, and her varicose veins had burst right through her skin. The corpse's lips were shredded, hanging from her face in gray-white strips. I let the dead woman wander by. She moved in silence. The only sound was the buzzing flies inside of her.

When the coast was clear, I continued on my way. Flames flickered in the night. I didn't see anyone else on the street. Either the mass exodus of survivors had gone another way, or the fires had trapped them, or they'd ended up as dinner for the dead. I moved cautiously, but quickly, too. Stayed mindful of what was behind me. Eventually, the smoke grew less thick. I passed by the burned-out shell of a car. A family of four had cooked inside the vehicle. They were just blackened shapes now, two adult-sized and two child-sized—a zombie's well-done Happy Meal. I wondered how it had happened. Was that horrible, agonizing death by fire preferable to facing whatever had trapped them inside? And what had burned them and their car? It couldn't have been the current inferno. The flames hadn't reached this street yet.

Eventually, I got far enough away from the fires to drop my washcloth. The smoke cleared and visibility improved. I immediately wished that it hadn't. More wrecked and abandoned automobiles choked the street and the bloodstained pavement was littered with body parts: severed heads, organs, and scraps of human meat. I recognized one of the heads. It was the guy who'd owned the liquor store around the corner. He was still functioning, despite the fact that he no longer had a body. His eyes focused on me, and his pale tongue slid across his dry, cracked lips. I tried kicking him across the street, just like Alan had done earlier that night, but his teeth clamped down on the toe of my boot. He didn't break the leather, but held firm just the same. I hopped around on one foot, trying to shake him off. His head came loose and soared through the air, shattering a storefront window. His teeth lay scattered on the pavement. They crunched beneath my heels as I walked on. It made me long for the days when the only thing littering the sidewalks in my hood was empty crack vials.

I passed by a Catholic church—a gothic-looking building with a cross-topped steeple and bell. Several of the stained glass windows were broken and neon red spray paint covered the front doors. The graffiti said GOD IS DEAD. Across the street was a pawn shop. Our neighborhood had plenty of pawn shops and liquor stores and check cashing places, but not many banks or factories. In truth, I was happy to see the liquor stores burn. They were blight. Cautiously, I peeked inside the pawn shop, hoping there were some weapons left, but the looters had picked it clean. The only things left were a few musical instruments, an old video game system, and a severed hand lying on the floor. Mopping sweat from my forehead, I continued along past a newsstand, another liquor store, and a row of houses. A blood-stained flyer advertising the Fourth Annual East Baltimore Black Singles Weekend fluttered by in the hot breeze. The rear end of a car stuck out of a barber shop. A pizza joint stood open to the elements, ransacked of everything, even the tables and fixtures. My stomach rumbled. Despite everything, despite the danger and the stench in the air and the body parts in the streets, I was hungry.

Shuffling footsteps caught my attention, followed by a low moan. Then came the stench. I ducked into a doorway and waited. Three zombies stumbled out of an alley. I could smell the rot wafting off of them, even from the other side of the street. I held my breath, waiting for them to pass and praying they wouldn't see me. My prayer went unanswered. The graffiti on the church doors had been right. God was dead now. Just like everyone else. God was a zombie and these were his children.

He must have smiled upon them.

They saw me, lurched toward the doorway, and I wondered how it was possible that dead men could still drool.

The first corpse was in bad shape: both his arms were missing, an ear hung by a thread of cartilage, and one empty eye socket festered with maggots. His face was expressionless. He showed no emotion, just blank hunger. His two companions followed close behind him; a teenage girl who barely looked dead, and a middle-aged man whose wrists were cut downward rather than across. He'd wanted to make sure he did it right. Too bad it hadn't kept him from coming back. The bite mark on his forearm, right in the middle of the cut, was proof enough of that. I wondered if he'd been bitten first and committed suicide in some effort to stop the infection or had cut himself before the zombie attack. It didn't matter. Either way, he was back now. Death was not the end.

"Damn, you guys stink."

If they understood me, they gave no indication. I tried to laugh, but my mouth was dry. It sounded more like a frightened whimper.

They were slow and stupid enough that I could easily get away from them. Just slip out from the doorway and run around them, making sure to keep a wide berth. But before I could do that, more creatures wandered into the street. None of them carried weapons or showed the slightest bit of cunning or tactical ability. If they had, I'd have been dead. One clutched a cell phone in its hand. When I took a closer look, I realized its arm had been burned somehow, and the phone had melded with its skin. Melted flesh stuck to the plastic like taffy left out in the sun.

Taking a deep breath, I raised the pistol and shot the first zombie—the one with the eye socket full of worms—in the throat. Blood, flesh, and maggots spun through the air. I'd been aiming for his head. That left me with one bullet, and the fucker was still coming. He staggered a few more steps, almost close enough to touch. His head tilted to one side because of the damage I'd done to his neck. It didn't matter. Cursing, I darted from the door and ran the gauntlet. The creature reached for me as I sped by him, his thick fingers clawing at my shirt. Fabric tore. I shook him off and danced away from his friends while he stuffed the torn piece of my shirt in his mouth. The girl spun and tripped over her own feet. The dead man with the cut wrists moaned unintelligibly, and then fell overtop her. The two corpses sprawled in the road.

Running for the other side of the street, I couldn't help but laugh again. They were so clumsy. So . . . *stupid.* All I had to do was keep moving and not let them touch me, and I'd be fine. Outthinking them was no problem. Neither was outrunning them.

Being outnumbered, however, had its disadvantages. And a second later, I found that out.

More of the creatures blundered into the area, attracted by the gunshot. Before I could reach the curb, they had me surrounded. The stench was brutal. My laughter turned to a scream. I glanced around, frantic, but there was nowhere to go. Just that quickly, the odds had changed. They swarmed toward me, grasping and clawing, gnashing their stained teeth.

And then the odds changed again.

"Hey, mister." A child's voice; sounded like a boy. "You'd best duck unless you want to get shot!"

I couldn't see the speaker. Hoping that my last bullet would be true, I raised the pistol and aimed at the closest zombie. Before I could squeeze the trigger, a thunderous blast rocked the street. I jumped. There was a flash from the second story window of a nearby row home. The creature's head exploded, splattering the creature behind it. The second zombie licked the gore from its lips. Luckily, none of it had landed on me.

A girl's voice shouted, "Malik, you could have shot him!"

"I told him to duck. It ain't my fault if he gets hit."

With a yell, I lowered my head and plowed through the zombies, shoving them aside. It was like pushing slabs of meat. Several toppled over. A few more grabbed at my clothing, ripping it further. I wrestled free of them and ran for the row house where the gunfire had come from. Another blast rang out. I heard something splatter behind me. It sounded wet. Dead footsteps padded after me. I waited for a third shot, but there was none.

"It's stuck!"

"Push down on it," the girl hollered.

"I can't."

"Give it here."

"Stop pulling on it!"

Wondering what they were yelling about, I jumped up onto the concrete stoop and tried the door. It was locked. I turned around and the zombies were drawing closer. Over their stench, I caught a faint whiff of smoke. The fires were getting nearer, too.

"Hey," I shouted, still unable to see the kids. "Unlock the door!"

"Can't," the boy hollered back.

"Why?" My voice cracked.

"You're a stranger. We ain't supposed to open up for strangers. You might be one of them child molesters."

The dead clambered onto the sidewalk. A few of them had trouble negotiating the curb. One of them fell over, sprawling in the street. When it got up again, I noticed that its foot was twisted all the way around, the toes pointing behind it. Some of the creatures moaned, but most of them were silent. There was no hint of intelligence in their expressions—just raw, naked hunger. *Need.* I fired my last bullet and the closest one dropped. My ears rang from the shot.

"Please," I screamed. "Let me in."

The children didn't respond, and I thought that was it. I was dead—and then I'd be undead. I pulled my knife, trying to decide if I had the balls to slash my own throat before the creatures reached me. Wondered if I could stab one hard enough in the head to penetrate the skull, and if so, if I could free the knife quick enough to do another one. But then I heard a rustling sound on the other side of the door. The first of the horde, a fat zombie with a broken rib poking out of his side, started up the steps. I slashed at him with the knife. It startled the creature. His mottled arms drew back, but then he started forward again.

The door opened a crack. A young girl, maybe eleven or twelve years old, stared out at me. Her eyes widened when she saw the zombies.

"Open up!"

"You promise not to hurt us?"

"Yes!" I had to strain to hear her because my ears were still ringing. "I'll promise anything you want. Just open the goddamn door right now!"

She removed the chain and I shoved the door open and pushed past her. She slammed it behind me and slid the chain back in place. Then she fastened the deadbolt. Finally, she slid a thick piece of wood across the middle of the door; each end fit into brackets that had been nailed into the wall. Someone had reinforced the building, and I doubted it was her.

"Thanks," I whispered, catching my breath.

A length of pipe lay propped against the wall. She picked it up, held it out in front of her, ready to strike, and looked me up and down.

"What's your name?" I asked.

"Tasha. Tasha Roberts."

"Thanks for letting me in, Tasha. My name's Lamar."

She glanced down at the empty pistol. "That thing got any more bullets?"

I shook my head. "No."

"We got a shotgun upstairs," she said. "Found it in Mr. Washington's apartment. But we're almost out of bullets and can't get it to work now."

Fists pounded on the door, slow and plodding. We both jumped.

"Will that deadbolt and plank hold?" I asked.

Tasha shrugged. "I don't know. This is the first time they've tried to get in. We've stayed quiet. Didn't let them know we lived here. They've left us alone until now."

I searched the hallway for something more to brace the door with—a potted plant, a bench, even a coat rack—but the corridor was empty. The hallway was dark. Ugly green wallpaper peeled away from cracked plaster, and the dusty floorboards creaked with every step I took. The building smelled of mildew and piss. Outside, the pounding grew louder. I turned back to Tasha.

"You said that you have a gun upstairs?"

She nodded.

"Show me."

We took the stairs two at a time. I had to run to keep up with the girl. Tasha ran through the darkened hallways with the confidence only someone who'd lived there could have. She was skinny, her hair beaded with multicolored beads. Gold earrings dangled from each lobe. She wore dirty red shorts and a pink-and-white striped shirt. Her shoes were old and worn out, and one of the back heels flapped as she ran.

On the second floor, she stopped in front of a door and raised her hand to knock. Before she could, I stopped her.

"Your parents? Will they be okay with me being here? Maybe you should warn them first that you're coming in with a stranger. I don't want to get shot."

Her voice softened and she stared at her feet. "We ain't got no parents. It's just me and Malik. He's my little brother. Momma, she . . ."

Hesitantly, I put a hand on her bony shoulder. She jumped a little, but that was all.

"I'm sorry," I said. "I didn't mean to stir up anything bad."

"I'll be fine." Sniffling, she knocked on the door. "Malik, open up."

"You okay?" the boy said from the other side of the door. He sounded defiant, but afraid. "That dude with you?"

"Yes, he's with me. His name is Lamar and he's okay. He ain't gonna hurt us. He just wanted help. Now do what I told you and open the door."

"Don't boss me."

"Malik . . ."

The door opened, revealing a small boy, maybe seven or eight years old, in a Spider-Man shirt and ragged black jeans. He frowned at me, refusing to step aside.

"You cool?" he asked.

I smiled. "Yeah, man, I'm cool."

"You better be. I ain't no punk. I'm hardcore, G. You try messing with my sister and I'll mess you up instead. And if you think I'm playing, just try me."

I choked down my laughter, careful not to offend him. The sincerity and ferocity in his voice was really something, and I had no doubts he'd try to do that very thing.

"Malik," I said, holding up my hands, "I promise, you're in charge. I just needed to hide out here for a second. Okay?"

"Okay." His attention was drawn to the pistol. "Cool. Can I try that out?"

"Can't. No more bullets."

"Damn. Well what good are you then?"

Tasha waved her hand, angry and dismissive. "Malik, get the hell out of the way and let us in."

"Don't boss me," he repeated. "What's that noise?"

"There's dead folks beating on the door downstairs."

Malik's eyes widened. "Oh, shit. I told you we shouldn't let him in. Now they know we're here."

"It'll be okay," I assured them. "Just give me a moment to catch my breath, and then we'll figure something out."

"Damn straight."

I shook my head. "Did your mother let you talk that way?"

"What do you mean?"

"Did she let you curse like that?"

"Shit, man. I'm eight years old. I can say what I want. Before she got sick, Momma said I was the man of the house."

"No she didn't," Tasha said. "Momma told you to mind me. If she'd heard you cursing like that, she'd have washed your mouth out with soap and then beat your ass."

"Nuh-uh!"

"Uh-huh!"

"Enough," I snapped. "Both of you knock it the hell off."

Tasha got quiet, but Malik frowned at me.

"You can't tell me what to do. You ain't my father."

Sighing, I laid the empty pistol on the coffee table. Then I knelt down and looked the boy in the eye.

"No, Malik, I'm not your father. You don't even know me. But I am a grown-up, and I do know things and I can help you and your sister, if you'll let me. I'd like to help. Would that be okay?"

He shrugged. "I guess."

"Good." I stood up and looked around the dismal apartment. It was small and cramped and dusty. Empty food wrappers and dirty plates littered the floor and coffee table. The furniture was threadbare. Soiled laundry lay heaped in piles. On one shelf was a picture of a heavyset woman: smiling, cheerful eyes beaming behind gold-rimmed eyeglasses, her arms around Malik and Tasha.

"That your mom?"

Tasha nodded.

"Anybody else left alive in this building?"

"No," Tasha said. "Everybody else is gone. They either left or . . ."

She didn't have to finish.

"Mr. Lahav helped us out after Momma died," Malik said. "He let us stay in his apartment. Cooked for us. Read us bedtime stories. I liked him, except when he made us brush our teeth. He said we got to be our own dentists now, so it was important to brush three times a day, even if we didn't eat. But he went out for water and never come back."

"And how long ago was that?"

The boy shrugged. "I don't know. Maybe five days?"

"He's dead by now," Tasha said. "Those things got to him."

"We don't know that," Malik insisted. "Maybe he got hurt, or trapped. We should go out and find him."

"Don't be stupid. He's one of them now, Malik. A zombie."

"No he ain't."

"He is too."

"Guys." I held up my hands. "Let's not fight, okay? That won't help us get out of here. Other than Mr. Lahav, is there anybody else in the building?"

They both shook their heads.

"Are there any zombies?"

Tasha shuddered. "No. Thank God."

"And this shotgun is your only weapon."

"Yeah," Malik said, holding it out to me, "but I can't get it to work no more."

"Let me see it." I took the shotgun from him and pumped it, the way I'd seen it done in the movies. An empty cartridge ejected from the side and bounced off the wall.

"I tried that," Malik said, pouting. "Wouldn't do it for me. Stupid gun."

Before this, I didn't have much experience with kids. One of my old boyfriends had a daughter (he'd been married for several years before finally coming to terms with the fact that he was gay), but I'd never really interacted with her, and had dumped her father after a few dates.

"Tell you what." I smiled. "Let me keep this one, and soon as we find more, I'll pick out one more your size. Sound good?"

He looked reluctant. "I guess so. You best not be tricking me, though. Just because I ain't strong enough to use this shotgun don't mean it don't belong to me."

"It's all yours, little man. I'm just borrowing it until we find a safer place to stay."

"Safer?" Tasha asked, confused. "Hold up a minute. We're not going nowhere. Malik and I are staying right here. Momma and Mr. Lahav both told us to—"

"Listen," I interrupted. "You hear that? They're going to get in. If they can't break the door down, sooner or later one of them will get lucky enough to bust a window. Then we're screwed. And there's something else, too."

"What?"

"The city is on fire. That's how you guys found me. I was running away from it when I got trapped down there."

"Fire?" Malik's eyes grew wide. "How bad is it?"

"My whole neighborhood is gone. It's spreading block by block and it's coming this way. It'll be here soon. We don't have much time."

"But if we go outside, the zombies will get us," Tasha said.

"And if we stay in here," I reminded her, "we'll burn to death."

"So we're screwed." Malik folded his arms across his chest.

I patted him on the head and smiled. "Not quite yet."

My knees popped as I stood up. Downstairs, the pounding continued. I glanced out the window and saw more zombies converging on our building. They were four deep around the door, clawing and shoving each other. More of them emerged from side streets and alleys. I didn't know how they communicated, or even if they did, but somehow they knew that dinner was inside this building. All they had to do was get inside.

The fires were spreading, too. The entire horizon was now glowing orange and yellow. As hard as it was to believe, it looked like the entire city was going up in flames. The rain we'd had earlier in the day had done nothing to slow it down, apparently. And it wasn't like there were firemen or other emergency personnel to battle the flames. I'd once seen a Civil War documentary on TV. In it, they'd talked about how General Sherman had burned Atlanta to the ground. At the time, I'd tried to picture that. It seemed inconceivable; unreal. But now, I had a good idea what that had actually looked like.

The kids had lined up the remaining shotgun shells on the windowsill. There were four of them; not nearly the amount I'd hoped for. I had no idea how many the shotgun could hold; indeed, I'd been surprised I was able to figure out how to pump it so easily. Rather than trying to load them into the weapon and risking jamming it or something, I scooped the shells up and stuffed them in my pants pocket.

Malik frowned. "Ain't you gonna put them in the gun?"

"Not now. Maybe later."

"Later? Nigga, do it now!"

"Hey," I scolded. "You shouldn't use that word."

"Nigga? Why not?"

"Because it's not a nice word. It means you're ignorant."

"I'm ignorant?"

"That's what it means."

He stomped his foot. "I'm not ignorant."

"I didn't say you were. But when you use that word, that's what you're calling other people—and yourself."

Malik frowned in concentration.

I turned to Tasha. "You got any other weapons in

the apartment? Anything you kids could use against the zombies?"

"No. But I think Malik is right. You should load the shotgun now. Might not have a chance later."

"Okay." I sighed. "I'll load it."

I pulled the shotgun shells out of my pocket. Then I fumbled with the weapon, wondering how they went in. There was a slot on the side, about the same size as the ammunition, but I wasn't sure which way the shells were supposed to face. The kids watched me in bewilderment.

Malik smirked. "You don't know how to load it, do you?"

"No," I admitted. "I don't know much about guns."

"And you calling *me* ignorant? Here, let me show you."

He took the gun from me and quickly inserted the shells with his little fingers. Then, with a smug, satisfied grin, he handed it back to me.

"Thanks."

"Mr. Washington taught me how."

"What happened to him?"

"He got eaten." The boy clammed up then, and stared at the floor. It was obvious that he was reluctant to say any more.

I checked outside again. The creatures were still coming. The pounding had grown louder and more insistent. We heard a cracking sound, like wood splintering. Tasha and Malik suddenly looked as scared as I felt.

"Okay," I whispered, "is there another way out of the building?"

Brian Keene

Tasha nodded. "The laundry room, down in the basement. It's got a pair of storm doors that lead up into the alley. And there's the fire escape. But it's broke. Don't extend all the way to the ground."

"Could we drop to the ground from it?"

"No, it's too high up."

"Which side of the building is the alley on?"

"The right."

"Do any of your windows face it?"

She pointed to a side room. "In there. That was Momma's bedroom."

"Stay here."

Their mother's room was still full of her presence. It smelled like perfume, lavender, baby powder, and vanilla body lotion. The scents were faint but lingering. It made me sad—in a few more weeks it would probably fade forever. The feeling surprised me. I thought of my own mother, and then pushed those emotions aside. No sense getting maudlin. Not while we were still in danger. The bedroom was dark, but the glow of the fires outside provided light. The bed was made up with a white, lacy comforter and light-green flannel sheets, two pillows, and a ratty old stuffed animal. Dust-covered picture frames and cheap knickknacks lined the top of the dresser. The kids were smiling in all the photos. There were a few books, mostly paperbacks by Toni Morrison, Chesya Burke, and some cheesy African-American romance titles, along with a well-worn copy of the Holy Bible.

I moved to the window and stared down at the alley—a narrow slice of pavement running between the apartment buildings. An empty paper bag fluttered by, but there was no other movement. So far, the alley was free of zombies. They'd stupidly clustered their forces at the front. It occurred to me that maybe I was giving them too much credit. They didn't know tactics or planning. The only knew hunger. Need. They'd seen their prey go in the front door, so that was where they'd gathered. In a way, it was kind of pathetic.

So the alley was clear. The question was if it would stay that way in the time it took us to get down to the laundry room. And even then, what was waiting for us down in the streets?

One step at a time, I thought. *Just get down to the laundry room first.*

I walked back into the living room. The kids stared at me expectantly.

"You guys still have water?"

"Yeah."

Tasha took me into the kitchen, where they'd lined up plastic buckets and jugs full of rainwater. Mosquito larvae squirmed in some of them. She explained that they'd been putting the buckets out on the roof. I had the kids wet down their clothes and I did the same again with mine. I also grabbed three more washcloths and soaked them down. I explained how they would help with the smoke if the fires got too close. Then we were ready. The kids still looked frightened, but they didn't argue or give me any lip.

"Okay," I said. "Stick close, but stay behind me. Breathe through your washcloths and duck down as much as possible. Smoke rises, and the air will be better lower to the ground. Try to keep quiet. You ready?"

They nodded. Tasha crossed her arms over her chest and shivered.

"You scared?" I asked her.

"No. Well, yeah. 'Course I'm scared. But that's not why I'm shivering. I'm cold. My clothes are wet."

"Sorry about that," I apologized. "We'll find you some dry clothes when we get to safety."

"Where are we going?" Malik asked.

I paused, not sure how to answer him.

"I don't know. Somewhere else. Somewhere other than here."

"Someplace where there's no zombies?"

"Yeah," I lied. "Somewhere without zombies or fires. Someplace where we can chill for a little while. Rest up. I don't know about you guys, but I'm tired. I'd like to stop all this running and fighting. I've had enough for one night. Let's get to where we don't have to do that."

Privately, I wondered where that place was— wondered if it even existed anymore, and if it did exist, how we'd get there.

We left the apartment, and Tasha locked the door behind us. I thought about asking her why, but then thought better of it. This was their home. It wasn't much. None of the homes here ever were. But it was probably the only one they'd ever known, and all their memories were here, and now they were leaving it with a stranger, while a bunch of dead people pounded on the door. Deep down inside, Tasha must have known that she'd never see the apartment again. I don't cry easily, but the look on her face damn near broke my heart.

The noise got worse as we reached the landing and started down the stairs. It kept growing louder as we neared the first floor, until finally it was almost overpowering. I wanted to scream at the dead, tell them to shut the fuck up. Glass broke somewhere, maybe in one of the first floor apartments. I couldn't tell for sure. It was hard to concentrate. The zombies' stink filled the hallway, and the smoke was getting stronger again, too. The front door shuddered with every blow, and long splinters of wood fell off the bottom of it. Cracks split open on its surface as the hammering continued.

"Which way?"

Tasha pointed toward the back of the hallway. We slipped down the passage, quick but quiet. I was in the lead, followed by Tasha and then Malik. Brother and sister were holding hands. I glanced back at them and smiled, trying to reassure them. I didn't feel very sure, but they smiled back.

And that was when the door burst open. It slammed against the wall with a loud bang, spilling zombies into the foyer. The first wave toppled to the floor, and more of the creatures rushed inside, clambering over the fallen ones. Their stench burned my nostrils. It felt like a thin layer of film in my sinus and throat. Tasha and Malik both screamed, but not as loud as me. They froze, staring at the onrushing hordes.

"Go!"

I pushed them behind me and raised the shotgun. The first zombie made it through the crowd and stumbled down the hallway after us. She'd once been a female. One swollen, purple breast had fallen out of her blouse. She moved in a series of spasms and twitches. There was hunger in her dead eyes, and I wondered how she'd eat me. Her jaw was hanging by only a few tendrils from her skull. With each jerking step that she took, her jaw swung back and forth like a kid's swing blowing in the breeze.

With one squeeze of the trigger, I solved that problem for her. The zombie's head just vanished. There was a spray of red and then nothing. The corpse dropped to the floor. My arm went numb from the shotgun's kick, but I managed to pump it again. I took down a second creature, which had once been a child about Malik's age. Despite the gruesomeness of it all, I got a thrill as I jacked a third shell. I was a much better shot with the shotgun than I'd been with the pistol.

Keeping the gun aimed at them, I retreated down the hall. Tasha was holding the basement door open for me. Malik had already run to the bottom of the stairs. I backed into the stairwell and pulled the door shut behind me. There was no lock.

"Shit."

"This way." Tasha tugged on my sleeve. She led me down the stairs and into a dark, wet cellar packed high with boxes and junk. A ten-speed bike. A damp mattress with wires poking out. Roller skates. A deflated basketball. A television with a broken screen. Mildewed clothes. Stacks of newspaper and magazines bound up with twine. The cement floor was cracked and uneven. Moisture spread in gray patterns along the walls. At the far end was another set of doors. They led into a small laundry room with three coin-operated washers and dryers. Two laundry baskets sat against the far wall. Clean clothes that somebody would never wear again spilled out of them and onto the floor. Beyond those was a small set of stairs and a pair of closed storm doors.

The doors were fastened with a bright, shiny padlock.

Above us, the dead began pounding on the basement door. It was in much worse shape than the front door had been. They'd be through it in a minute— maybe less. I stared at the padlock, my mouth hanging open. Then I turned to Tasha in disbelief.

"Why the hell didn't you tell me it was locked?"

She dismissed me with a wave of her hand. "You think we're stupid? We're the ones that locked it. Mr. Lahav had us lock all the doors. We just didn't have a padlock for the front door, so we used the plank."

The pounding grew louder, in time with my pulse rate. Over in the corner, behind a pile of boxes, something skittered in the shadows. I wondered if there were rats in the basement, and if so, if they were the dead kind.

I turned back to the lock. "You have a key for this one? If not, stand back and let me shoot it off."

Smiling, she pulled it out of her pants pocket and held it up. She started for the storm doors, but I stopped her.

"Wait. There might be some of them in the alley by now. Let me go first."

She stepped aside. My fingers were sweaty and it was hard to hold the key and the shotgun. Plus, my hands were shaking, which made turning the key even more difficult. When it clicked open, I breathed a sigh of relief. Slowly, I opened the storm doors and stuck my head out—shotgun barrel first. The coast was clear.

"Come on."

I helped them up into the alley, and then shut the doors behind us. The kids put their wet washcloths over their faces and waited for me. After hunting around for a moment, I found an old skid and managed to tear a board loose from it. I wedged the board between the door handles.

"That should slow them down."

Malik squeezed my hand. "What now?"

I checked both sides of the alley. The front led out into the main street, where the zombies had surrounded me earlier. The rear intersected with another alley running along behind a bail bondsman's office. We went that way as carefully and quietly as possible. Behind us came a muffled thump. The zombies in the basement had discovered the storm doors.

"This way," I whispered, hurrying the kids along.

We turned left, and then right, and then left again, working our way toward the waterfront, more out of need than any sense of direction. I wasn't trying to reach the harbor. That was never my plan. We were just trying to stay ahead of both the fires and the zombies. Several times our progress was blocked by one or the other. I preferred the flames. Didn't have to waste ammo on them. Whenever possible, we stuck to side streets and back alleys.

We'd made it a few more blocks before we were attacked again. We were behind a used sporting goods store and I was trying to get a bearing on the fires. The smoke was getting thicker again, making it hard to tell how close the flames actually were. Every time the wind shifted direction smoke billowed toward us.

Without a sound, a corpse lurched out from behind a Dumpster. The only reason we noticed it was because it accidentally kicked an empty forty-ounce while stalking toward us. Its face was concealed by a hockey mask. The zombie clutched a hockey stick in its hand but never tried to use it as a weapon. I think it held the stick more out of instinct than anything else. With its free hand, it reached for my head, trying to pull me toward its gaping mouth. I ducked, sidestepped, and swung with the shotgun. The stock crashed against its jaw. The corpse stumbled backward. Gripping the shotgun barrel in both fists, I clubbed the creature's legs, breaking both of its kneecaps. As it collapsed, I smashed its head in. The zombie's face imploded behind the hockey mask. Black sludge that must have been curdled blood squirted out of the mouth and eyeholes like wet clay. It lay on the pavement, twitching.

"Hit it again," Malik cried. "Smack that son of a bitch."

I did. I struck the zombie on the side of the head,

and its mask flew off. Its face looked like a bowl of spoiled spaghetti. Black mold grew on its skin. I slammed the shotgun down again and the skull cracked. The zombie quit twitching and lay still. Bending over, I picked up the hockey stick and wiped the mud and gore off of the handle.

"Here." I tossed the stick to Malik. "Think you can use this?"

"Hell yeah, I can." He grinned like a kid who'd just unwrapped his Christmas presents. Then he swung the stick around in a circle, making a sound like a light saber.

"Knock it off, Malik," Tasha said. "You're gonna get blood on me."

"No I ain't. I know what I'm doing. Next zombie we see, I'm gonna crack it in the head just like Lamar did."

"Now you're talking," I said. "Just don't hit me or your sister with it."

"You should have given it to me," Tasha said. "He's too little to hit anything with it."

Malik frowned. "Say's you."

"It's not fair."

"We'll find something for you," I promised Tasha. "Don't worry."

After I'd cleaned the gore off the shotgun butt so that I wouldn't accidentally infect myself, we continued on. I wiped the sweat from my brow and wished for a cold beer or just some water. The hot summer temperatures combined with the heat from the fires had made it pretty much unbearable. Add to that the fact that we were running and then fighting and then running again—I was exhausted. Sweat dripped from the tip of my nose and soaked my already wet clothes.

We came across some other survivors as we neared Fells Point, an area of the city where mostly rich, white college kids from the suburbs went to drink on weekends. It was full of bars and music stores and vintage clothing shops—stuff like that. (They called it vintage clothing, and paid top dollar for the shit. Meanwhile, you could buy the same pair of pants at the Goodwill store for a dollar). Every night, you'd see Eminem wannabes stumbling around drunk, shouting to each other, groping their girlfriends or even strangers passing by, pissing in alleys and puking all over the brick sidewalks.

Now Fells Point was a battleground. We'd cut through a very narrow alley, the old kind with crumbling brick archways over it. We heard the gunshots and the screams but they were muffled by the buildings on each side of us. It wasn't until we'd reached the end of the alley that we really saw what was happening. There was a riot going on in the central market area—human versus zombie and even human versus human. It was hard to keep track of anyone. Hard to focus. I held out my hand, motioning for the kids to stay behind me. Then I stared in disbelief.

The street was littered with body parts and unmoving corpses, and the gutters ran with blood. Gunfire echoed off the buildings and smoke filled the air. It was a nightmare. The stench, the screams—

the chewing sounds. Even over the explosions, you could hear the zombies as they fed.

I saw a car that was upside down, its tires sticking up in the air like the legs of a dead animal. It must have just wrecked right before our arrival because there were people still inside it. They screamed as the zombies pulled them out through the shattered windows and ripped into them, tearing their flesh with teeth and hands. Another corpse staggered by a burning antiques store. Its arms were missing. Someone shot it from inside the store. The store's display window shattered, and the zombie crumpled to the sidewalk. Then the store's roof collapsed with a roar, sending fiery embers soaring into the night sky. Someone, probably the shooter, screamed inside the burning building.

In the street, a pack of undead dogs chased a woman and her baby. A zombie pit bull ripped the infant from the fleeing mother's arms and tore it apart, shaking the screaming baby like a rag doll. A wayward bullet took down the mother a second later. At least I hope it was wayward. Maybe the shooter had been aiming for the dogs and hit her instead. Or maybe they were aiming for her after all; a mercy shot. There were a lot of zombie animals among the chaos. Mostly rats and dogs, but I also saw a few dead cats and what I think was an iguana. The dog zombies moved faster than their human counterparts, and I wondered why that was. Maybe it was because they had four legs instead of two, or maybe they hadn't been dead long.

A man stumbled by us, close enough for me to reach out and touch if I'd wanted to. He wasn't dead yet, but he was certainly dying. His hands were clasped around his bleeding stomach, trying to hold his guts in. Half-dollar sized drops of blood speckled the pavement behind him. A child zombie in bloodstained rags trailed after him, chewing what looked like a length of intestine. The man seemed oblivious to his pursuer and the zombie seemed in no rush. I shot it in the back of the head as it passed by us. The man never paused. Just kept walking. I ducked back into the shadows, worried that my Good Samaritan act may have given away our hiding place.

But it didn't matter because a second later things got even worse.

Civilians in a commandeered half-track barreled through the crowd, crushing both the living and the dead beneath the vehicle. A teenaged corpse in a Slipknot shirt tried to climb up onto the half-track, but one of the men kicked him back down with a boot to the face. Another of the men opened fire with a mounted machine gun. Bodies—both living and dead—jittered and danced as the rounds punched through them. I gasped. These guys didn't care who they shot. They were just as bad as the zombies—maybe even worse. The dead couldn't use guns. Clearing a path, the vehicle rolled on. The humans they'd just killed stayed dead. They were the lucky ones.

Another man ran by us. He was carrying a rifle.

"Hey," I shouted, trying to get his attention.

"Get the fuck out of here," he gasped, and kept running.

I started to tell him that we didn't know where to go. Figured he might know of a safe place. But he rounded the corner and disappeared.

The median in the middle of the brick-lined street was carefully landscaped, full of trees, flowers and shrubs. As I watched, the treetops burst into flames, fed by the fire in the antiques store. More stray bullets chewed up the pavement. Something shattered a car's windshield nearby us, and chunks of cement sprayed through the air. The stench grew stronger; decay, cordite, burning fuel and flesh. The screams got louder.

"What are we going to do?" Malik asked. He didn't sound brave anymore. He sounded like a scared little boy on the verge of tears.

That was when the idea of making it to the harbor actually occurred to me. I was pissed off at myself for not thinking of it earlier, when we'd been fleeing in that direction anyway. Fells Point bordered the Inner Harbor area. The Inner Harbor was Baltimore's main tourist attraction. It had the National Aquarium, the big Hard Rock Cafe, the three-story Barnes and Noble store, Port Discovery, the World Trade Center, Fort McHenry, the Maryland Science Center, the Pier Six Concert Pavilion (I'd seen Erik B and Rakim along with some other old-school hip-hop acts there last year), tons of shops and restaurants and bars, and quick access to hotels, the stadium, and the convention center. But Inner Harbor was also just what its name implied—a fucking harbor. It emptied out into Chesapeake Bay. The open water—someplace where the zombies couldn't reach us, just like I'd promised the kids.

There were ships and boats all along the waterfront. The *Pride of Baltimore II*, which was a reproduction of an 1812-era clipper ship. The *USS Constellation*, the last Civil War vessel still afloat in America, built in 1854 and still seaworthy. Both of those were out of the question. I didn't know the first thing about sailing one, but I knew that you needed a whole crew just to get underway. There was a coast guard vessel, the *USCGC Spratling*, which they let tourists tromp around on. It had permanently replaced the *Cutter Taney*, which had been sent out for repairs and restoration a year or so ago. Before that, both coast guard vessels had been open to the public. Again, the *Spratling* was out of the question, just like the other big ships. But there were smaller boats, too; ferries, water taxis, and tour boats. Hell, there were even paddleboats, and I certainly knew how to operate one of those. There were also several marinas nearby full of yachts and fishing vessels and pleasure cruisers.

I didn't know shit about boating, but how hard could it be—especially given our alternatives? If we could reach the Inner Harbor or one of the marinas without getting killed or eaten, and manage to steal a small boat, we'd be well away from land before the entire city burned to the ground. Even if I could just cast off from the dock, we'd at least be able to drift far enough out into the bay to where the zombies couldn't touch us. Maybe even into the ocean. Drifting on the open sea was better than staying here.

The Inner Harbor was only a few blocks away. No telling how many zombies and crazy fuckers with guns we'd encounter between here and there. It would be tough, but what choice was there? We had to try.

I ushered the kids even farther into the shadows and then I knelt down. The smoke was really getting bad, and when I spoke, my throat felt raw and dry.

"Listen," I croaked. "I have an idea, but you guys are going to have to stick close to me and do exactly as I say. We're going to try to get to a boat—"

Tasha interrupted. "What boat?"

"Any boat. There's hundreds of them at the harbor. All we have to do is get there."

"How?"

"Well, we're gonna have to make a run for it. That's why I'm—"

"Run?" Tasha looked stunned. "Out there? Into that mess? Are you crazy?"

"I know it's dangerous, but there's no other way. Everybody is fighting each other. If we're quick, the zombies might not even notice."

"I ain't afraid," Malik said—but his eyes said different.

"I am," Tasha admitted. "I don't want to go out there, Mr. Reed. Please don't make us."

I squeezed her hand, hoping to calm her down. Instead, she began to cry.

"I don't want to go. They'll get us. Just like everyone else. All our friends. Momma . . ."

Sobbing, Tasha flung herself against me, her arms wrapped tightly around my neck. Malik started to sniffle, and then he began crying, too. I pulled him to us in a three-way hug. I held them while their tears and snot soaked into my already wet shirt. From the street came more shots and screams, followed by a volley of nearby machine gun–fire.

"Guys," I said softly, "I don't know what else to do. The city is on fire. Don't you see? It's reaching here already. We just can't stay put, and we can't fight them all. All I know to do is run. The water is our only chance. I promise—I promise you that I won't let those things get us. I'll die first."

I knew deep down inside that I meant it. I'm no hero. Earlier that night, I'd watched a woman get slaughtered outside my apartment and I'd done nothing to help her. A few moments before, when I'd shot the child zombie, it had been more out of instinct than any desire to help the creature's prey. But in the short time I'd known Malik and Tasha, I'd grown fond of them. They seemed like good kids. Brave. Resourceful. Didn't deserve the crappy hand life had given them. They deserved something better; a fighting chance at least. Besides, they'd saved my life. Figured I should return the favor.

I meant what I said. I'd die before I let the dead claim them. But my promise was a lie, because the minute I was dead, there'd be nothing I could do to protect them. Instead, I'd be hunting them, just like the other zombies.

Malik pulled away from me and wiped his nose

on the back of his hand. Then he wiped that on his shirt. After a moment, Tasha stepped back as well.

"How many bullets we got left?"

I shrugged in defeat. "I don't know, Malik. I've lost count."

"Don't matter," he said. "I've still got my stick. If they come at us, I'll take them down while you two run."

Grinning, I stood up.

"Okay, here's the plan. We run out into the street and turn right. Stay on the sidewalk if possible and stick close together. Next street up, we're gonna go left. That will take us out to the old Sylvan Learning Center building. There's a marina near it—some kind of private yacht club for rich folks. If the gates are locked, we'll have to climb. If I remember correctly, the fence is like twelve feet high. Are either one of you scared of heights?"

They shook their heads in unison.

"Can you climb?"

They nodded.

"Good." I nodded. "Once we're over the fence, we should be good to go."

"Smooth sailing?" Tasha asked.

For a second, I didn't realize she'd made a pun. Both of them began to giggle, elbowing each other and laughing at the joke. Then I laughed with them—until a low growl made the sound dry up in my throat.

It was a zombie dog, a pit bull, the one who'd killed the baby only a few moments before. Apparently, it was still hungry and looking for dessert. It stood at the mouth of the alley, blocking our way into the street and making all my planning and pep talks pointless. It took another step forward, its claws clicking on the bricks. It didn't growl again; just watched us silently with black, staring eyes. A pale white tongue drooped from its mouth. A broken rib jutted from its rancid flesh, and there were large patches of fur missing from its maggot-infested hide. Guts hung out of its open stomach. A big metal tag around its collar said the dog's name was Fred. Despite my terror, I almost started laughing when I saw that. Fred wasn't what you named a pit bull. The people in my neighborhood gave their pit bulls names like Killer or Butcher or Satan. Fred was what you named a good dog, a shy and timid dog, the type to inch toward a stranger with its tail tucked firmly between its legs and its ears drooping down.

Fred was none of those things. Fred was teeth on four legs. Sharp teeth.

There was a crackling sound from above us as the roof of the nearest building caught fire. The flames spread quickly, racing along the power lines connected to the roof and then jumping to the next building. The power lines fell to the ground. Luckily, there was no electricity running through them. Another gunshot rang out.

The dog inched closer. Behind it, at the entrance to the alley, two more zombie dogs appeared. Then another. And another. I raised the shotgun. Fred the pit bull tensed, his haunches flexing beneath matted fur. The other four dogs in the pack filed into the alley and lined up on each side of him.

I tensed. "Kids . . ."

Fred leaped, trailing his guts behind him like streamers.

"Run!"

I squeezed the trigger. Nothing happened—just a heavy, metallic click. The shotgun didn't fire. It must have been jammed. Shouting, I bashed Fred in his snapping jaws with the barrel while he was still in midair. Canine blood and teeth flew through the air. The dog landed on the bricks. I turned around and ran, shoving the kids forward, not daring to look over my shoulder. Malik dropped his hockey stick but kept running. Behind us, I heard the pack giving chase. Their feet padded along the alley and their nails tapped the bricks, but other than that, they were silent. No growls or barks. Not even panting.

If we trip, I thought, *we're done for. That's it for us.*

"The shotgun," Tasha gasped. "Shoot them!"

"Can't—it doesn't work. Keep running!"

We dashed from the alley and into another side street, free from all the fighting and chaos. Another building burst into flames beside us. We weaved our way around wrecked and abandoned vehicles. The pursuing dogs drew closer. Already I was winded, and both of the kids were gasping for breath. All the smoke in the air and the stench of decay made it even worse. There was no way we could outrun the pack. Even though they were dead, four legs still moved faster than two.

"High ground," I shouted. "We need to find higher ground. Some place where they can't climb."

Tasha darted toward a parked SUV and scrambled up over the hood. She held her hand down for her brother and pulled him up behind her. The hood buckled under their combined weight. They climbed up over the windshield and onto the roof as I jumped up onto the vehicle as well. Flipping the useless shotgun around in my hands, I gripped the barrel and used it as a club, swinging at the dogs. They jumped and snapped but couldn't reach me. Fred clumsily leaped into the air and his front paws landed on the hood. I smashed them with the shotgun and he slipped back down again, his nails scratching the paint with an awful shrieking sound, leaving furrows in the paint.

We huddled together on the SUV's roof as the pack surrounded the vehicle. My throat burned. I tried to work up some saliva so I could talk.

"What—what do we do now?" Tasha asked.

"I don't know."

"Can they get up here?"

"I don't think so. We're safe."

"How are we gonna get away?"

"I don't know, damn it. Let me think."

The dogs attempted a few more leaps and then gave up. Refusing to leave, they sat back on their haunches and waited. Their dead, black eyes never left us. Death was patient. Desperate, I examined the shotgun, trying to figure out what was wrong with it. I didn't know if I was out of ammo or if it was jammed or what, and like I said earlier, I didn't have much experience with guns until the robbery.

"Can you fix it?" Malik asked.

"I don't think so," I admitted. "But I can still bash their goddamn brains in with it."

Tasha watched the pack with wide, terrified eyes. "Are you sure they can't get up here?"

"I don't think so. We're okay for now."

"But how are we gonna get away from them?"

"Maybe they'll lose interest in us," I said. "Go off and find an easier meal. Or somebody might show up and help us."

"What about the fires?" Malik asked.

I didn't have an answer for that. The flames leapt from building to building, turning night into day. The kids had both lost their washcloths and their faces were dirty with soot. I wondered if smoke inhalation would kill us before the zombies did.

A dead man emerged from a burning bookstore. His shirt sleeve was on fire. As we watched, the flames engulfed the creature's entire body, spreading from its arm to its head and chest, and finally its legs. The corpse kept walking until its brain boiled. Then it collapsed in the street.

Several more zombies appeared from farther down the block. One was missing a leg and it crawled along the sidewalk, pulling itself by its hands. Its fingernails were gone and the tips of its fingers had split open like squashed grapes. Another one didn't even look dead. Could have just been a pizza delivery man out for a stroll, but its slow-moving, jerky gait was a giveaway. Seeing us up on the roof of the SUV, the zombies lurched toward us. The undead dogs didn't acknowledge these new arrivals. They simply kept watching, drool dripping from their jowls.

When I heard the shot, I didn't think much of it at first. Figured it was just more of the same from the main battle. But then I noticed that one of the creatures had fallen over face-first onto the pavement. It jittered and then lay still. A second later there was another shot, and one of the dog's heads blew apart. One of its pointed ears careened through the air and skull fragments clattered onto the street. A third shot slammed into the side of the SUV, causing all three of us to gasp. The vehicle rocked gently back and forth. With the fourth shot, the shooter found his mark again, and another dog collapsed.

"Where's it coming from?" Malik glanced around.

"I don't know." I studied the buildings and rooftops. It was hard to see any gunfire flashes because of all the smoke and fire. When the fifth shot came, I followed the sound, and on the sixth, I spotted the shooter. I couldn't tell if it was a man or a woman, but they were crouched down between a mailbox and some newspaper vendor boxes on the corner. Slowly, the person stood upright and walked toward us, still firing. It was a man, and as he got closer, I could make out the details. Caucasian. Good-looking guy. What some of my friends would call a "bear." Not my type, but handsome just the same, despite the fact that he'd been living the same way we had—without a shower or a clean change of clothes. He appeared to be in his early forties but in good shape, well over six feet tall, and

wearing blue jeans and a leather biker vest. He had
no shirt on underneath, and thick curls of black
chest hair poked out from beneath the vest. His
arms were covered in tattoos, and several gold
hoop rings dangled from his ear. Several weeks'
worth of beard covered his face. He had a pistol in
his hands, the barrel still smoking from the rounds
he'd just drilled into the zombies. A rifle was slung
across his shoulder, as well as a small backpack,
and he had two holsters (one of them held another
pistol) strapped around his waist, along with some
kind of ammo belt. Round objects dangled from the
belt. After a moment, I realized they were grenades.
Whoever he was, this guy wasn't playing.

He moved swiftly, his eyes roving and watchful.
One of the dogs ran toward him. The pistol jerked in
his hands. The dog dropped. Another human zombie closed in on him from the right. The pistol
roared and the creature's head exploded. One by
one, he brought them down until the street was littered with corpses. Then he looked up at us and
smiled.

"Come on down. Coast is clear."

Hesitant, I eyed him warily. The kids hid behind
me. If he meant harm to us, I knew there wasn't anything I could do to stop him. He must have sensed
our suspicion, because he holstered the handgun.

"I'm not gonna hurt you," he said. "I just saved
your sorry asses. So climb on down from there and
let's go while we can. There'll be more of them on
the way any second."

As if on cue, another group of zombies lurched

into view. They headed straight for us. With one fluid movement, the biker yanked a grenade from his belt, pulled the pin and tossed it toward the zombies.

"You folks might want to duck."

There was a massive explosion, louder than anything I'd heard that night. I could actually feel it push against my eardrums. Dirt and shards of brick and mutilated body parts rained down onto the street.

"Hey," Malik said. "Can I have one of those grenades?"

The biker laughed. "Better ask your father first."

Malik glanced up at me. "He ain't my dad. Mr. Reed's just been helping us."

"We saved him earlier," Tasha added.

The biker arched and eyebrow and looked at me.

I shrugged. "Yeah, they did. I would have been a zombie dinner if they hadn't helped me. And now you saved us all. Thanks."

"Don't mention it."

I climbed down off the SUV, and then helped the kids down. The biker stuck out his hand and I shook it. His grip was strong, his palms callused and sweaty. I checked out the tattoos covering his arms—a winding snake, a half-naked woman, the Harley-Davidson logo, and several tribal designs.

He squeezed my hand harder. "Mitch Bollinger."

"Lamar Reed. And this is Tasha and Malik Roberts." I paused, unsure of what to say next. Living like a hermit, with only Alan for company, had apparently affected my conversational skills.

"Let's get out of the street," Mitch suggested, releasing my hand, "and away from these burning buildings. We stand here jawing and the smoke will kill us before the dead do."

"We were going to try for the harbor," I said. "No zombies in the water. You know anything about boating?"

Mitch nodded; his expression was excited. "A buddy of mine at work had a boat. We used to take it out fishing on the bay all the time. Don't know everything there is to know, but I can navigate, if that's what you mean."

"Figured if we got out into the bay, we'd be safe from the fires and the dead."

"Good plan," Mitch said. "Can I tag along with you?"

In truth, I was surprised he asked. He didn't need us, but we needed him. I think he knew that, too. Maybe he was just being polite.

I grinned. "I was hoping you would."

"Then follow me. I know a shortcut to the marina."

He strode off onto a side street and we followed him without question. Still didn't know anything about him, but what choice did we have? My gut told me he was okay. If he'd wanted to rob us, or do something to the kids, he could have just gunned me down in the street. He'd drawn his pistol again and held it at the ready as he guided us toward another alley. Malik was fascinated with Mitch's weapons, and asked again for a grenade. Mitch promised him that when we got to safety, he'd teach him all about them.

"You out of ammo?" he asked, nodding at my shotgun.

"I don't know," I admitted. "Tell you the truth, I don't know shit about guns. It quit working. Jammed up or something."

"I'll take a look at it later, if you want. In fact, I think I have some shells in my bag that should fit it. Meanwhile . . ." He reached behind him and grabbed the rifle slung over his back. Then he handed it to me. I gave the shotgun to him and took the rifle. It was gray and heavy and had a black scope attached to the top of it.

"That's a Remington seven-ten," Mitch told me. "Looks a lot like the seven hundred, but it's more reliable. At least *I* think it is. I used to argue about that with people on the gun message boards online. I rescued it from a pawn shop a few days ago, along with the rest of this stuff. It's got a single-stage trigger, better lock time, and a sixty-degree bolt throw so you can be quick with your follow-up shots. Not that you'll need them with that scope. It's boresighted, but you may need to adjust it for yourself a bit. Nice gun, though. The three rings really do make a difference. Your magazine box holds four rounds. After that, you'll have to reload. Cool?"

I stopped walking and stared at him, speechless.

"Mitch, I don't understand a fucking thing you just said. You want to try it again—in English?"

He paused, and then laughed. "Sorry, man. Sometimes, I forget that some people don't know as much about guns as I do. My wife used to tell me the same thing when I started going on about them. I'll give you a crash course. The safety is off. Set the rifle against your shoulder, sight through the scope, line up the crosshairs, and squeeze the trigger. Try aiming at something right now."

While I sighted on a glass bottle lying in the gutter, he handed the second pistol to Tasha. She needed less instruction than me, and my ears and cheeks burned with embarrassment.

"What do I get?" Malik asked.

Mitch looked at me and I shrugged. He stroked his salt and pepper beard, considering the request.

"Can you throw a softball?"

"Yeah," Malik said. "Better than anybody on my street."

"Can you throw it really far?"

"Damn straight I can."

"Here." Mitch handed him a grenade. "Now listen to me. This is really, really dangerous. You pull this little pin here and throw it as far and as fast as you can. Then get behind something. Can you do that?"

Malik puffed his chest up proudly. "Find me some dead people and I'll show you."

"Hopefully," I said, "you won't get that chance. If we can get to the marina without running into any more of those things, that would certainly be okay with me."

We started walking again, going slowly, all four of us watching for more of the undead. Behind us we heard the crackling roar of flames as the fires continued spreading, punctuated with the occasional gunshot or scream. The smoke wasn't as bad, though—maybe because the buildings in Fells Point were mostly two-stories high and the smoke could rise into the sky easier, instead of getting trapped in the city's concrete canyons.

"You must have owned a gun store, right?" I asked Mitch.

"Nope."

"A gun salesman, then?"

He shook his head. "No, but you're close. I was a salesman, but not guns. I'm just a firearms enthusiast. I always liked hunting and target shooting."

"So what did you sell?"

Mitch grinned. "Bibles."

"Get the fuck out of here. You look like a Hell's Angel."

"I'm serious, Lamar. I was a Bible salesman; sold to Christian bookstores and churches and private academies, mostly. I covered my tattoos up with sleeves when I needed to, and took out my earrings. Bibles were my business. Guns are just my hobby."

I frowned. I don't know what it's like for other gay people, but in my experience, the Christians I'd known had been less than understanding when it came to my sexuality. Of all the people to fall in with as we escaped the city, it looked like we'd joined forces with a possible fundamentalist who would judge me based on some old book supposedly written by the world's most omnipotent bigot.

Mitch must have been able to read the expression on my face. "Don't worry. I'm not a believer in the product. I'm just a spokesman."

I snorted. "You don't believe in God?"

He waved the pistol around. "Do you, after all this shit?"

"No. But you *sell Bibles*."

"Sold," he corrected. "Somehow, I don't think I'll have much business anymore. Yeah, I sold them. I sold lots of things—televisions, cars, computers, insurance, and vacuum cleaners. There was just more money in Bibles."

Laughing, we continued on our way.

Behind us, the fires spread, driving the dead forward.

CHAPTER FOUR

After fifteen tense minutes of sneaking through alleys and side streets, staying out of sight of the zombies when we could, we finally emerged at the waterfront. We smelled seawater. To our right was an old factory that had been converted into a nightclub. It took up the whole block. Past the nightclub was the old Sylvan Learning Center building and several luxury hotels that towered into the sky. In the distance was the Inner Harbor itself, along with the stadium and downtown Baltimore's skyline. Buildings were on fire there, too. On our left was the private yacht club. We could see all kinds of little boats and pleasure crafts tied up at the docks. Leftover yuppie toys. There was no movement inside the club. We heard a bell toll once; probably mounted to someone's mast. It was the loneliest sound in the world. A twelve-foot high wire mesh fence surrounded the yacht club. The gates were chained and padlocked. Curled lengths of razor wire stretched across the top of the fence. Security cameras were stationed every ten feet, along with floodlights. The cameras and lights were dead, of course, just like everything else.

"What is it with fucking padlocks tonight?" I fingered the lock and then turned back to Mitch. "Don't suppose you got a pair of bolt cutters in your backpack?"

"No. Wish I did. I take it this isn't the first time you've been stymied by a lock tonight?"

I shook my head. Above us, a pigeon took flight with an angry squawk. I envied the bird. Found myself wishing we all had wings so we could fly above the city. Mitch stared up at the bird, too, and then turned to the fence.

"We can't climb it either," he said. "The kids would cut the shit out of themselves on that razor wire."

"I can climb," Malik said. "I ain't afraid of no wire."

"I am," Mitch replied. "And you should be, too. It'll cut the hell out of you. Slice your arms and legs to ribbons."

Malik appeared doubtful.

I stared at the boats—so close and yet so far away. "Couldn't we just shoot the lock off?"

"Not one that big. That's high-end, American-made steel. A smaller lock, yeah, it would work. A round or two from the forty-five and we'd have no problem. But we don't have the firepower to even dent that fucking thing. We could use a grenade, but that would attract too much attention." He kicked the fence in frustration. "The owners really made sure no one could get in."

"Doesn't surprise me," I said. "There were a lot of homeless people in this area. Used to beg off the tourists and college kids, and the folks over in the office blocks. No doubt they'd have slept on the boats if they could have gotten in."

Instead of responding to me, Mitch raised his pistol and fired a shot past us. The empty shell clattered onto the ground. Tasha, Malik and I all jumped in surprise. I turned around. A zombie lay in the street, blood spreading in a pool from its head. It had been creeping up on us in silence.

"We'd better figure something else out," Mitch said. "And quickly. That shot is sure to bring more of them."

I pointed at a small, cinder block building next to the nightclub. A sign outside indicated that it was a machine shop. "Maybe we could try in there. Find something to cut this chain with?"

"Good idea."

"Come on, guys." I motioned for Tasha and Malik to follow us and they did.

We ran across the street to the machine shop. The only entrance from our side of the building was through a large, graffiti-covered garage door. I figured it would be locked, but when Mitch bent over and tugged at the handle, the door rose a few inches. Maybe the owners had not had time to lock it, or maybe someone else had already broken in. Unoiled pulleys screeched. A horrible slaughterhouse stench drifted out.

Tasha grabbed my arm. "That smells like . . ."

Grunting, Mitch yanked on the door. It rose higher.

"Mitch," I whispered. "Wait."

My warning was too late. Mitch let go of the handle and the door shot upward, disappearing into the ceiling. The interior was pitch-black, but something moved in the shadows. We saw feet. Then legs. Zombies lurched out of the darkness—two; then six; then a dozen. The machine shop was full of them. Guess they'd been trapped inside for a while, unable to open the door. Just standing there rotting, waiting for someone to free them. A few of them had exploded abdomens. Others suffered from swollen, leaking limbs. Mitch jumped backward and the dead spilled out into the street. There were more inside, stumbling toward the light.

Mitch stayed cool. He raised his pistol with both hands. Keeping his feet spread apart at shoulder-width, he opened fire, squeezing off six shots. Each one was true, and six zombies fell to the pavement. Tasha screamed as one of the corpses lunged for her, but then she raised her pistol and fired. The handgun jerked upward, and the bullet missed. She fired again, blowing a hole in the creature's shoulder. The zombie reached for her and I slammed it in the jaw with the butt of my rifle. It toppled backward, sprawling on the ground. Tasha stepped forward and shot it in the head at point-blank range. The corpse's hair caught on fire. Blood and brains and skull fragments splattered upward. Tasha gagged.

"Good girl," I said softly. "You didn't get any blood in your mouth or eyes, did you?"

"No," she answered. Then she leaned over and threw up on her shoes.

Malik, meanwhile, clutched his grenade in one hand and darted back and forth in front of us, dodging zombies and staying out of Mitch's line of fire. The boy seemed excited. Frantic, even, but he showed no fear. Despite everything, I smiled.

"There are more of them inside," Malik shouted. "Too many for you guys to shoot."

"Lamar!" Mitch called as he changed magazines. "Don't just stand there. Shoot the fuckers!"

I grabbed Tasha's arm. "Are you okay?"

"No," she said, shaking me off and raising her pistol again. "I'm wet, I'm cold, I smell like smoke, and I just threw up all over my shoes."

My reply was drowned out as she squeezed the trigger again. It didn't matter if she was fine or not—she was okay enough to start shooting again. That was good enough for me. Turning, I set the rifle's stock against my shoulder, closed one eye and sighted through the scope, picking a female zombie with a ragged bite wound on her cheek as my target. I pulled the trigger. The rifle's stock slammed against my body, making my arm go numb. Watching through the scope, I saw the creature's head explode in magnified color. Grinning, I picked another target and did the same. Then another and another. My shoulder ached, but it was a good pain. Despite the seriousness of the situation, I felt more confident than before. With the scope, I was a much better shot. Then, the fifth time I squeezed the trigger, nothing happened. Remembering that Mitch had said the rifle held four bullets, I cried out for more. At the same time, Tasha clicked empty, too.

"Mitch," I yelled. "We need more ammo."

More dead poured from the building and into the street, forcing us backward. A few of them moaned with hunger, but they were mostly silent. Some of them had decomposed so badly that there wasn't much left of them—just arms and legs and gaping, toothless mouths. Another large group of corpses appeared farther down the street. I recognized a few of them from the battle we'd witnessed earlier. Still more of the creatures exited the nightclub, drawn to the sounds of conflict.

A man ran out into the street. I don't know where he came from, but we immediately knew he was one of us—alive—just from the way he was screaming. An undead rat hung from his face, tiny claws digging into his flesh, yellow incisors ripping at his cheek. Infecting him with the disease. Poor bastard was dead already. He just didn't know it.

"Help me," he begged. His voice was slurred—reminded me of Alan. The rat dug deeper, shredding flesh. "Help me, please!"

Mitch fired one shot, killing both the rat and its victim. When Mitch looked up again, his eyes widened at the number of zombies slowly homing in on us.

"Mitch," I hollered again. "We need more bullets!"

"No time," he said. "There's too many of these things. Let's get the hell out of here."

Malik stepped forward. "Ya'll are forgetting something."

He pulled the pin the way Mitch had shown him and tossed the grenade overhand. It soared over the creatures' heads and through the open garage door, disappearing deep inside the building.

I froze. "Oh shit . . ."

"Move!"

Mitch shoved us forward, sprinting back toward the fence. Tasha and I started to follow him, but Malik refused to move. I don't even know if he heard us. His attention was focused on the machine shop. His eyes shone with anticipation, and he licked his lips. Just like any other boy his age, he wanted to see something blow up, and know that he'd done it. I'd been the same way as a kid, when we used to buy penny sticks and M-80s from the guy at the Korean grocer.

I grabbed his arm and pulled. "Come on, Malik."

"But I want to—"

"Now!"

We ran. Seconds later, the grenade went off behind us. There was a brief flash and a muffled *thump*. I heard debris rain down, clattering on the pavement. Something hot zipped by my ear. When we reached the fence, the four of us turned around. Smoke and flames poured out of the machine shop, but no more zombies exited the building. But that didn't matter. Malik may have destroyed the zombies inside the building, but there were plenty more. At least four dozen were in the street now, and coming for us in that slow, determined way.

"Shit," Mitch said, grabbing another grenade off his belt. "Somebody rang the dinner bell."

"What are you doing?" Tasha asked.

"What we should have done in the first place. I'm going to blow that lock off. You three get back."

We stepped back out into the street, but the zombies swarmed toward us. Their stench grew with every faltering step. More and more of them kept coming: humans, dogs, cats, rats, and something that had been skinned—something so pink and glistening that I couldn't tell what it used to be. Whatever its origin, now it was just one of them— an eating machine.

"Forget it," I said. "Another minute and they'll be on us."

"Bullshit," Mitch argued. "They're slow. I'm gonna blow the gate and then we'll be home free."

"Mitch. Look behind us. We can't get out of the grenade's range without running into them. *There's no time!*"

"Please, Mr. Bollinger," Tasha pleaded. "Let's just go."

Malik stuck close to Mitch. He watched the approaching hordes with wide eyes. "Yo, give me another grenade. I'll take care of them."

Mitch looked at the locked gate; then at the zombies, and then turned to me.

"Goddamn it. You're right. Let's go."

"Stick close to the fence," I told the kids. "Don't let them box you in. They may be slower than us, but if enough of them fill the street, we'll be trapped."

"Where are we going?" Tasha shouted as we ran.

"The harbor," I choked. "Maybe we can hole up inside the aquarium for a while."

I knew how stupid that sounded. How hopeless and futile. The National Aquarium was the centerpiece in Baltimore's busiest tourist area. No way was it free of zombies. But I didn't know what else to do, and Mitch wasn't offering up any alternatives.

"What about a paddleboat?" Tasha suggested. "We rode on one last year when we took a field trip to the Inner Harbor. They hold four people."

I nodded, gasping for breath. "Good idea."

The undead followed after us with single-minded determination. Their feet echoed on the street and sidewalks. Their stench went before them like a cloud.

"Give me your guns," Mitch said. He still had my useless shotgun. It was wedged between his backpack and his shoulder blades. I raced along beside him, watching as he ejected my magazine and loaded in a fresh one that he pulled from the backpack. I was impressed. He did it without pausing, found the bullets without having to search through the pack. Mitch tossed the rifle back to me and then did the same for Tasha.

My lungs burned, and my legs were starting to feel like rubber. It felt like I'd been running for hours, and in truth, I had. Since leaving the kids' apartment, we'd been on the run, chased by one zombie after another without a chance to catch our breath. I was amazed the kids were holding up as well as they were. Personally, I felt like dropping. Mitch was panting, too. He'd seemed like he was in good shape. I wondered just how heavy his back-pack was and what he had inside of it.

Tasha turned around and raised her pistol. I guess she'd wanted to take a shot, lessen the pursuit. But instead of doing that, she froze, staring at the onrushing corpses.

"There's so many. Look at them all."

She didn't sound afraid; just stunned.

I nudged her. "Keep running, Tasha. Don't look back anymore. Just run."

Three mangled corpses lunged out of the shrubs in front of the Sylvan Learning Center building. Mitch snapped off three shots, dropping them before they could cut us off.

Three down, I thought. *How far can we get before the rest of them catch us?*

I had four bullets left—one for each of us, if it came to that.

Mitch darted down an alley between a travel agency and a Whole Foods grocery store.

"This way," he called.

"No," I insisted. "We have to head for the harbor. That way takes us back into the ghetto."

"Hope you're right." He paused. "I'll lay down some cover fire."

Mitch changed course and followed us, now bringing up our rear. His heavy biker boots pounded the pavement, his footfalls punctuated with pistol fire as he chose targets over his shoulder. It was like pouring a glass of water into the ocean. The creatures continued their slow-moving charge.

They don't get tired, I thought. *We're staying ahead of them, but they're like the goddamned Energizer Bunny. They keep going and going and going. But we don't. Sooner or later, we ain't gonna be able to run any more. And then they'll catch up. . . .*

Malik and Tasha pulled ahead of me. I stared at the backs of their heads and shifted my grip on the rifle. Could I do it? If it came down to it, could I shoot them, shoot Mitch, and shoot myself? I didn't know. And then it didn't matter.

Because we found salvation.

We rounded the corner. The National Aquarium was on our left and the Hard Rock Cafe and Barnes and Noble store were behind us. In front of us, tied up along the waterfront, was the *USCGC Spratling*. I'd expected that, of course, but what I hadn't counted on was that the ship was apparently operational. Seemed that way from where we stood. The lights were on, the engines thrummed, and there were people onboard it—living people, not zombies. They moved too fast to be dead, and some of them carried guns. Several of them were casting off the big ropes that kept the ship tied to the cement pier. Heavy chains clanked as the anchor slowly rose out of the dark water. One man leaned over the railing and shouldered his rifle, bringing down a corpse on the steps of the Barnes and Noble.

"Holy crap," Mitch panted. "We're saved. . . ."

He'd pretty much summed it up.

We stood there sweating and gasping for breath, momentarily forgetting about the zombies and the inferno behind us. Tasha began to cry. I put my arm around her, and then realized that I was crying, too.

"They're casting off," Mitch shouted. "Come on!"

We stumbled after him, with the dead right on our heels and the flames consuming everything in their path. The stench of decay grew stronger, which meant the zombies were closing the gap.

Mitch waved his arms, pistol still clutched in one hand. "Hey! Over here. Hey, onboard!"

If they saw us, the crew gave no indication of it. Maybe from that distance, they thought we were just four more zombies. Two more of the big ropes were hauled onto the deck, and the anchor completed its ascent with a thunderous clang. The engines roared louder and the water at the rear of the boat began to churn.

"Motherfuckers!" Mitch hollered. "Wait for us! Over here. Wait!"

A steel gangplank connected the ship to the concrete walkway. My stomach sank as I watched them begin to raise it.

"They're leaving," Tasha whimpered. "They're leaving without us. Why don't they wait?"

I stopped running, raised my rifle into the air and fired off all four rounds.

That got the crew's attention.

Immediately, all hands on deck turned in our direction. We still weren't close enough to make out their expressions, but I can guess what they were. Because when I turned around to see how close our pursuers were, I screamed. Before Hamelin's Revenge, Baltimore had a population of just over

700,000 people. Now, with the exception of the people on the ship, it looked like all of them were dead—and coming for us. I don't know if it was the fires or just the sounds of us fleeing, but the zombies' numbers had grown during the chase. Every mobile corpse in the area seemed to now be converging on our location. Not just humans, either. There were animals in the mix, too. Lots of dogs and rats. Another creature stepped out of the throng. A tiger. A dead fucking tiger. Probably escaped from the Baltimore Zoo, and was now prowling around the city.

"Fuck me running," I whispered. Then I turned and chased after the others. "Mitch, I'm gonna need more ammo again."

"Yeah," Malik echoed. "And I'm gonna need another grenade."

Another human zombie emerged from behind a trash barrel, cutting us off from the ship. It wore the bloodied remains of a blue work shirt. Something moved beneath the fabric, almost as if he were pregnant. The creature took another step and the shirt parted. Where his stomach had once been, there was now a hollow cavity, empty—except for the dead rat squirming inside it. Mitch fired one shot into the abdomen, pulverizing the rat. Then he drilled another round into the zombie's head.

"Drop down, now!" The command came from the *Spratling*, the speaker's stern and impatient voice magnified through either a bullhorn or public address system. Whoever he was, the guy was in no mood to mess around. We did as he said and dropped to the ground, flat against the concrete pier. A volley of shots rang out as the ship's crew opened fire. The entire harbor echoed with gunshots. Bullets slammed into the cement and blew out the windows of the nearby buildings as the shooters found their range. Behind us, we heard wet meat slap against concrete as the dead fell.

When the volley ended, the voice boomed, "Get up and run. Quickly. We can't wait for you."

Each of us found our second wind, and we sped toward the ship. I spared one quick glance over my shoulder. The next wave of creatures was clambering over the ones on the ground, but it was slowing them down. Although the human zombies had trouble getting around their fallen comrades, the animals were quicker. The dead rats scampered over their bodies and swarmed after us. The tiger charged forward, faster than the others.

We reached the pier's edge and dashed up the gangplank. Steel banged beneath our feet. As we crossed the threshold, Mitch saluted a pudgy older man in a coast guard uniform. The man had a pistol holstered on his hip.

Mitch grinned. "Permission to come aboard, sir?"

"Permission granted. Now get the hell out of the way."

I recognized the man's voice as the one who'd given us the warning. I stuck out my hand. "Thanks for saving us. My name is—"

"Mister, I suggest you find a safe place for yourself and these kids and stay there. There'll be plenty of time for introductions later, if we survive this.

And if we don't, then I don't need to know your name anyway."

He brushed past me and began shouting orders.

Malik and Tasha glanced around the ship in amazement. People ran all over the decks, some of them armed and shooting at the zombies, others helping get the ship underway. I noticed that except for the man who'd spoken to us, none of them wore uniforms, but instead were dressed in civilian clothes. Many of them seemed unsure what to do, and kept shouting questions.

"This isn't a crew," I whispered to Mitch. "They're just like us—survivors."

"Maybe they're all reservists," he said.

"No. They're confused. And look at the hair lengths on some of them. That ain't military regulation."

"Well, get the kids to a safe spot. I'm gonna see if I can help. Find out what's going on and who exactly our saviors are."

"Be careful."

"You too."

I guided the kids over to a wall—what sailors call a bulkhead. There was another walkway above us and it provided a sort of roof over our heads. We leaned up against the steel bulkhead and watched as the people around us prepared to cast off. There were two ropes left and a swarm of undead rats climbed up them. Mitch and another man leaned out over the railing, shooting the rats off the ropes one by one. One of them reached the top and scurried over the railing. A third person stepped forward and pushed it back into the water with a mop. Before the rest of the creatures could reach the deck, the ropes were loosened and dropped into the black, dirty water. The rats fell with them.

And then we began to move.

"Full ahead," the man in the uniform bellowed. "Take us out, just like I showed you. I'm on my way up."

It was a really weird sensation. Felt like we were standing still and the land was moving. We cruised farther out into the bay, leaving the harbor and the city behind us. The zombies stood on the pier watching us go. Some of them stepped forward, plummeting over the side and sinking beneath the surface. The others simply stared, their faces expressionless—except for that look of constant hunger. I wondered about the ones that had fallen into the water. Zombies didn't need to breathe. Didn't require oxygen. They were dead. So what was to stop them from hunting along the bottom of the Chesapeake Bay the same way they hunted through the city's streets? Couldn't they just walk along the bottom, feeding off fish and crabs until they reached the ocean itself? And then what? Sharks versus zombies? The image was ridiculous, but what if? What if . . .

What if Hamelin's Revenge spread to the sea life?

"They can't reach us now," Malik shouted. "Nothing can get us out here!"

Tasha hugged him and he hugged her back. Both of them smiled. I turned back toward the land and watched the city burning. Stared at the orange-and-red skyline. By morning, there would be nothing left. Baltimore would be a smoldering pile of ashes. Port Discovery and the section of the city that housed popular bars like Ramshead and Howl at the Moon were obscured by smoke. The trade center and the Harbor Place shops belched flames. Yesterday, the skyline had been made up of tall buildings: offices, parking garages, banks, museums and apartment complexes. Now, it was composed of towering torches, each of them a blazing inferno. The city skyline looked like a row of Roman candles. And below them, growing smaller with every minute as the *Spratling* picked up speed, were the dead. The people onboard the ship cheered as we left the harbor. There was lots of hugging and clapping and fists in the air—a real celebration. And when the Domino Sugar factory exploded a few minutes later, we even had our own fireworks. Flaming debris rained down from the sky, splashing into the water.

"I'll tell you one thing, kids."

Tasha looked up at me. "What's that, Mr. Reed?"

"Lamar. Call me Lamar."

"Okay. What are you thinking, Lamar?"

"That this was the longest getaway I've ever seen."

"Doesn't matter," Tasha said. "We're safe now. Like Malik said, they can't get us out here."

The dead watched us leave. More of them tumbled into the water. Birds squawked above us. The sky was full of smoke, obscuring the moon and the stars. The ocean itself seemed lifeless. No fish leaping from the water or dolphins following the boat. Just the waves, and even those seemed small. The ship's engines throbbed as we picked up speed. The bay's surface was black, but the full moon lit a silvery path for us. The flames reflected off the waves. Then a cloud passed over the moon and the gradually lights vanished. Under the cover of darkness, we sailed out onto a dead sea.

CHAPTER FIVE

I don't remember much about that first night on-board the *Spratling*. We were all dehydrated, exhausted, and stressed from our ordeal, and after a while, things just kind of blurred together. When the ship was safely away from the city, and far enough out into the Chesapeake Bay that the fires were just a dim glow on the horizon, everyone relaxed a little more. But there was still a lot to do. Mitch and I had to find sleeping quarters for the kids—the older man in the coast guard uniform called them "berthing areas"—and a place for ourselves as well. We ended up together in a room with six racks—bunk beds—three on each side. The mattress on each rack lifted up to reveal a small, narrow storage space. Each of us also had a small footlocker to store things in. We didn't have many belongings. I pulled out my wallet and my keys and put them in-side a locker. It seemed weird. Might as well have tossed them over the side for all the good they'd do me now. The keys were all for a life I'd left behind, a life I'd never return to. And the wallet was empty— no pictures, no money. I'd never had much use for snapshots. And money? Well, I'd never had much of that, either. And now, I didn't need them. What good was money when there was nothing to buy? What good were photographs of friends and family when all of them were dead? I didn't have many people that I cared about, but those I did I could remember in my head. If I looked at their pictures now, I'd just see them as zombies.

Mitch pulled a small rifle cleaning kit out of his backpack and went to work on the guns, using long cotton swabs to get the debris and residue out of the barrels, and then oiling them down. He explained each step to the three of us as he went along, so that we'd be able to do it, too. When he was finished, he stowed our weapons beneath his mattress and slid one pistol under his pillow. He didn't unload his backpack; instead, he stuffed it between his rack and the bulkhead. Then he took off his boots and lay down. We all did the same. Each bed had a tiny feather pillow, one sheet, and a thin gray blanket that felt like it was made out of horse hair—very rough and scratchy. They smelled musty and mildewed.

"This pillow stinks," I complained.

"Mine does, too." Tasha wrinkled her nose. "Smells like a zombie."

"They should," Mitch said. "They've probably been sitting on this boat for the last twenty years."

I propped myself up on one elbow. "What do you mean?"

"This is a museum ship," he explained. "The *Spratling* is a piece of American history, so rather than sending it to the scrap yard to be cut up into razor blades, the maritime museum preserved it and turned it into a floating tourist trap, just like all the other ships at Inner Harbor."

"Okay," I said, "but what's that got to do with why these pillows smell funky?"

"Think about it, Lamar. This is a museum. A tourist attraction. How long have you lived in Baltimore?"

I shrugged. "All my life."

"And in all that time you never took a tour of the ships? Not even when the *Taney* was here?"

"No. I mean, I knew about them. Knew a little of their history. But I never toured one."

"Damn. Well, I guess I can't say anything. All the years I lived in Towson, I never came downtown and visited Edgar Allan Poe's grave."

That told me something about him. Towson was the suburbs, way out on the edge of the city. I wondered what had brought Mitch down into Fells Point.

"Were you a fan of Poe's?" I asked.

"Sure. Read the shit out of him when I was in the ninth grade. My grandfather gave me a big collection of all his stories. My favorite was always 'The Narrative of Arthur Gordon Pym.' " He chuckled. "It takes place on a boat, now that I think about it—a ship sailing to the South Pole."

"So if you dug the man's work, why not visit his grave?"

"Didn't feel like getting shot. That's a bad area of town, isn't it?"

I shrugged again. "When you actually live down here in the city, all of it's a bad area, Mitch. That's just how things are. You get used to it."

"Yeah," he said. "I guess I can see that."

But I knew he'd never really understand it. He couldn't. He had no frame of reference; only what he'd watched on episodes of *Homicide* or *The Wire*. Tasha and Malik knew it, too. They didn't say anything. Didn't have to. The expressions on their faces said enough. Mitch was from a different world.

"Well," Mitch continued, "the *Spratling* has always been a pretty popular attraction. Not just with tourists, either. They do weddings and stuff onboard, too. So there are a lot of people that have tromped through here over the years. When people come aboard this thing, they want to experience exactly what it was like for the men who served. They'd board via the gangplank, just like we did. Then, the tour guide would take them around above deck and show them everything. Answer all their questions. Then they'd go below, down the original stairways—except on a ship they're called ladders—just like the crew would. And just like any other museum, there'd be stuff all around on the tour: old photos, the captain's log, shit like that. And of course, they'd keep the racks made up just as they would have been when the *Spratling* was still on active duty."

"You mean—"

"That's right. Your pillow stinks because thousands of tourists have walked through here over the years and got their funk on it. Housewives from Illinois saying, 'Hey, George, lay down on the bed just like a sailor would and I'll take your picture with the kids.' Think about it."

My nose wrinkled. "That's gross."

Exhausted from our ordeal, Tasha and Malik fell asleep soon after. Mitch and I lay there in the darkness, not speaking, not wanting to disturb them. The kids had the top racks on each side. Mitch and I had taken the bottom bunks. The other two beds remained empty, and I figured there must be enough berthing areas that we wouldn't have to share our quarters with two more strangers. Tasha snored softly, and Malik cried out once, and then was still. I wondered what they were dreaming about. Were they reliving the day or creating zombies out of loved ones in their sleep? I'd done that in the past—pondered the dreams of various partners as they slept beside me, presuming to know and understand their dreams and nightmares since I didn't have any of my own.

Eventually, Mitch crawled out of his bunk and flashed a pack of cigarettes, indicating that he was going outside for a smoke. I nodded, and he tiptoed to the door and opened the hatch. Despite his efforts to be quiet, the steel door clanged when he shut it behind him. The kids didn't stir.

The ship rocked gently back and forth. You didn't really notice it unless you tried to walk around or if you were lying on your back. That was when the sensation became strongest. It was a constant, steady swaying. My stomach lurched each time it rolled. Sour bile burned the back of my throat. My eardrums throbbed. I wondered if it was just sea-sickness or some kind of delayed shock from the night's events. I was exhausted, but didn't think I'd be able to sleep. And then I did. Fell asleep thinking about Alan and the supermarket and the bitch I'd shot in the head.

If I dreamed, I don't remember it.

I never did.

The next day, I saw for myself what Mitch had meant. The *Spratling* really was nothing more than a floating museum. All of the ship's original interior features had been restored, but much of the equipment was inactivated. I wondered what worked and what didn't. Luckily for us, it was still able to sail. Throughout the ship were framed mementos of its years of service: uniforms, replicas of weaponry, old photographs, pages from the ship's logs, menus, and other things. Many of these were set up behind glass displays complete with recorded sound effects and narration, and red velvet ropes to keep the tourists from getting too close.

We found the showers easily enough, but they weren't working. A white guy named Murphy was standing at the sink, peering into a cracked mirror as he shaved with no soap, water, or shaving cream. He winced with each scrape of the dry razor. His big nose was lined with the red veins of alcoholism. After introducing himself, he gave us a bottle of spring water so that we could at least brush our teeth. Mitch had a tube of toothpaste in his backpack. Tasha, Malik, and I used our fingers for toothbrushes. We didn't have any clean clothes, either. My pants felt crusty and stiff. If I'd leaned them up in the corner, they could have stood by themselves. A middle-aged white woman in the next berthing compartment, who introduced herself as Joan Barnett, lent Tasha a T-shirt, but Malik and I were shit out of luck. Mitch had one spare pair of clean underwear in his backpack, but that was all. I noticed that after he'd washed up and dressed, he holstered a pistol at his side. The other weapons were still stashed in our berthing compartment.

Most of the people onboard the ship had gathered in the galley. A guy named Cleveland Hooper and an Asian dude named Tran were serving breakfast—little boxes of cereal, canned pineapple, granola bars, and Jell-O. No bacon or eggs or pancakes or fresh fruit; that would have all spoiled by now. There was coffee but no milk; just the little packets of sugar and powdered creamer. They had plenty of bottled water, though, and concentrated orange juice, which tasted better than anything I'd ever drunk in my life. I couldn't remember the last time I'd had orange juice.

"Good to see you, brother," Hooper said as he put some pineapple chunks on my tray.

"Why's that?" I asked.

" 'Cause we the only two niggas onboard this ship. Everyone else is white, except for Tran here, and he don't speak no English. It's just you and me, player. We can divide up the women. Show them some *good* dick."

"Yeah?" I feigned heterosexuality and tried to sound interested, but all I really wanted to do was eat. The sooner I could get out of this conversation, the better.

"Hell, yeah, man. It's pussy central, brother. There's some honeys onboard. Just hope half of 'em ain't dykes. Know what I'm saying?"

My expression hardened. "No, I don't know what you're saying. And I'm not your brother. Don't call me that again."

Hooper put down his ladle. "What's your problem, dog?"

"You. You're my fucking problem."

I walked away, rather than let it turn into a fight. Behind me, I heard him muttering that I was an Uncle Tom. I sat down next to Mitch. Tasha and Malik sat on the other side of us. My shoulders felt tense, my jaw tight. The ship continued to roll.

"All the people left alive, and that homophobic asshole had to be one of them. We should have left him behind."

Malik stopped chewing and looked up at me. "What'd that word he used mean? *Dyke.* What is that?"

"It's a bad word," I said. "People use it when talking about women who are gay, but it's not very nice."

"Gay?" Malik nibbled his granola bar. "So a dyke is like a girl fag?"

"Malik, don't say that."

"Say what?"

"Fag. Faggot. It's not a nice word. Do you know what it means?"

He shrugged. "Yeah. It's when two guys is kissing and hugging on each other."

"That's one way to describe it, I guess." I shook my head. "In any case, you shouldn't say it."

"Why not? All my friends say it."

I sighed. "Remember when we were at your apartment last night?"

Both of the kids' faces grew sullen for a moment. I immediately felt guilty for stirring up bad memories.

"Yeah," Malik said. "I remember."

"Do you remember when you said nigga and I told you not to? Told you what it really meant?"

"Uh-huh. I felt bad after it. You ain't ignorant, and that's what it meant. I ain't gonna say it no more."

"I bet your friends called you nigga, right? But they probably didn't know what it meant, either. But has anyone ever called you a *nigger*?"

"With an 'r' on the end?"

I nodded.

His expression hardened. "Once, a long time ago. There was this white dude on the light rail when we was coming back from the grocery store. Tasha and me and our momma was all in the same seat and he couldn't find one. Had to stand and hang on to the rail. He said under his breath, 'No seats except for the niggers.' I don't think he meant for us to hear it, but we did. It pissed me off. I wanted to kick his behind, but Momma and Tasha said not to."

"Yes, we did," Tasha agreed.

"How did it make you feel when he called you that, Malik?"

"Bad. It hurt my feelings. I . . . I wanted to cry, but I didn't."

"Well, the same thing happens when you say fag. It hurts gay people's feelings."

"Yeah, but there ain't no gay people around here, Lamar."

I turned to Mitch and winked. He frowned in confusion. Then I turned back to Malik.

"How do you know there aren't any gay people around here?"

He shrugged. "I don't for sure, I guess. There just ain't."

"Malik, I'm gay."

He stared at me, mouth open in astonishment, half-chewed granola bar stuck to his tongue.

"Y-you're gay, Lamar? You like other guys?"

I nodded, smiling. "I sure am, and yes, I do. And when you say fag or faggot, it hurts my feelings just as bad as when someone calls us niggers. Faggots were bundles of sticks that people used to start fires with. When you call someone a fag, you're really saying that you want to burn them alive, even if you aren't aware of it. So don't do that anymore, okay?"

"Okay. I'm sorry. I didn't know that's what it meant."

"That's all right, buddy. Now you do."

"Damn straight, and I won't say it no more."

The kids went back to eating. I picked up my coffee cup and noticed that Mitch was staring at me.

"What?" I asked. "Don't tell me you have a problem with me being gay."

He held up his hands in mock surrender and laughed. "Hey, man, like I told you before, I just sell the Bible. Doesn't mean I believe what it says—especially the bit about men lying down with other men. I couldn't care less. Too much hate in the world. Nothing wrong with a little more love."

"So then what are you smiling at?"

"You, man. I was just thinking that you're pretty good when it comes to kids. You must have been a teacher or a coach or something. Am I right?"

"Not even close," I told him. "I worked at the Ford plant, until it shut down."

I didn't tell him the rest, didn't mention the robbery at the dealership or the money I'd gotten away with—money that was gone as soon as I paid the bills.

"Yeah," he said. "I remember reading about that in the *Baltimore Sun*. Lot of guys lost their jobs."

"It was tough," I agreed, then switched topics. "So, Mitch—how did you end up in Fells Point? You were a long way from Towson, weren't you?"

When he answered, his voice was thick with emotion. "I'd rather not talk about it. You cool with that, Lamar?"

"Sure, man. That's okay."

"Thanks."

Sounded like we both had secrets that we didn't want to share. I figured that was okay. Maybe being on this ship, sailing away from our homes, was a chance to reinvent ourselves—find out who we really were. The past was behind us. The past was dead—or maybe undead.

We went back to eating. I studied Hooper and Tran, tried to figure out if they'd assigned themselves as the ship's unofficial cooks or if they'd just decided to help out for the morning because nobody else would. There were a dozen people in the room, not counting the two of them and us. None of the people eating breakfast looked military. Judging from their conversations, most of them had been in the same situation we were in the night before—fleeing the flames and the zombies, and then happening upon the boat. Apparently the guy we'd met in the coast guard uniform had been hiding out on the ship at the time. When he saw what was happening, he'd decided to pull out to sea. Same plan I'd had. Great minds think alike and all that shit.

Joan, the woman who loaned a T-shirt to Tasha, joined us at our table. While she was there she told us her story. She'd been trapped in a bathroom for the last two weeks. Two zombies had chased her inside, but when they finally lost interest and left, the door was jammed and she couldn't get it open. The creatures had battered the doorknob till it was useless. The bathroom had no windows and no other exits. She drank water from the toilet bowl and survived by eating toilet paper and cough drops. She'd considered eating a bottle of ibuprofen as well, but decided to save them instead in case she needed to commit suicide. Lucky for her, she didn't have to. Three other survivors found her while they were looting the house, and freed her from the bathroom. Two of them were killed later on—one by a zombie and the other by a sniper. The third had run away during the sniper attack and she didn't know what had happened to him. If he'd stayed in Baltimore, he was probably dead by now.

We didn't talk much after she told us her story. Too busy eating. Joan was ravenous, and so were the rest of us. I'd had nothing since the fruit cocktail at my place the evening before. Already, it seemed like long ago, but in reality, it had been less than twelve hours. Malik asked me if he could have seconds and I told him I didn't see any trouble with that. When he'd left the table, Mitch took a sip of coffee and shifted uncomfortably.

"What's up?"

"Just thinking." He set his coffee mug down. It slid about a quarter of an inch as the ship rolled. Mitch's complexion paled.

"Seasick?" I asked, trying not to let on that I felt the same.

"A little, maybe," he admitted. "But that's not what I'm thinking about. Just wondering how much food we have onboard. I mean, I can't imagine any of this is the ship's stores. Must have been brought on after Hamelin's Revenge."

"I'm just happy for anything," Joan said.

"Me, too," Mitch agreed. "So is there anyone in charge of inventory or rationing?"

Before Joan or I could answer, there was a sudden burst of electronic feedback, and the ship's public address speakers crackled.

"Good morning, ladies and gentlemen, this is your captain speaking. Chief Maxey is my name.

You can call me Wade or Chief or Captain—whatever you like. I'd like all hands to muster on the flight deck, located aft, at oh-nine-hundred hours. If you have companions still sleeping in their racks, please wake them and have them join us. I thought a brief orientation might be in order, since we all seem to have been thrown together like this. Thank you."

There was another burst of static and then the speaker cut off.

"What's he mean by muster?" Joan asked.

Tasha shrugged. "And where's the aft deck?"

"What time did he say," a man called out from across the room. "Oh nine what?"

"Folks, if I could . . ." An old man stood up. He was short, and his thin white hair was disheveled. He wore a dirty suit and thick trifocals that kept sliding down his face. He pushed them back up and said, "Hi."

"Hi," someone shouted back. Then more people joined in.

The old man blinked, grinning sheepishly, clearly embarrassed. The he cleared his throat and continued.

"My name is Professor Williams. Well, actually, my real name is Steven Williams, but my friends and family have always called me Professor, since I am one. Was one, I mean. Before retirement and before—well, before what happened to all of us. Anyway, just to clarify what our captain said, aft is the rear of the ship. I believe if you exit out of that hatch back there, what you call a door, and work your way along the catwalk on this side of the ship, you'll come to the aft deck. Can't miss it, really— big, black, flat area. The requested time was nine o'clock, which is about ten minutes from now."

"Thanks, Professor," another man called out. There was a sarcastic edge to the stranger's voice, and the old man blushed. He sat down quickly and stared at his tray.

I stood up and emptied my tray in the garbage can. Then I stopped at his table and tapped him on the shoulder. He was busy packing a pipe, and he jumped when I touched him, spilling tobacco onto the table. The professor looked up at me. He seemed very small.

"Sorry," I apologized. "Didn't mean to make you spill."

"Oh, it wasn't you. My hands aren't as steady as they used to be."

"Well, I just wanted to say thanks for that explanation, man. I was never in the military, so it all sounded like Greek to me until you spoke up."

He smiled, flashing a set of false teeth. "Thank you, Mister . . . ?"

"Reed. Lamar Reed." I stuck out my hand and he shook it.

"Professor Steven Williams. Just call me Professor. But of course, you already know that."

"Hey Lamar," Malik yelled across the galley. "Can I get thirds?"

"Save some for everyone else," I said.

"But I'm still hungry."

"Don't be a pig." Tasha elbowed him in the ribs.

I turned back to the old man while Mitch quieted the kids down.

"They're lovely children," the professor said. "It's actually nice to see children again. Nice to see anyone, really, I suppose. I've spent the last month sequestered in a storage room at the public library. I had plenty to read but no one to talk to. It was a very lonely existence."

"Yeah," I agreed. "That would be tough."

"They seem very well-behaved."

"They're pretty good kids."

"Are you their father?"

"No. No, I'm just watching out for them. We crossed paths last night. They helped me out so I took them under my wing."

He smiled again. "Ah, so you are the protector, then. The hero archetype."

"Excuse me?"

"The hero. Are you familiar with the works of Joseph Campbell?"

"Can't say that I am."

"Well, then you must read *The Hero With a Thousand Faces*. It's all about mythic archetypes. Understand those and you have the key to unraveling the riddle of life itself. Fascinating material, really. Most scholars prefer his other books: *The Mythic Image* and *The Masks of God*, but I was never one for popular convention. Come find me later and I'll explain all about it. You're on a quest, Mr. Reed, and you are fulfilling a role."

"I'll do that," I said. Meanwhile, I had no clue what he was babbling about, and no time to wonder. There were more important things to worry ourselves with. Such as Mitch's idea of food rationing and exactly what destination—if any— Chief Maxey had in mind for us.

I found out soon enough. When we were done eating breakfast, the four of us filed outside, joined once again by Joan. Slowly, the rest of the passengers assembled on the flight deck. The sun hung high in the sky, bright and hot. Sweat beaded on my forehead. I shielded my eyes against the glare and studied our companions. I counted eighteen of us total, and I learned that there was one more person, a guy named Tum, who was piloting the ship while the rest of us had our little powwow. Apparently Tum was a retired harbormaster, and Chief Maxey had made him second-in-command.

Mitch sniffed the air and breathed deep. "Smell that salt air? Man, I love that sea breeze."

I grinned. "Know what else?"

"What's that?"

"For the first time in over a month, I don't smell rotting corpses."

He shuddered. "You're right. I hadn't even noticed. As horrible as it sounds, I guess I'd gotten used to it."

Another hatch banged open and Chief Maxey walked out onto the deck. His stride had purpose, and the expression on his face was all business. He wore the same uniform he'd had on the night before, and a pair of black sunglasses. He had us gather around him in a circle and silently studied each of us for a moment.

"Good morning." He didn't raise his voice. Didn't shout over the waves or the engines or the screeching birds that followed the ship, hoping for a hand-out. He didn't have to. The man had presence. Even though he was an overweight, middle-aged white guy in a dirty coast guard uniform and hat, and even though he smelled like he hadn't showered in days and had salt and pepper stubble on his face, the man commanded our attention. There was no doubt that he was in charge.

"I'd like to welcome each of you onboard the United States Coast Guard Cutter *Spratling*. I'm sorry that it can't be under better circumstances. We weren't properly introduced last night, and I'm sorry for that, too. If I was gruff with you, just ignore it. We were in a tense situation and I didn't have time for pleasantries. My priority was getting us away from the harbor. Also, I want to thank those of you who volunteered to help last night. Your will-ingness to chip in probably saved all our lives."

The crowd murmured thanks and then Maxey cleared his throat and continued.

"We've got a lot to cover, so make yourselves comfortable. I figure that first we—"

A man in front of me put his hand up. He was short and balding, and his scalp was beet red from sunburn. I wondered where he'd spent his time hid-ing from the zombies. Maybe a rooftop somewhere?

"Yes?" The chief pointed at him. "You have a question?"

"Sure do, Chief. If this is gonna take a while, why

don't we move back inside to the galley where it's a lot more comfortable and cooler?"

Maxey's smile was tight. "I'm sorry, Mister . . . ?"

"Basil. My name's Basil Martin."

"Well, Mr. Martin, the reason we're not going inside is because I need your attention. If you're too comfortable, then chances are your attention will drift. You might even nod off. I wouldn't blame you, of course. I'm sure each and every one of you has been through quite an ordeal. But if you quit paying attention, then you might as well jump overboard right now. Because I intend to stay alive. And as captain of this vessel, it's my job to make sure you folks do the same. I can't protect you unless you help me, and to do that, I need to make you fully aware of our situation. So I need your full attention. Clear?"

Blushing, Basil nodded, and then slipped past us to the back row.

"Now," the chief continued, "as I was saying, I figured we'd start with the basics. I'll tell you who I am and a little bit about the *Spratling*. Give you an overview of our situation. Then I'd like to know a little bit about each of you—especially any skills or trades you might have, or military or law enforcement experience. Let's start with a head count."

He paused, surveying the crowd. Then he nodded at Hooper.

"Where's the other guy? Tran? Wasn't he helping you with breakfast?"

"He's in the galley doing dishes. Don't matter none. Motherfucker can't speak English anyway."

The chief frowned, but continued with his count. I got the impression that he felt the same way about Cleveland Hooper as I did.

"Okay," Chief Maxey said. "So, counting the absent Mr. Tran, and our second mate Tum, who is piloting the ship while we're down here, there are twenty of us onboard."

Joan timidly raised her hand.

"Yes?"

"I'm sorry," she apologized. "But last night, after we'd gotten underway, I thought I counted twenty-one."

"Yes ma'am, you did."

"But you said there were twenty, counting the two men who are absent. Aren't we missing somebody else?"

"There *were* twenty-one. One member of our party was bitten sometime before he came aboard. He tried to hide it from us, but we discovered it early this morning, before most of you were awake. We removed him from the ship immediately."

Joan stuttered. "W-who? Who did that?"

"Tum and I, and Mr. Runkle.

"Mr. Runkle?"

"Yes, he's standing there to your left."

We all looked at Mr. Runkle, a large man, probably in his late thirties, physically fit and hair cropped short. I made him for a cop right away. It was in the way he carried himself. Chief Maxey confirmed my suspicions a second later.

"Mr. Runkle is a Baltimore City police officer. We

asked for his help as soon as we were aware of the situation."

"Hi. Steven Runkle. Just call me Steve."

A few of us nodded at him, but our attention was on the chief. I noticed the professor step away from the group. Frowning, he lit his pipe and puffed on it. The smoke smelled like cherries. In the sudden silence, the roaring waves seemed to grow louder. Seagulls squawked above us, perched on one of the antennas.

"I'm sorry," a redheaded woman said, "but what exactly do you mean when you say you 'removed him from the ship'? Weren't we already out to sea by then?"

Chief Maxey nodded. "That's correct. And what is your name, Ma'am?"

"Never mind my name! You threw him over-board? *You killed him?*"

"No," Runkle said. "We didn't kill him. The bite did that. He was already dying. You've all seen how fast the sickness works. The times vary depending on the person, but the end result is the same. Unless you totally incinerate the body or destroy its brain, it comes back after death. He'd have been dead in a few more minutes, and then . . ."

He didn't finish. He didn't have to.

"If it's any consolation," the chief muttered, "we made sure that he didn't suffer."

I braced myself for the expected outcry, but surprisingly there was none. A few people looked unhappy about it, a few more looked queasy, but nobody objected out loud. This was a new world with new laws. You did what you had to in order to stay alive. All of them had survived this long—they new what it took. To remain human, you had to give up a little bit of your humanity. I'd done stuff I wasn't proud of—shooting Alan, for example. But something else was bothering me, too. If the guy had been bitten but was still alive when they threw him overboard, what happened after he drowned? Did he still turn into a zombie? Hamelin's Revenge was already in his bloodstream. Did he wake up on the bottom of the ocean and start attacking the fish? I wondered again if the disease could transfer to marine life.

"So there are twenty of us," Chief Maxey said once more. "That should give me a better idea of how long the ship's stores will last. Not that we really have any. But we'll get to that in a minute. First, let me tell you about myself and about your new home. If you didn't hear me before, my name is SMC Wade Maxey, United States Coast Guard, retired. Specifically, I was a signalman. SMC stands for Signalman Chief. I actually served onboard the *Spratling* in the eighties, and when she was finally decommissioned in 1987 and turned into a historic attraction, I was hired by the Maritime Museum to serve as a curator and tour guide. Believe me when I tell you that nobody knows this ship better than me. I'm a part of her and she's a part of me, and I'm glad they saved her from the scrap yard. Usually, when they're no longer seaworthy, those old ships are cut up and sold for scrap by their owners before they become completely worthless. Only a few of the really old ones have survived. Most of the time, that's because of dumb luck. And sometimes, they escape the scrap yards because of their historical significance, as was the case with the *Spratling*. The coast guard felt it was an important vessel."

As Maxey talked, I wondered how much of his speech was from his normal tour recital and how much was for our benefit. I had to give him credit. Despite his warning about putting us to sleep, he held everybody, including the kids, spellbound.

"The USCGC *Spratling*," he continued proudly, "is significant because she is one of the last of the fleet's high endurance cutters. With the exception of our polar ice breakers, these are—or were—the largest class of vessel in the coast guard's fleet. The *Spratling* is just under four hundred feet long, has a beam of forty-five feet, and weighs a little over three thousand, two hundred and fifty tons. She was a sister vessel to the USCGC *Taney*, the only ship that was left floating during the Japanese attack on Pearl Harbor. As you might remember, the *Taney* was also docked at the Inner Harbor until a year ago, when she was sent to the shipyards in Norfolk for major refitting and preservation work. The *Spratling* became the sole military vessel attraction after that. The *Spratling* was named for former Secretary of State William B. Spratling, who was a former college roommate of President Jeffrey Tyler. Please do not hold that against her."

The crowd laughed politely, and Joan applauded.

"She is one of the last three treasury-class coast guard cutters still left afloat. The *Spratling* and her various crews have served our country proudly for over sixty years. During that time, she's been through a lot. She saw combat in both World War Two and Vietnam, and was also called upon to assist civilians during Hurricane Agnes in the seventies and more recently, along the Gulf Coast after the devastation of Hurricane Katrina. During my service aboard the *Spratling*, she was a vital asset in drug interdiction, search and rescue operations, border enforcement, and fisheries protection. While these may sound mundane to you, they are anything but. They can be—and were— very dangerous operations. She also participated in the search for John F. Kennedy, Jr. after his plane crashed. She's seen a lot of history, and I'm proud to serve aboard her. I hope that you're all proud to be here, as well. Now, if you look forward, you'll notice that big dome on top of the pilot house. While we're doing that, everybody wave to Tum."

We did, and behind the pilot house window, Tum waved back. He looked embarrassed.

"That dome," Chief Maxey explained, "is a special storm-tracking antenna. In addition to its other duties, the *Spratling* also helped track storms for many years, until the use of more sophisticated storm-tracking satellites and radars became common. The antenna was reinstalled for posterity when she became a museum. Sadly, it is not active."

I stared at the dome. A seagull was perched on top of it, watching us with interest.

"Now," the chief continued, "for the nuts and bolts. We are powered by two diesel engines and two gas turbines with controllable-pitch screws. We have enough fuel onboard to last us about two weeks. Our top speed is just over twenty-one knots per hour. Not too shabby, folks. We also have two Boyle and Snyder boilers—a very dependable manufacturer. Luckily, the boilers are still operational and I know how to operate them, or else we'd still be sitting at the harbor. In truth, there's not much that I *don't* know how to do onboard this ship.

"As you can see, we are equipped with a helicopter flight deck. You're standing on it, in fact. We also have a retractable hangar, which is still operational even though we no longer have the facilities to support helicopter deployment. The weapons systems are still functional, too. After years of service and several tours of duty, the *Spratling* was totally refitted and relaunched in 1965. One of the showcase displays in the galley contains newspaper clippings of the event. She was modernized again through the fleet rehabilitation and modernization program in 1979. Actually, she was one of the first coast guard vessels to undergo that upgrade. During that time, the original caliber big guns were replaced with much more modern versions. They do a lot more damage."

Mitch and another man both whistled in appreciation.

"Finally," the chief said, "she's also equipped with both a seventy-six millimeter cannon and twenty millimeter Phalanx Close-in Weapons System, or CIWS, in military-speak. Sadly, though all of the weapons are still operational, we have no armament for them. After September Eleventh, the museum frowned upon keeping explosives onboard the ship, as I'm sure you can understand. I said before that the *Spratling* was a big ship."

Professor Williams exhaled a cloud of cherry-scented pipe smoke and interrupted him. "That's all very impressive, Chief. But what's the bad news?"

"I was getting to that. To be honest, there is all sorts of bad news. The *Spratling* hasn't actually been out to sea in years, and I'm afraid to push her. We're doing okay so far, but the truth is, we could break down at any time. If that happens—well, let's just say we'd have a difficult time getting replacement parts. But the engine and boilers are in good shape. As I said, we have two diesel engines and two gas turbines, and I estimate we have enough fuel for two weeks, if we conserve it. But if we run into trouble, we don't have the weaponry to fight a sea battle, and we'll have to run. The faster we go, the quicker we deplete our fuel supply."

"What kind of trouble could we run into?" Mitch asked. "It's not like the zombies can pilot a boat. They can't touch us out here."

"No, they can't. But it's not just the dead that we have to worry about. With no law and no coastal patrols, I'm afraid the seas may be just as dangerous as the cities were. There are bad people who will take advantage of situations like this. They thrive on it. I'm sure all of you encountered them on land over the last few weeks. We could encounter them out here, as well. We might run across pirates or raiders at any time. And if that happens, we'll have to run. We have no heavy armaments. We don't have the means to defend ourselves, unless they board us and it comes down to small arms fire. I'll come back to that in a minute, but first we need to talk about supplies."

He turned to Hooper. "Cleveland, when we're finished here, I'd like you and Tran to inventory our food supply. Obviously, we didn't leave port with a full complement. This was a museum, not an active duty vessel. What little food we do have is stuff I managed to sneak onboard during the first few days of martial law."

"You stayed here during the collapse?" Murphy, the man who'd lent us toothpaste earlier, asked.

Chief Maxey nodded. "I had nowhere else to go. I'm not married. I have no children. I don't even have a pet. My apartment was just where I went to sleep. All of my free time was spent here onboard the *Spratling*. This was where I wanted to be. And by then, it wasn't like we were open for tours. anyway. Early on, I raided the Whole Foods store, the aquarium's cafeteria, and some of the restaurants at the Inner Harbor. But I was alone and couldn't carry much at once. And to be honest, I wasn't counting on feeding twenty people. Food and water will be our number one concern. The good news is we have fishing tackle onboard—I used to fish in the evenings after we closed to the public. And one of the displays has deep sea rods that previous sailors used. So we can supplement our rations with fish. We can catch and collect rainwater, as well. The ship has a small supply of fresh water. It was used for the water fountains and the head—that's a restroom for you civilians who don't speak military. But the water tank isn't at full capacity. I've shut off the showers and sinks so that we can better conserve it. The toilets and urinals are shut down, too, but I kept the head in the engineering compartment operational. We'll show you how to get there later on. But that is the only functioning head and I ask that when you use it, you adhere to the following rule— if it's yellow, let it mellow. If it's brown, flush it down. That will help to save water."

We laughed at the joke, and then he continued.

"The showers in that head are also functional. Again, I ask that you adhere to a strict time limit. No longer than two minutes per person to shower. Once we fill our tanks, I'll lift that rule. My plan is to find a base or station where we can take on supplies. Maybe we'll try the naval base in Norfolk, or Hampton Roads or Portsmouth. There are a number of bases and commercial docks we could try. We could possibly even anchor off Ocean City or one of the other seaside resorts along the coast, and take a lifeboat in to shore."

"But the situation in those places will be just like it was in Baltimore," Mitch said. "Do we have enough people to fight our way into and out of a storage depot or fueling station if it's overrun with zombies?"

"I don't know," the chief admitted. "But I'm glad you brought that up, Mister . . . ?"

"Sorry. My name's Mitch Bollinger."

"Well, Mr. Bollinger, you raise something else that we need to talk about. Officer Runkle and I were talking earlier this morning about law and order on-board ship. Like it or not, this is our home for the foreseeable future. Now, I'm sure that all of you are very nice people, but the fact of the matter is, I don't know for sure. Neither do you. With the exception of Mr. Bollinger and his three friends," he nodded toward me and the kids, "all of you boarded the ship on your own last night. None of you were traveling together. It was simple luck—and the fires of course—that brought you all to the harbor at the same time. So even though we might all seem nice, we really don't know each other. Many of you brought weapons onboard: rifles, pistols, knives—I think I even saw some grenades, though I can't re-member who had them. Officer Runkle and I feel that our best course of action is to lock all of those items up in the ship's armory. It's for your safety as well as everyone else's onboard. We have children present, and it wouldn't do for one of those weapons to find its way into their hands."

"Hey," Malik said, "I know how to use a gun. Grenades, too. I blew up a whole bunch of zombies last night."

A few people in the crowd laughed, and that just

made Malik angry. Glaring at them, he leaned against the rail and scowled.

"I'm sure you're very brave, son," Chief Maxey said. "And if you used a grenade last night, then I think it's safe to assume it was your father or Mr. Bollinger who brought them onboard?"

I started to tell them that I wasn't his father, but before I could, Mitch spoke up.

"I did," Mitch said. "And I'm not too happy on the idea of giving them up, even temporarily. Like you said, we don't know each other that well. And what if we do get attacked by marauders? How would we defend ourselves if we got boarded?"

"If we were attacked," Runkle said, "we'd know in advance. The chief has a key to the armory. He could distribute the weapons."

Mitch didn't seem assured. "Is it the only key?"

"Yes." Chief Maxey nodded. "I have a complete set of keys for the ship. The duplicates are back at the Maritime Museum offices."

"So, no offense, Chief, but if something happened to you—if you fell overboard or lost the keys or something, and we were attacked, what would we do then? Cut through the armory door with a torch?"

"Well," the chief admitted, "that wouldn't be very feasible."

"No, it wouldn't," Mitch said. "And we don't have the means to copy your key. Look, I don't like the idea of all of us roaming around with guns either, but the simple fact is I'd feel more comfortable holding onto mine."

I noticed that Officer Runkle was eyeing Mitch's holster, as if he were contemplating making a grab for Mitch's pistol. I tried to stay inconspicuous, but slid between the two of them, just in case. Runkle glared at me, but stepped backward. I smiled. He didn't smile back. Must have been straight. Shame. He was a good-looking guy. I would have enjoyed getting to know him better, but the vibe he gave off was definitely a warning. Plus, I never dated cops. The world may have ended, but I still had my standards.

Runkle spoke up. "With all due respect to Mr. Bollinger, I don't think we can—"

"He's right," Chief Maxey interrupted. "I hate to admit it, but he's absolutely correct. What if something does happen to me or to the key? You'd all be shit out of luck if we really were attacked. But it doesn't sit well letting everyone carry them around, either."

"If I could make a suggestion,"—the professor stepped forward—"why don't we agree to confine our personal weapons to our private quarters, and not carry them at any time while onboard ship, unless of course it's during a general quarters situation."

"What is general quarters?" the redheaded woman asked.

"An emergency," the chief explained. "If we were attacked, you would hear an alarm bell over the PA system. That's called general quarters."

"I like the professor's idea," Mitch said. "How about the rest of you?"

"Sounds fair to me," Murphy agreed. "I've only got a little twenty-two pistol, but I'd hate to give it up. It's kept me alive so far."

"Ditto," said Basil.

Officer Runkle looked unhappy with the decision, but all of the others agreed.

The chief finally nodded with obvious reluctance. "Okay," he said. "I guess that's fair. A ship isn't exactly a democracy, but then again, you folks really didn't have much of a choice but to come aboard. If you want to store them in your compartments, that's fine. However, I think we need to agree that there will be penalties for anyone who breaks that rule."

Mitch frowned. "Such as?"

"The *Spratling* is also equipped with a stockade. It's down on the lower level, right between the ship's laundry and the boiler room."

"And who's in charge of that?"

Smiling, Officer Runkle stepped forward. "I am. Unless anyone has a problem with that? It makes sense. I was a cop, after all."

He was going to be trouble—an inferiority complex with a badge, desperate for others to recognize his authority. I knew his type well. Had seen it before and hated motherfuckers like him. I'd been exposed to them all my life.

The conversation continued. We discussed the ship's routine and schedule, and Chief Maxey gave everyone some tips about how to cope with things like seasickness, the proper way to stow our belongings, surviving inclement weather, what to do if someone fell over the side or if we had to abandon ship, and other factors of life at sea. He said that he and Tum would look over the maps and charts and try to pick a port with a minimal surrounding population. That way, there was less chance of it being overrun with the dead when we conducted our supply raid.

After answering more questions, the chief wanted to know more about each of us and any specific skills or abilities we might be able to offer. We already knew that Runkle was a cop, and he didn't offer any other personal details. Basil Martin was a Web designer. He refused to tell us anything about his personal life, other than he'd been in the National Guard before going to college. Professor Williams told us that his fields of specialty were English literature and mythology. He was a widower—his wife had passed two years before, and his children were grown. His son lived in Thailand and his daughter in California. He hadn't heard from either since the nation's communication grid went down. Our new friend Joan Barnett went next. She was a dental hygienist. Turned out her spouse had passed away, too—dying from lung cancer in a room at Greater Baltimore Medical Center as the dead first began to stalk the streets. He'd died alone. She'd been unable to get to him because of martial law. The hospital had confirmed his passing. She never made arrangements because soon after, arrangements no longer mattered. Murphy's first name was Ollie. He was a boiler operator. Chief Maxey got excited by that news. He'd spent the last few weeks holed up in a bar on Pratt Street, which was no surprise, judging by the telltale alcoholic veins in his nose. Cleveland Hooper had been a cook at a diner. Twice divorced, he'd been hiding out from deputies looking to serve a warrant for nonpayment of child support, and hadn't even been aware of the zombies at first. Hooper had also served a four-year stint in the navy. Nobody knew anything about Tran, and even if he hadn't been washing dishes, he wouldn't have been able to tell us about himself. Mitch told everyone he was a Bible salesman and firearms enthusiast. Then it was my turn. I introduced myself and then the kids.

After that, we met the other passengers. The red-headed woman was Carol Beck. She was a quality control manager at an injection molding plant and had been trying to flee the city. Stuck in a traffic jam on Interstate Eighty-three, she'd gotten out of her car to get a better cell phone signal. As she stood there, zombies had swarmed the on-ramp, forcing drivers to flee. She'd hid inside a factory. Next was Cliff Shatner, a young kid in his early twenties. He'd been a student at Towson University, majoring in journalism, and was partying in Fells Point when everything fell apart. He'd been trapped downtown, hiding inside the basement of the Soundgarden music shop. Stephanie Pollack didn't look so well when she introduced herself. Her skin was pale and dripping sweat. Her pupils were dilated. At first I thought it was the heat, but we soon learned that she was diabetic and had run out of insulin. The fires had forced her to flee quickly, and her supply of insulin had burned up with her apartment. We were concerned for her, but there wasn't much we could do. It was a hopeless, demoralizing feeling. It seemed so unfair—to survive the fires and the zombies, only to have your own body turn against you. And yet she was a trooper. She'd stood on the flight deck the whole time, baking in the heat, listening patiently as we talked and debated, and not once had she complained. Basil and Hooper, on the other hand, had done nothing but bitch since we'd got there. The chief told Stephanie to go lie down, promised he'd do anything he could to make her more comfortable, and had Joan escort her back to her compartment. He promised that if we could get to a port quickly, the first thing he'd look for was insulin. I thought the chances of that were pretty slim, but I kept that to myself.

We had two teenagers in the group: a boy and a girl. The boy's name was Nick Kontis. His father had owned a Greek restaurant just off President Street. He'd watched his entire family get slaughtered by those things. He'd survived by hiding inside the restaurant's walk-in freezer. The night of the fires, he'd crept out, looking for water. He'd stumbled, literally, over a zombie a few minutes later. Legless, it had been crawling around in the dining area, munching on rancid, spoiled meat. The girl was Alicia Crawford. She was shy and soft-spoken, and we didn't learn much about her other than her name. She stared at the deck the whole time and kept cleaning her eyeglasses on her shirt. The last two passengers were Chuck Mizello and Tony Giovanni. Chuck was a forklift operator with four years of army experience, including a tour in Iraq. He'd taken shelter in a warehouse and survived on the contents of the vending machines. Tony was a tow truck driver. He barricaded himself in a hotel room across from the Inner Harbor. Like Mitch, he was a firearms enthusiast. I noticed that he scored points with my friend when he complimented the pistol at Mitch's side.

Once the introductions were finished, each of us were assigned duties. According to Chief Maxey, the biggest danger at sea was boredom, so each of us needed a task to perform. Keep our minds occupied. Hooper and Tran were in charge of the galley, and Nick volunteered to help them since he had a restaurant background. Runkle was going to help Chief Maxey and Tum on the bridge. Murphy was the obvious choice for engineering, since he'd been a boiler operator. Chuck, Tony, and the college kid, Cliff, volunteered to help him. Cliff didn't look happy when Murphy warned him it would be hot, dirty work, but he didn't change his mind either. Guess he wanted to fit in, make a good impression. Mitch, Basil, Professor Williams, and I pulled fishing duty. Carol suggested that someone should work with the kids, a shipboard school of sorts. Chief Maxey was hesitant about the idea, but she finally convinced him it was important. He didn't look thrilled. Neither did Tasha and Malik. I guess the one nice thing about the end of civilization was that they didn't have to go to school anymore. Carol would teach them in the mornings, assisted by Alicia. In the afternoons, they'd perform other duties, as would the kids. Joan was temporarily assigned to care for Stephanie.

After we had our assignments, the chief excused us all, promising to give us an update as soon as he and Tum decided on a safe destination. The group separated, some of them moving off together, others leaving by themselves. Chuck had a tennis ball (I don't know where the hell he'd found it) and gave it to Malik and Tasha to toss around. I warned them not to get too close to the edge of the flight deck, and then let them run off. Felt good to see them having fun, if only for a little while. They tossed the ball back and forth, bouncing it off the flight deck's black, sun-baked surface. I pulled away from the others and stood by myself against the railing. Gazed out at the sea. I'd never been on the open water like this, and despite the seasickness and the memories of what had led us to the *Spratling* in the first place, I was enjoying it. When I looked out at the water, there was nothing in all four directions. No buildings. No mountaintops. No land at all. There was just an endless, flat sheet of gray and white, broken only by the rolling waves. It was easy enough for me to imagine that there was nothing else beyond the horizons—no cities or countries or people. No dead. As I watched, something—I think it was a dolphin—jumped from the water, spun through the air, and then splashed back into the ocean, disappearing beneath the surface. I smiled. Three more appeared and did the same thing. It was one of the coolest things I'd ever seen.

"Dolphins," a voice beside me said, confirming what they were.

I turned. It was Tony Giovanni, the tow truck

driver. He'd moved next to me along the railing while I was watching the waves, but I'd been distracted and hadn't noticed.

"I wasn't sure what the hell they were," I admitted. "Sort of look like sharks."

"Sometimes it's hard to tell," he said. "Especially when all you can see is their dorsal fin sticking out of the water."

"You been around them much?"

Shrugging, he patted his pockets till he found a half pack of cigarettes. He put one in his mouth and then offered the pack to me.

"No thanks. I don't smoke."

"I don't guess I'll be smoking much longer, either. It's gonna be ugly when I run out. Not as ugly as if that Murphy guy runs out of booze, but still . . ."

He thumbed his lighter, shielding the flame with his hand so that the wind wouldn't blow it out, and then continued.

"My wife and I used to take trips—you know, those whale watching or 'Swim with the Dolphins' things? She loved nature. So do I. Paid sixty bucks a month for cable TV and the only thing either of us watched was the Discovery Channel. So yeah, I've seen them up close. Usually, they just follow the boat, looking for handouts. Same way the birds do."

He pointed upward. A flock of seagulls circled overhead, squawking at one another.

"They'll follow us for days, just waiting on any scraps we throw them. They're trained, almost. Fuckers love to eat. If the birds ever caught Hamelin's Revenge, we'd all be fucked."

I nodded, and then turned my attention back to the sea. The dolphins were gone.

He exhaled smoke. "You ever been on a boat?"

"No," I said. "First time. Still a little seasick."

"Next time you go down to the galley, see if that Hooper guy has any crackers. Saltines work best. Eat a bunch of those and try not to drink much, and you'll be okay. They soak up all the liquid in your stomach."

"Thanks. I'll try that."

The tennis ball rolled over to us, bounced off Tony's shoe and almost went over the side. Tony bent down, picked it up, and tossed it back to Tasha.

"Thanks," she shouted.

He smiled, watching them play.

"Cute kids," he said. "Got to tell you, until we introduced ourselves, I would have sworn you were their daddy."

I laughed. "Not me. It's funny, though. You're not the first person that said that. The professor thought the same thing, and the chief brought it up just a few minutes ago."

"You must look alike."

I wasn't sure what to make of the comment. Was it innocent or was he implying that all black people looked the same? He must have known what I was thinking.

"Hey, man, don't get the wrong idea. That's not what I meant."

"Sorry," I apologized. "Old habits die hard, I guess."

"Yeah, I hear you. No sweat. Just didn't want you to get the wrong idea. All I meant is that you guys looked like family."

"I don't have much of a family. Just a brother, and he's long gone."

"Well," he said, "you do now. Those kids dote on you. Can see it in their eyes, the way they look at you when you talk. My kids used to . . ."

Tony couldn't finish. His Adam's apple bobbed up and down, but no sound came out. Tears welled up in his eyes.

"Sorry," he said after a moment. "Every time I think I can talk about them . . . Shit. Guess I should get down to the boiler room and let Murphy show me what to do. If I can even find it, that is. This ship's like a damn maze. Nice talking to you, Lamar."

"You too, Tony."

I watched him go, shoulders slumped, head to the deck. He didn't look at anyone as he passed them, especially the kids. I felt sorry for the guy. Sorry for us all. We'd survived. We'd beat the odds. We were still alive. But was it worth it?

I watched Tasha and Malik as they played and decided that it was; if only for them.

I closed my eyes and leaned back against the rail, letting the ocean breeze cool my skin. I listened to the roar of the waves. Listened to the screeching birds. Listened to the kid's laughter. It all blended together.

With my eyes shut, it sounded like screams.

* * *

Stephanie died in the middle of the night. Weak and dehydrated, she'd slipped into a diabetic coma shortly before sundown. Wasn't much any of us could do for her. Joan kept her warm and wiped her forehead with a cool washcloth. Held her hand and talked to her. Watched her go and made sure she didn't do it alone. Sometimes, that's the best you can hope for in this world.

Stephanie Pollack had lived in an apartment in Baltimore and was diabetic. That was all any of us knew about her. Joan said that before she'd slipped into the coma, Stephanie had whispered some names. But those names had died with her. No tears were shed. We hadn't known her long enough. It was sad. Demoralizing and depressing. We were still human after all, and another human's passing, even a stranger's, was cause for reflection. But what was there to reflect on, except our own fucked-up situation? How to remember her? Stephanie had no purse, no identification, nothing that would give us a deeper glimpse into her life and who she'd been. Her locker was empty, as was the storage space beneath her rack. Was she married? There was no ring on her finger, so probably not. Divorced, then? Widowed? Gay? Did she have children, and if so, were they still alive somewhere out there, or had they joined the ranks of the others? Brothers or sisters? She must have had parents, at least. Were they alive or dead? We would never know.

Again, I found myself wondering what the fucking point was. Why continue fighting, continue struggling to survive? In the end, you died with a bunch of strangers who couldn't even eulogize you properly because they didn't know shit about you. When you died, you were supposed to live on in the memories of others. That's what I'd always been told. Didn't matter what you believed, which religion you subscribed to, what god you worshipped. The simple fact was that none of us knew what lies beyond. Immortality and eternal life? The only sure shot at that was the memories of those you left behind—your friends and family. But if you had no one, if you were alone in this world, who would remember you when you were gone? If memories were your only shot at eternal life, and there was no one to remember you, what then? If there was such a thing as a soul, what happened to it? Maybe death was all there really was. Maybe there was no such thing as eternal life. But now, even death wasn't the end, thanks to Hamelin's Revenge. Did the zombies still have their souls or were they just hollow shells? Could the person who'd once inhabited their bodies still be alive inside, conscious even after death, and if so, did they scream?

Why not just go outside, climb over the rail, let go, and fall into the ocean? After all we'd seen and done in life, and all that had happened to us, both good and bad, all the triumphs and tragedies and everything associated with them, what was the fucking point? Was it all just to die among a bunch of strangers who barely knew your name? Or to end up inside a zombie's stomach or worse yet, to walk around like one of them, putrefying on the go?

Word of Stephanie's death spread quickly through

the ship. Murphy woke Mitch and me to tell us. He'd stood in the passageway, leaning through our hatch, silhouetted in red light. His breath smelled like cough syrup and his voice was slurred. If he was down to drinking cough syrup already, what would he do when he ran out of that? I wondered if there was any rubbing alcohol onboard.

After Murphy left, Mitch and I didn't talk. The kids hadn't woken up and we didn't want to disturb them. Soon I heard Mitch softly snoring again. It amazed me, how quickly he'd fallen asleep. I lay there in the darkness, hands behind my head, and stared at the ceiling. My rack swayed with the ship, but I wasn't queasy. Tony's suggestion had worked. During dinner, I'd wolfed down a bunch of saltine crackers. They'd done the trick. No more seasickness.

Heartsickness—there was no cure.

I didn't fall back asleep.

The others slept like the dead. I wondered if they dreamed and wished that I could, if only to escape this world for a little while. Even a nightmare would have been welcome. It certainly couldn't have been as bad as reality.

The next morning, we buried Stephanie at sea. She'd died of natural causes, so she didn't come back. No worries there. She did what dead people were supposed to do. Old school. Just slipped beneath the waves and passed from this world.

She was the lucky one.

Before we committed her body to the sea, Chief Maxey asked if anybody would like to say anything. Perhaps a prayer or a Bible verse. Everyone looked at Mitch. Embarrassed, he explained that he only sold Bibles and didn't actually know much about them. Cliff eventually volunteered.

After it was all over and she'd sunk beneath the surface, Cliff approached Mitch and I. He touched Mitch's shoulder.

"I don't mean to be rude, Mr. Bollinger, but you should get in touch with God again. It's obvious you believed at one point in your life."

Mitch brushed him away. "How's it *obvious*?"

"Well, you're probably a very good salesman, and a good salesman always knows his product. Try reconnecting with the Lord. It might bring you comfort, with all that's happened. It does for me. He can be a mighty pillar of strength."

Mitch exhaled. "Let me get this straight. With all that's happened you still believe in God?"

"Of course. Now more than ever."

"Well good for you, kid. Now fuck off."

Cliff flinched as if Mitch had slapped him. "I'm sorry?"

"You should be. Congratulations."

"Look, exactly what is your problem?"

Mitch's smile held no humor. "You've still got your faith. Meanwhile, I got nothing. So get the fuck away from me before I throw you over the rail and we find out once and for all if the Lord is watching over you."

Cliff stomped away in a huff. When he was gone, I nudged Mitch.

"You think you were a little too hard on that kid?"

Mitch shrugged. "Hell with him. Look, I don't

care if he's a Christian. Seriously, I'm cool with everyone. Good for him. There's nothing wrong with that. But he's got no right to try proselytizing me. I hate that shit. Just because he's still a believer, doesn't mean I've got to be one, too."

"Maybe it's his faith that keeps him going."

"I'm sure it is. And you know what else? I'll admit it—I'm jealous as fuck."

I nodded in understanding. "Yeah, I know what you mean. What keeps you going, Mitch?"

He stared out at the water, smoking his cigarette down to the filter. It was a long time before he spoke, and when he did, I had to strain to hear him over the seagulls and the waves.

"I don't know, Lamar. I don't know what keeps me going. And sometimes, I wish that whatever it is would just stop."

I nodded again. Once more, I empathized all too well.

CHAPTER SIX

"Norfolk is definitely out," Chief Maxey muttered around the stub of his cigar. "You have any idea how many personnel were assigned to that base?"

"No," Mitch said. "How many?"

"Well, I'm not sure exactly. But it was a lot. Thousands. The naval base is the size of a small city."

"Damn straight it is," said Hooper. "Hell, the base *is* Norfolk. Everything else in the city is just there to support the base. It'll be crawling with zombies."

We were standing inside a shack on the ship's signal bridge, planning our excursion to the mainland; me, Mitch, Chief Maxey, Tum, Officer Runkle, Basil, Tony, and Hooper. Chief Maxey had given Chuck a crash course on how to pilot the ship and put him in charge of the pilothouse while we met.

"Just steer it straight," he'd said. "There shouldn't be any other vessels out here for you to hit. And if an alarm goes off, call us."

The chief and Tum were there because they

knew the coastline and could read the maps and charts. The others were there because they had military or law enforcement experience and knew guns. I was there only because Mitch had insisted I come with him. I was cool with that. Fish weren't biting anyway, and Tasha and Malik were busy with their studies—something they'd warmed up to after a few days. I think they liked having something to do, a challenge to occupy their minds, even if it was just school. Carol had found some paper and pens and had created study guides, since we had no books onboard. The kids took to her right away, and Tasha seemed especially fond of Alicia—and Alicia of Tasha as well. The night before, Joan had commented that the only time the teen seemed to open up was when she was with the kids. After three days at sea, things had begun to gel for all of us. One dysfunctional little family.

Runkle sipped water from a plastic bottle. "Before everything went to shit, FEMA had set up an aid station in South Point. I remember hearing about it on the radio. It was supposed to provide food, water, and medical assistance. South Point is pretty rural, so maybe it didn't get overrun. Could we try for that?"

Chief Maxey shook his head. "South Point is in the Chingoteague Bay. I'd have to circle all the way around Assateague Island. That puts us close to Ocean City, which would have been packed with tourists this time of year. Too many potential zombies, especially given the way they roam. Plus, if the wild horses on Assateague got the disease, we'd have zombies on both sides. The horses were used to crossing the bay—chances are they'd do the same after death. I'd rather not risk it."

"But horses are immune to Hamelin's Revenge," I said. "I saw it on the news, before we lost power. Sheep caught it, but not pigs. Horses were immune, but cattle were not."

"Perhaps they were," the chief said. "But the disease must have adapted later on because I saw a dead horse running around downtown. It was one of those police horses and it was chasing a live dog."

"Are you sure it was a zombie?"

"Its broken ribs were sticking out of its flesh and its tail had been torn out by the roots."

"Something else to consider," Tum said. "Wherever we dock, even if there are relatively few zombies, we might want to wear gloves and some type of face mask to breathe through. Maybe we can make something up with what we have on hand. One of the museum displays has cheesecloth. We could make a mask out of that."

Basil, who had only been paying half-attention, sat up. "Why would we need to do that?"

"Disease," Tum answered. "Think about it. Even if the army or somebody had killed all the zombies, they wouldn't have been able to burn all the bodies. There's simply too many of them. The fire pits worked early on, but once the situation got out of control, those failed, too. So now you've got thousands, maybe millions, of dead bodies lying around—or walking around. Corpses carry disease. Every zombie is nothing more than a walking biohazard."

"Good point," I said. "But if that were the case, then why aren't any of us sick yet? We've survived this long. Wouldn't we have caught whatever disease they're carrying by now?"

"Not necessarily. I don't know for sure because I wasn't on deck when you guys shared your stories. But I'll bet almost all of us survived by staying holed up somewhere and avoiding the zombies whenever possible. The fires were what forced us out of hiding, and we had limited contact with the dead before boarding the *Spratling*."

Basil still wasn't convinced. "You guys remember Hurricane Katrina, right? In New Orleans, people waded through the floodwaters, and there were bodies floating in the streets. There wasn't a massive outbreak after that."

"Lot's of people got sick in New Orleans," Tum said. "But the difference was that there were aid stations and medical help on hand soon after."

Tony lit a cigarette. "Maybe we're immune to Hamelin's Revenge. Maybe we've already been exposed and it just didn't take."

"Maybe," Hooper said, "your ass should go first when we land. Let one of them fuckers take a bite out of you and then we'll see if you're immune."

"No thanks."

"I think we should keep an eye on each other," Mitch suggested. "Make sure nobody is getting sick."

"I agree," Runkle said. "And if they do show signs of disease, we should quarantine them."

None of us argued with him. Runkle may have been a prick, but he was right. No way could we risk everyone onboard the ship coming down with hepatitis or the bubonic fucking plague.

Chief Maxey tapped the laminated map. "That's all the more reason why we need to find a place to resupply ourselves soon. In addition to food and water, we need medicine and first aid supplies. If we'd had insulin, maybe that poor woman would still be alive."

"No sense beating yourself up over that, Chief," Tony said. "It was just bad fucking luck on Stephanie's part. There wasn't anything we could have done."

"I suppose not," the chief admitted, "but I'll be damned if we're going to lose anyone else because of something like that. We've got one little bottle of aspirin and Murphy's cough syrup supply—and he's drinking through that like it's a bottle of Knob Creek. If somebody does get sick or hurt, we're going to need a lot more than those."

"Okay," Mitch said. "So Norfolk and Portsmouth are out. Same with Virginia Beach, Hampton Roads, Little Creek, and Ocean City."

"Virginia Beach is a possibility," Chief Maxey corrected. "Down from the tourist area, there's a stretch of national forest. There's a small station there we could try."

"What's up north?" Runkle asked.

"The Isle of Wight." Chief Maxey traced the coastline with his finger. "And up in Delaware, there's Rehobeth Beach, Bethany Beach, and South Bethany—all of them are going to be packed with zombies."

Tum said, "What about the lighthouse at Fenwick

Island? That should be fairly deserted. I think the lighthouse itself is on automatic, so there'd only be a maintenance man, if anyone."

"That's a long way to go," Chief Maxey sighed. "We're closer to North Carolina and points south. I think we should consider one of those or the station near Virginia Beach—keep Fenwick as a last resort. Maybe we could try one of the islands off the Carolina coast."

"I don't know, Chief," Tum said. "Those islands are all inhabited, and they had regular contact with the mainland, which increases the chances of infection. I think Fenwick Island is our best shot."

While they were talking, I noticed a little red dot on the map, positioned farther out in the Atlantic Ocean. It looked like it had been drawn with a dry-erase marker.

"What's this?" I asked, pointing to it.

"Oil rig," Chief Maxey grunted.

I was surprised. "There are oil rigs off the East Coast?"

"Sure," Tum said. "There wasn't a lot of drilling going on off Florida because of political stuff, but there are lots of operations elsewhere in the Atlantic. Most of them are way off shore. The one you're pointing at is a jack-up. It's mobile, which is why we drew it on the map in erasable marker. That was its last known location."

"What's a jack-up?" Basil asked.

Hooper grinned. "It's when I run up to Lamar and jack his ass up."

"You're welcome to try," I said, keeping my voice

low and steady. Things had not calmed between us since our initial introduction. He thought I was an Uncle Tom and had since learned that I was gay—two strikes against me. In turn, I thought he was a lazy, ignorant, punk-ass motherfucker.

"I'd like to see him try it, too," Mitch said.

"Ya'll are tripping," Hooper muttered, backing down. "I'm just fucking around."

"A jack-up is a shallow water rig," Tum explained, ignoring Hooper. "Basically, it's just a big barge with a drilling rig and living quarters attached to it. The oil companies float it wherever they need to drill and then there are literally jacks that extend down, raising the platform and stabilizing it on the surface. It's a little smaller than a full-blown drill ship. They've got motion compensating motors and all that shit. But anyway, yeah, they're out there. Not just confined to the Gulf. The oil companies are forever drilling test wells just to see what's down there beneath the ocean floor."

Mitch asked aloud what I had been thinking. "So why couldn't we just go to that rig?"

"There would still be zombies," Chief Maxey said. "Even a small platform would have a crew. The company man, the tool pusher, driller, derrick man, floor hands, cooks, and roustabouts. Unless they evacuated the crew before everything on the mainland collapsed, they'd still be there."

"Yeah," Mitch said slowly, "but they wouldn't necessarily be zombies. If they had no connection to the mainland, then there's no way they'd have caught Hamelin's Revenge. You've got to be exposed to it—bitten or come into contact with infected blood—to turn into one of them, right? Only thing that could get them would be the birds and the fish, and neither of them are carriers. Those crews could still be alive. They could help us."

"He's got a point, Chief," Tum said. "In the Gulf, it's pretty common for shrimp boats and the like to pull up and trade their catch for diesel. Stands to reason the same would go for Atlantic platforms. We could trade for supplies. They'd probably welcome us, especially now."

"But we don't have anything to trade."

"We've got transport," Tum said. "I doubt the oil company is sending a helicopter to pull them off the jack-up anytime soon. But we can. We're their ticket off the rig."

"Okay," the chief argued, "but what if they don't want to leave? What if they'd rather stay? Then what? What else do we have to trade?"

"The women," Runkle suggested. There was no hint of humor in his voice. The guy was serious.

We stared at him in disbelief.

"Fuck that," Hooper said. "The women are ours. We ain't trading them. Need them for breeding purposes."

"What the fuck is wrong with you two?" Mitch slammed his palm down on the map. "Do you hear yourselves? You're talking about fucking slavery— like the women onboard are something to be used for barter or a harem."

"You mean they ain't?" Hooper grinned wide enough to expose his missing teeth.

My hands curled into fists. I kept them at my sides. It was hard to do. I noticed Mitch tense up, as well. He was shaking with anger and his face turned red. Chief Maxey interrupted, defusing the mounting tension.

"Knock it off, all of you. Officer Runkle. Mr. Hooper. While your contributions to this ship are valuable and needed, I won't stand for that nonsense. I don't ever want to hear either of you talk like that again. Not while you're on my ship. Do I make myself clear?"

Hooper shrugged. "Whatever, man. I was just fucking around."

"You've been doing that a little too much," Tum said.

"Runkle?" Chief Maxey glared at him. "Do you understand me?"

Runkle nodded, but said nothing.

"So what's the plan, Chief?" Tum turned back to the map. "We need a decision."

"We'll try for the small station near Virginia Beach—the one surrounded by the national forest. It should be fairly deserted. If we have no luck there, then we'll consider Mitch and Lamar's suggestion and try the oil rig. Fair enough?"

We all agreed that it was. Then we began planning the expedition. According to Chief Maxey, we'd have to take the lifeboat into shore, because the water at the station was too shallow for the *Spratling*. After some discussion, we decided that six people should be enough to make up the shore party. That would leave enough space in the lifeboat to haul back supplies. Chief Maxey and Tum were the only two people onboard qualified to operate the lifeboat, so Tum was picked to go ashore. Mitch, Tony, and Runkle volunteered right away. Hooper reluctantly agreed to go as well.

"We need one more," Chief Maxey said. "Basil, how about you? Want to join the shore party?"

Basil looked startled. "Me? Why?"

"You've got National Guard training. It would be helpful."

"Yeah," Mitch agreed. "You know how to use a firearm, right?"

"L-look," Basil stuttered, "thanks for the vote of confidence, but I can't do it. No way. I just spent the last two weeks hiding out in a fucking restroom stall at the Baltimore Zoo. I barely made it out alive. There's no way I'm going back into that shit again."

"Pussy," Hooper teased. "Chicken shit mother-fucker."

"Fuck you, man!"

Basil charged him, fists raised, jaw clenched. Runkle stepped out of the way. He looked eager to see them fight, and he licked his lips. Tum and Chief Maxey intervened, stepping between them. Basil tried pushing past the chief, but Maxey refused to budge.

"Come on, pussy," Hooper shouted. "What you got for me, huh? You ain't got nothing. Bring it. I dare you. Fucking bring it."

Tum shoved Hooper backward. Hooper took a swing at him but Tum sidestepped. Suddenly, Mitch had his pistol out of the holster and pointed at Hooper's head.

"Back the fuck down." He motioned with the pistol barrel. "Right now."

Hooper's eyes grew wide, but he backed down. "You gonna pull a gun on me?"

"Sure looks that way, doesn't it?" Mitch turned to the chief. "See why it's a good idea not to lock up all the guns?"

Chief Maxey wiped his sweaty forehead with the back of his hand and then stubbed out his cigar. "I don't give a shit who is at fault here. Each and every one of you will stand down right now, or I'll throw you all in the brig. This is not a democracy, goddamn it, and I am in charge. What is wrong with you? Fighting? Pulling guns on each other? If I'd have known it was going to be like this, I would have left all of you back on the pier."

"I'm sorry." Mitch holstered his weapon. "Didn't think you'd want your first mate getting the shit beat out of him."

"Thanks," Tum muttered.

"I'm sorry, too," Basil said. "But I'm not going ashore and I don't care what anyone thinks. I can't do it."

"Why?" Tony asked. "What happened to you at the zoo, man? We've all been through shit. What's your story?"

Basil shuddered. "You don't want to know."

"Yeah," Tony said. "I do want to know. Think we *deserve* to know. Every one of us on this goddamn shore party is risking our necks for the lives of everyone else on this ship. I think you owe us an explanation why you can't do the same—especially since you'll benefit from the raid, too."

Basil didn't respond. He walked over to the round window, put his hands behind his back, and stared out at the sea. When he finally spoke, we had to strain to hear him.

"I always loved the zoo. It was my favorite place to go when I was a kid. I grew up in Glen Burnie. Every weekend, I used to beg my parents to take me. We went maybe four times a year. When I became an adult, though, I got one of those lifetime memberships and went every chance I got. At least once a month. And when my wife and I first started dating, I used to take her to the zoo, too. She loved it as much as I did. I proposed to her in front of the monkey exhibit. It was our place, you know? Every couple has a place. Ours was the Baltimore Zoo."

None of us spoke. The only sounds were the constant cries of the seagulls and Tony's lighter as he lit another cigarette.

"So," Basil continued, "we've got a good life. I'm doing Web stuff for Northrop. My wife, Kelli, is working for Southwest Airlines at BWI. We've got a nice house in Glen Burnie, near where we both grew up. Everything's fine. Then her period is late. She takes one of those home tests where you pee on the stick, and it says she's pregnant. And then, along comes Hamelin's fucking Revenge. You guys remember how it was, when it first started. It was happening elsewhere. Localized. New York City is a long drive up Ninety-five, right? It wouldn't spread to here. But it did. The last time I saw Kelli was when I left for work. She was going to be late coming home that night. She had a doctor's appointment after work—they were going to tell her if the pregnancy test was correct or not. I got home and made dinner for us. Even stopped off at the store and got a bottle of that sparkling cider, because if she was pregnant, I didn't want her drinking wine. Lit some candles and then I waited. She called from the car—the cell phone connection was bad. She was on the inner loop of the beltway, stuck in traffic. There was some kind of accident with an ambulance. She wasn't hurt, wasn't even involved, but the highway was shut down and she couldn't go anywhere. That was the last time I talked to her."

"The inner loop," Mitch whispered. "Wasn't that where the—"

Sniffing, Basil nodded. His voice was choked with emotion. "Yeah. There was a zombie in the ambulance. It got free. Killed somebody. More zombies came out of the woods and onto the highway. You all saw the footage on WBAL. My wife was there."

"Sorry to hear that," I said, and I was. Basil had been kind of a jerk in the short time I'd known him, but still—you don't wish ill of someone when he's telling you how his wife died.

"I didn't know," he said. "I kept looking for her on television. Kept looking for her car as the news chopper did flybys, but I didn't know what had happened to her. Her cell phone wasn't working. Kelli never came home. I waited all night but she never came home. I fell asleep around four in the morning. When I woke up, I thought she'd be there. She wasn't. I tried calling in sick to work but by then all the phone lines were down. So, I decided to find Kelli myself. Figured I'd check the highway and if I didn't have any luck there, then I'd check with the hospitals. Hopped in the car and made it to the highway before the National Guard turned me back. I got caught in the detour and ended up downtown. After that, I went to the zoo. You've got to understand—I couldn't find her. Thought that maybe she was looking for me, too. So I went to the zoo and I waited. It was closed, but I hopped the fence and waited for her to show up. She never did. She's out there somewhere still, along with our baby."

"Basil," Tony said. "I'm really sorry that happened to you and your wife, man. Seriously, I am. But that doesn't explain why you're afraid to go ashore. You need to pull your weight if you're gonna be part of this group. I lost my whole fucking family. I had to smash my daughter's head in with a goddamn shovel. . . ."

His voice cracked. Basil looked at him with red-rimmed eyes.

"At least you know what happened to them. I don't. I have no idea! Do you understand what that's like? I hid in a restroom at the zoo. It was too late to leave—the zombies had already broken in. You can't imagine it. I know, I know. All you guys hid out, too. All of you saw zombies. But you didn't see anything like what I saw. The animals . . . the elephants and the zebras and the monkeys. They all turned. The rats got through the bars of their cages and attacked them and then they turned into zombies. They rotted inside their cages. And the lion, when it got loose . . ."

Runkle frowned. "There was a zombie lion on the loose?"

Basil nodded his head. "Yeah. Some gang members let it loose. I think they were looking for somebody. They had guns, and I didn't have shit, so I hid from them. I heard one of them say they'd let the lion out of its cage by accident. And then it showed up and it was horrible. The way it smelled . . . the sounds it made. How it looked. While the lion was killing them, I managed to escape. I ran. . . ."

He paused again, and asked for water. Tum gave him a sip from his bottle.

"Thanks," Basil said. "As I was escaping the zoo, I saw a woman. She was dressed like a prostitute or something. Very skinny. Track marks on her arms. She was a zombie, but it looked like she'd just turned. You know? She still looked fresh. She had a baby with her. It was dead, too—and it was nursing."

"That's impossible," Runkle said. "Are you saying these things are smarter than we thought?"

"I don't know," Basil admitted. "Probably not. But one of her nipples had been bitten or cut off and she held the baby to her breast and it . . . it *nursed*. Do you have any idea how bad that fucked with me? My wife and baby were missing, but these . . . fucking . . . *things* . . . "

He closed his eyes and shuddered.

"After that, I ran. Managed to get a pistol off one of the gang members. I was out of ammo by the time I reached the Inner Harbor. There were zombies all around by then—I guess the fires were flushing them out. But so many of them were children. So many . . ."

He stared at Tony, unflinching.

"If I go back out there and I see another dead child, I'll kill myself. It's that simple. I don't want to die, but I know my limits. I can't do it. Does that answer your question, Mr. Giovanni?"

"Yeah," Tony said, placing an arm on Basil's shoulder. "Yeah, man. You don't need to say any more. It's okay."

"That's bizarre," Mitch said. "All the zombies I saw before boarding this ship, I didn't see any of them displaying traits like that. Maternal instinct? Does that mean they can learn? Evolve?"

"If it does," I said, "then we are truly fucked."

"Like I said," Basil whispered, "she was fresh. Maybe she still had some rudimentary instincts left in her."

Chief Maxey cleared his throat. "So who replaces Basil on this mission?"

I raised my hand. "I'll go."

"You?" Hooper snorted. "I don't want you watching my back."

"That's a shame," I snarled. "You've got such a nice ass."

"Motherfucker . . ."

"Knock it off, Hooper," the chief warned. "Lamar, are you sure about this?"

I nodded. Mitch slapped me on the back. The others seemed okay with it.

"Okay," Chief Maxey said. "Then let's take inventory. Mr. Bollinger, how many weapons did you bring aboard?"

Mitch gave him a rundown of his guns and grenades, and how much ammunition he had left for each. In addition to those, Runkle, Tony, Hooper, and many of the others also had weapons. There was also Basil's empty pistol, which Mitch said he had ammo for. We divvied up the firearms and agreed that Runkle should act as team leader.

And then we were ready.

"Okay," Chief Maxey said. "Tum, you prepare the lifeboat. The rest of you arm yourselves. I'll go relieve Chuck on the bridge and take us in."

We should have smelled them first, but the breeze was blowing toward the shore. We saw them soon enough, though. Lined up along the ship's port side rail with several pairs of binoculars that we'd taken from the ship's displays, we stared in horror and disgust. The summer heat and exposure to direct sunlight and the elements had done a job on them. The dead looked like bloated, oversized ants shuffling along the beach. They crawled through the sand and sprawled in the surf, wandering aimlessly in search of prey. Seagulls darted down out of the sky and plucked away bits of rotting flesh and the insects that burrowed inside the zombies. Then they'd take flight again and fight each other in midair for the choicest morsels. Decaying ears, cheeks, eyeballs, and noses dangled from their beaks. Occasionally, a bird moved too slowly or sat on a zombie's shoulder for a second too long. Then, dead hands lashed out, seizing the birds—ripping and chewing in an explosion of blood and feathers. As we stared through the binoculars, we saw more zombies on hotel balconies and patio decks. Virginia Beach's boardwalk was actually off the beach, hidden behind a row of hotels and restaurants and stupid trinket shops. We caught glimpses between the buildings as we sailed by. Both the boardwalk and the streets were choked with corpses. I couldn't believe how many of them there were. We saw no signs of anyone still alive—the zombie's food source had to be running out. Why didn't they move on?

"Look at them all," Chuck gasped. "If you didn't know they were dead, it would be like a regular day at the beach."

Joan paled. "I can't watch. I'm going to be sick."

She handed her binoculars to Nick, and then leaned out over the rail and threw up. Nick adjusted the focus, peered through the binoculars, and then closed his eyes and turned away.

"Jesus." He sounded like he might be getting sick, too.

"I want to see," Malik said, reaching for my pair of binoculars.

"No," Carol admonished. "You don't need to see that."

"Damn straight I do. Let me get those binoculars, Lamar."

"Malik." Carol's voice grew stern. "What did we agree in regards to your cursing?"

"You said I shouldn't use swear words, but I don't remember agreeing to it."

Tasha slapped him on the head. "Quit being a dork."

"Stop hitting me! Lamar, Tasha hit me."

Sighing, I handed my pair of binoculars to Basil. Then I bent down and put an arm around each of the kids.

"Listen, guys. Mitch and I have got to go with the others to the mainland, so while I'm gone, you need to behave. Don't fight. Don't give Miss Carol or Miss Alicia any shit."

Carol pursed her lips and scowled at me.

"Um, I mean, trouble."

"Why do you and Mitch have to go?" Tasha asked.

"Because we need stuff. Food, water, medicine. We don't want what happened to Stephanie to happen to anyone else."

Malik pulled away. "Can I go, too?"

I shook my head. "Not this time."

"But I can fight zombies. I'm good. Just give me another grenade."

"I know you can, but we need you here, Malik. We need somebody that we can count on to stay behind and keep everyone on the ship safe. Can you do that for us? Protect everyone?"

He nodded. "You can count on me."

"Okay." I gave them one more squeeze and they hugged me back.

Eventually, we passed beyond Virginia Beach.

The hotels and developments vanished, replaced by trees and dunes. Within a few more miles, the forest grew thicker. Tall pine trees towered over the shoreline. The only sign of civilization was a cell phone tower sticking up above the treetops. Then the rescue station came into sight. It wasn't much—just a small cove with a single dock, and a few white, cement block buildings and a long, tin-roofed warehouse. There was also a tiny chapel. Someone had mounted a basketball hoop in the parking lot. A single vehicle, a dark green Ford Explorer, sat beneath it. A tattered American flag fluttered in the breeze at the top of a pole in the compound's center.

The *Spratling* slowed to a halt and Chief Maxey dropped the anchor. Tum, Mitch, Tony, Runkle, Hooper, and I boarded the lifeboat and took our seats. Chuck and Chief Maxey lowered us down to the surface and then we cast off. Tum started the motor and we cruised toward the cove. While en route, he turned on his battery-operated radio and checked communications with the ship. Chief Maxey answered him, his voice loud and clear.

The shoreline was deserted. The flag slapped against the pole. A few birds perched on the roof of the warehouse, but there was no other movement. I sniffed the salty breeze but smelled no sign of zombies. Tum pulled alongside the dock and shut off the motor. Hooper stood up carefully and tied us off. He glanced around, nervous. After confirming the coast was clear, the rest of us climbed up onto the dock. We agreed that Tum would stay with the boat just in case we had to make a quick getaway.

"Mitch," Runkle said, "you take point. Hooper, you bring up the rear. The rest of us will move spaced ten feet apart. Everybody with me?"

We nodded.

"Good. We'll start with the closest building. Once it's clear, we'll move on to the next. We do this as a group. I don't want anybody going off by themselves. And if we do get into some shit, watch your shots. Last thing we need is to catch each other in a fucking crossfire. Understood?"

We nodded again. In the trees, a flock of crows suddenly took flight, startling us all. I nearly squeezed my trigger.

"Weapons check," Runkle said. "Everybody make sure you're locked and loaded."

Once that was completed, we moved forward. Mitch approached the Explorer first and peered inside while the rest of us hung back. He opened the door and checked the interior. Then he popped his head back up.

"Empty."

"Anything we can use?" Runkle asked.

"Not unless you guys are into Fallout Boy, John Tesh, or gospel music. There's a bunch of CDs in the console, but they're all shit. End of the fucking world and Fallout Boy is all that's left for our descendants to find."

Tony and I snickered. Runkle motioned toward the first cement block building. Mitch crept toward it, weapon at the ready. We followed. My palms

GET UP TO 4 FREE BOOKS!

You can have the best fiction delivered to your door for less than what you'd pay in a bookstore or online—only $4.25 a book! Sign up for our book clubs today, and we'll send you **FREE* BOOKS** just for trying it out...with no obligation to buy, ever!

LEISURE HORROR BOOK CLUB

With more award-winning horror authors than any other publisher, it's easy to see why CNN.com says "Leisure Books has been leading the way in paperback horror novels." Your shipments will include authors such as RICHARD LAYMON, DOUGLAS CLEGG, JACK KETCHUM, MARY ANN MITCHELL, and many more.

LEISURE THRILLER BOOK CLUB

If you love fast-paced page-turners, you won't want to miss any of the books in Leisure's thriller line. Filled with gripping tension and edge-of-your-seat excitement, these titles feature everything from psychological suspense to legal thrillers to police procedurals and more!

As a book club member you also receive the following special benefits:

- **30% OFF** all orders through our website & telecenter!
- **Exclusive access to** special discounts!
- **Convenient** home delivery **and 10 days to return any books you don't want to keep.**

There is no minimum number of books to buy, and you may cancel membership at any time. See back to sign up!

*Please include $2.00 for shipping and handling.

YES! ☐

Sign me up for the Leisure Horror Book Club and send my TWO FREE BOOKS! If I choose to stay in the club, I will pay only $8.50* each month, a savings of $5.48!

YES! ☐

Sign me up for the Leisure Thriller Book Club and send my TWO FREE BOOKS! If I choose to stay in the club, I will pay only $8.50* each month, a savings of $5.48!

NAME: _____

ADDRESS: _____

_____

TELEPHONE: _____

E-MAIL: _____

☐ **I WANT TO PAY BY CREDIT CARD.**

☐ VISA   ☐ MasterCard   ☐ DISCOVER

ACCOUNT #: _____

EXPIRATION DATE: _____

SIGNATURE: _____

Send this card along with $2.00 shipping & handling for each club you wish to join, to:

Horror/Thriller Book Clubs
1 Mechanic Street
Norwalk, CT 06850-3431

Or fax (must include credit card information!) to: 610.995.9274. You can also sign up online at www.dorchesterpub.com.

*Plus $2.00 for shipping. Offer open to residents of the U.S. and Canada only. Canadian residents please call 1.800.481.9191 for pricing information.

If under 18, a parent or guardian must sign. Terms, prices and conditions subject to change. Subscription subject to acceptance. Dorchester Publishing reserves the right to reject any order or cancel any subscription.

JOIN NOW!

were sweaty, and I had to keep switching the pistol from hand to hand so that I could wipe them on my shirt. My armpits grew damp. My ears felt hot and my pulse pounded in my temples. A headache started to bloom behind my eyes.

Mitch flattened himself against the wall of the first building and listened at the door. He looked back at us, nodded, and then reached out and tried the handle. It was unlocked. Taking a deep breath, he lunged forward and threw the door open. Runkle and Tony ran through it, their pistols extended. Hooper and I followed. Mitch came in behind us. The room, some type of communications center, was deserted. A massive, dust-covered two-way radio sat on a shelf behind the front desk. A microphone dangled from it, swinging by the cord. There were two telephones, a box of what looked like replacement parts for the radio, and several maps and charts. Taped to the wall were a list of maritime distress signals and important emergency phone numbers. There was a single closed door at the back of the room.

Hooper picked up one of the phones and held it to his ear. The rest of us looked at him hopefully.

"Dead," he told us. "Didn't figure it would be working, but it never hurts to check."

Mitch inched to the second door, listened carefully, and then tried the handle. The door swung open, hinges creaking. Mitch reached inside, found the light switch and turned it on. Then he whistled.

"Got some stuff we can use here, I think."

Runkle told Tony to guard the entrance, and the

rest of us filed into the room. Cardboard boxes were stacked against the walls. Mitch pulled out his pocketknife and sliced one open. It was full of D-sized batteries. The next one contained AA batteries. We continued going through the supplies, and found more batteries, emergency flares, portable two-way radios, extension cords, rope, steel chain, shovels, rakes, brooms, and other assorted tools. There were also cases of spark plugs, engine oil and bearing grease, and several marine batteries for a small boat.

"Haul the batteries out and set them on the sidewalk," Runkle ordered. "The flares, walkie-talkies, and oil, too. We'll wait and see what's in the other buildings before we grab any of this other stuff."

We carried the boxes outside and stacked them against the wall. There was a stack of magazines near the front desk—months' old issues of *Time*, *Newsweek*, and *Outdoor Life*. I flipped through one of them and sighed wistfully.

"What's up?" Tony asked.

"I used to read these all the time. I was a news junkie."

"Not me, man. I never bought into stupography."

"Stup-what?"

"Stupography. Media that makes you stupider the longer you watch it. Everybody talks about how biased the media is. Either for the left or the right. What they don't realize is that it all comes from the same source. They wanted us to stay asleep, and look what happened."

He went back to work. I dropped the magazine

back on the pile. Then I noticed four comic books amidst the stack—*New Avengers*, *Spider-man*, *The Simpsons*, and *The Walking Dead*. I stuffed the first three in my back pocket, thinking Tasha and Malik might like them. I left the last one lay where it was. Didn't think the kids would want to read about more zombies. But then I changed my mind. Judging by how much Malik liked blowing them up, a comic about destroying zombies might be exactly what he'd enjoy. Wasn't like it would give him nightmares. Real life could do that just as easily.

Then we moved on to the next building, where we hit the fucking jackpot. It was a bunkhouse and living quarters, and in the rear were a small kitchenette and a walk-in pantry. The metal shelves were lined with cans and dry goods, bags of flour and noodles, snack food, and cases of soda and bottled water.

"Holy shit!" Tony gaped at the rows of canned goods. "Green beans, peas, corn, peanut butter, kidney beans, succotash, fruit fucking cocktail—we are good to go."

"I can't believe they left all this stuff behind," Runkle said. "Doesn't make sense."

Mitch nodded. "I was thinking the same thing. If you knew this stuff was here, and the zombies were on the march, wouldn't you hide out here? Makes sense, right? But it looks deserted. No people and definitely no dead. Can't even smell them nearby. There's no blood, no signs of a struggle anywhere."

Runkle picked up a jar of jelly. "Maybe the personnel assigned to this station went out to perform a rescue at sea and didn't get the chance to come back?"

"Could be," Mitch agreed. "Sucks for them. Good for us."

"Let's check the rest of the compound," Runkle said. "Make sure it really is free and clear. Then we'll start hauling this stuff back to the boat."

The next building was a small infirmary, and we found a large stockpile of medicine. Since none of us were doctors, we didn't understand what a lot of it was, but we grabbed the stuff we recognized and set it by the door. The warehouse was full of vehicles and equipment—lawnmowers, a forklift, tractor, several old pickup trucks, and a speedboat sitting atop a trailer. Another boat was suspended on jacks. It looked like someone had been working on the hull at one point. Now it would probably sit here for all time. Outside, behind the warehouse, we found skids with fifty-five gallon drums of motor oil, gasoline, diesel fuel, and kerosene, along with propane bottles, a pump, and several empty plastic gas cans.

"The chief will flip when we bring all this back," Runkle said. "Unbelievable."

I tapped a drum. "How are we going to get these down to the boat?"

"The forklift." Tony laughed. "We should have had Chuck come with us. He drove a forklift for a living. But I can run it, okay, long as there's keys and fuel in it."

For a moment, I thought that I heard Tum's voice, calling out for us. When I glanced around, I didn't see him, and nobody else mentioned it. I figured it was my imagination.

"I got to take a piss," Hooper said. "Be right back."

"Wait a second." Mitch grabbed his shoulder. "We still need to clear the chapel."

Hooper brushed his hand aside. "Man, ain't nothing in the chapel. Look around. This place is deserted. Anybody that was here ain't here now."

"Well," Runkle said, "you still shouldn't go walking off by yourself."

"I got to piss, and I ain't pulling my dick out in front of Lamar. Fucker might try to molest me and shit."

"Trust me, Cleveland—I'm not interested."

He scowled at me, and then stalked off into the trees, muttering under his breath. We watched him go, shaking our heads.

"Asshole," Mitch said.

"He may be a dick," Tony said, "but he's right. We're all on edge. But this place is zombie free, man."

A crow flew overhead. Something pink dangled from its beak. I thought I knew what it was. Before I could say anything, the wind shifted, blowing from inland out to the sea.

Mitch cringed. "Oh yeah? Well if that's so, then what's that smell?"

Deep inside the forest, Hooper screamed.

CHAPTER SEVEN

We ran into the forest and pushed our way through the thick undergrowth. Vines and thorns tugged at our clothing. A few yards beyond the tree line, the foliage abruptly cleared. Sand gave way to a thick carpet of pine needles, and the trees were spaced far enough apart for us to move freely. Hooper screamed again, his voice closer.

"Cleveland," Runkle shouted, "where are you?"

He answered with another shriek.

"Hooper!" Mitch cupped his hand around his mouth. "Sound off, man. Let us know where you are."

"I'm over here! Oh, fuck me. Fuck me running! Ya'll get over here, right now."

We followed his cries and emerged in a circular clearing. Hooper was in the middle of the clearing, staring upward. We brushed past the branches and stood beside him. Each of us froze, gaping in horror. I felt my gorge rise. I ran to the edge of the clearing and puked.

Except for the section where we'd entered, the outer edges of the clearing were lined with crosses. Somebody had made them out of fence posts and logs. A zombie hung from each cross, nailed through the wrists and ankles, their legs, arms, and waists tied down with thick coils of bare copper electrical wire. The stench was terrible, but even worse were the flies. Their buzzing filled the clearing. Maggots writhed inside the corpses and fell out of various orifices. They squirmed on the ground. Birds sat on the creatures' shoulders and heads or perched on the crossbeams. They'd stripped the crucified zombies of most of their skin. What remained were pink, wet, human-shaped *things*—internal organs, lips, tongues, and eyeballs missing. Their nerves and veins hung like limp strands of spaghetti and bones poked through the glistening tissue. One of the zombies raised its blind head, as if sensing our presence, and moaned. Worms burrowed in the empty eye sockets. Bird shit covered an exposed section of skull. The creatures' stench made my eyes water.

"Jesus fucking Christ . . ." Mitch bent over and threw up all over his boots.

I wiped the bile from my lips and rejoined the others. My stomach lurched again. The comic books in my back pocket brushed against my spine. I'd forgotten all about them. I was surprised they were still there.

The buzzing flies grew louder. Another bird flew off with some intestine. The grayish-purple strand looked just like a big, fat worm.

Runkle gagged. "Somebody . . . somebody did this. The zombies couldn't have crucified their own. They're not that smart. They don't function that way. A human being did this."

"How"—Tony choked—"How did they get them up there? If the bodies were already dead and infected, they'd have turned into zombies before they were finished with the crucifixion."

"And if they were still alive when they were crucified," Runkle said, "then how did they turn into zombies? How did they get exposed to Hamelin's Revenge from up there?"

"Maybe they were exposed and then nailed to the crosses before they actually died," Mitch said, gasping for breath. "But that still doesn't tell us why."

"It was God's will."

The voice came from behind us. Hooper screamed again, his voice growing hoarse. We all whirled around, weapons raised and ready. A man slowly stepped out of the forest. He was short and thin, and looked to be in his late forties. A few wisps of white hair clung to the sides of his head. The rest of his scalp was bald and shiny. He was dressed in black pants, a white short-sleeved dress shirt, and had a dirty preacher's collar around his neck. A small silver cross was pinned to the collar. Sweat stains covered his shirt and there was mud on his pants. His dirty yellow fingernails were long and ragged.

Mitch stepped forward and pointed his pistol at the stranger's head.

"Don't you fucking move."

The man held up his hands and smiled sadly. "You have no reason to fear me, son. I am a man of God." He had a Hispanic accent.

"What the hell happened here?" Runkle patted the man down, carefully searching for weapons. "Who did this?"

The man's smile remained. "I told you. It was God's will. This is the Lord's work. Only he can grant life after death."

"He's fucking crazy," Hooper muttered. "Just shoot him and be done with it, Runkle. The hell with this shit."

"Please," the man said. "As I already told your other friend, I mean you no harm."

"Our other friend?" Runkle stepped away and holstered his weapon. "What are you talking about? You better start making sense."

"The man on the boat. He was your friend, yes? He said his name was Tum. He told me all about your trials, how you escaped from Baltimore and traveled here, looking for a safe harbor. I spoke to him while the rest of you were here in the forest. I explained to him what has actually happened— told him all about the resurrection and the life. He's in the chapel right now. Come, I'll take you to him."

Mitch's finger tightened on the trigger. "Have you hurt Tum?"

"No," the man said, as if speaking to a child. "Why would I do that? I am a man of peace. I merely told him about the glory of God."

"I'm telling ya'll," Hooper said. "We should shoot this crazy old fucker right now."

"Shut up," Mitch snapped, not taking his eyes off the preacher.

Cursing in frustration, Hooper kicked the base of the nearest cross. The ground around it must have been soft, because the post shook and the zombie nailed to it shifted in its bonds. Before we could cry out a warning, the copper wire that had been holding the corpse to the beams sliced through the rancid meat. The zombie slumped forward, now cut into sections. The feet and hands remained nailed to the cross. Everything else tore loose and exploded, spilling down onto Hooper and showering him in gore. It reminded me of a bursting water balloon. Shrieking, Hooper flailed his arms and legs. Blood and half-liquefied tissue dripped from his nose, chin, and fingertips. Putrefied slime ran into his mouth and eyes.

"Oh shit," he squealed. "Got it on me, motherfuckers. Got it on me, got it on me, *got it on me. . . .* "

The zombie's head and shoulders were still attached to each other by a cross-section of rotting musculature, sinew, and tendons. The creature's gaping mouth worked soundlessly. Hooper danced around, slapping at his gore-covered body and stamping the corpse into mush beneath his heels. The creature's head split open, spilling maggot-ridden brains.

"Oh, shit," Tony gasped, staring at Hooper. "Oh, fuck me. Somebody do something. Help him!"

Runkle and I could only stare at the grisly site. Hooper leaned over and vomited blood. He shook his head like a dog, spraying droplets of gore. The stranger didn't seem affected by what had happened. He just watched with a blank expression, his hands folded in front of him as if in prayer.

"Oh, motherfucker . . ." Long, ropy threads of red spittle hung from Hooper's mouth. "Somebody get me a hose. I got to wash this shit off before I get infected."

Mitch walked toward him. Hooper looked relieved.

"Mitch. Yo, man—help me out. Fucking shit is all over me. Get me some water and disinfectant. Got to wash this shit off. Damn, it stinks!"

"I'm sorry, Cleveland."

"I'm sorry, too, motherfucker. Now help me out."

"No," Mitch whispered. "I mean that I'm sorry."

Mitch raised his pistol. Hooper's eyes widened. In the space of a second, Mitch turned his face away, closed his eyes and mouth tightly, and squeezed the trigger.

And then we couldn't tell which parts were Hooper and which parts were the zombie. They both looked the same.

Mitch ran over to me. "Is there any on me, Lamar? Did I get splattered?"

It was hard to hear him clearly. The gunshot still rang in my ears. I looked him over carefully, and made him turn around in a circle.

"No," I said. "You're clean, man. You're okay."

On their crosses, the rest of the zombies wiggled harder, stirred up by the noise.

"You shot Hooper," Tony said. "You didn't even hesitate. Just walked up and . . . bang. You killed him."

"No," Mitch replied. "He was already dead. You saw what happened."

Tony nodded. "Yeah, I did. No problem there. I'm just saying—I'm glad you had the balls to do it. He was an asshole and everything, but I still don't think I could have done it."

Mitch turned to Runkle and nodded at the man in the preacher's collar. "What about him?"

Runkle grabbed the man's arm and twisted it behind his back. The man yelled in surprise and pain.

"He's going to tell us what the fuck happened here," Runkle growled in his ear. "Aren't you, pops?"

"Please," the man pleaded. "You don't have to hurt me, young man. Please let me go. I'll be happy to help you, just as I helped your friend. That is what the Lord wants—what he asks of us all. And my name is Daniel, not pops. Reverend Daniel Ortega."

Runkle released his arm and spun him around. Then he leaned close, his nose almost touching the preacher's.

"Okay, Reverend. You said that you'd met our friend, Tum. Where is he now?"

"He's resting in the chapel. I administered Holy Communion to him and then came out here to fetch you all. Follow me. I'll take you to him. We can break bread together."

Runkle moved aside and let him pass. Ortega slipped into the forest. We glanced at each other and then followed him; Runkle, then Mitch, and then me. Tony brought up the rear. Behind us, the crucified thrashed helplessly on their crosses.

Ortega spoke calmly as we shoved our way through the underbrush. He seemed unaffected by what had happened to Hooper. True, the preacher hadn't known him, but it was just so fucking grisly. He should have had some reaction.

"Corinthians, chapter fifteen, verse twelve, tells us: 'Now if Christ preached that he rose from the dead, how can some of those among you say that there is no resurrection of the dead? But if there is no resurrection of the dead, then is Christ not risen; and if Christ is not risen, then is our preaching in vain, and your faith in vain?' That's always been a favorite verse of mine."

"That's wonderful," Runkle said. "But I don't think any of us are in the mood for a sermon right now. How about you tell us what's been happening here? Who crucified those zombies back there in the woods?"

"I did."

"You?"

"Yes. You see, gentlemen, with the power of the Lord, I can bring people back from the dead. Just as Christ brought back Lazarus; just as our savior was delivered on the cross."

Mitch stopped walking. "You're insane."

"Am I?"

Ortega turned and winked; then he continued on his way. We emerged from the tree line and approached the back end of the warehouse.

"You saw for yourselves," Ortega continued. "Back there in the clearing. You saw them rise. You beheld the mystery. They were asleep—dead—and now they are changed. They live again in death. Christ told us, 'I am the resurrection and the life.' He is working through his faithful, giving the gift of eternal life to all. This is happening all across the world. We shall not all sleep, but we shall all be changed!"

Mitch shook his head in disbelief. "You crucified them by yourself?"

"Well, it wasn't easy. I'm not as young or as strong as I used to be. But the Lord is my strength. My sword and my shield. He gives me the power to do his will."

We approached the chapel door. The preacher reached for the handle, but Runkle stopped him, motioning with his pistol for the man to step aside.

"I'll go first."

Reverend Ortega smiled. "As you wish, young man. This is the Lord's house. All may enter freely. I told your friend the same thing before I administered Communion."

This was the second time Ortega had mentioned giving Tum Communion. I didn't know Tum very well, but he hadn't seemed like a religious sort. The statement didn't ring true to me.

"What do you mean?" I asked, stepping forward. "What's this Communion shit?"

Ortega frowned. "You aren't familiar with the rite of Holy Communion? It symbolizes Christ's pact with man. He gave us his flesh and shed his blood. It is through his blood that we are born again. It is his blood that's responsible for what you have seen. That's why the dead return to life—because of his blood."

"They're zombies," Tony shouted. "You and your God didn't have anything to do with it. Everybody is coming back from the dead because of a fucking disease. Don't you know that?"

The preacher's expression darkened. "The Lord has shown you proof. He has shown you miracles—the miracle of the resurrection. And still you don't believe. You're just like the first one I crucified. I removed his eyes and tongue before I nailed him to the cross. 'If thy eye offends thee, pluck it out. If thy tongue offends thee, cut it out.' Those aren't my words. They're God's. Who am I to disagree?"

Flinching, Runkle shoved the chapel door open. Mitch ran after him. They both shouted for Tum. Meanwhile, Tony and I held Ortega at gunpoint and warned him not to move.

"I'm not going anywhere," the preacher said. "Not until I die. Then I will—"

"Would you shut the fuck up?"

Tony slapped him with the back of his hand. Ortega collapsed to his knees. Blood trickled from the corner of his mouth. His eyes narrowed, and when he spoke again, his kind tone had vanished.

"You struck me. I came to you in peace, ready to share the glory of God, and you greeted me with violence. But you will see that I'm right. Even now, your friend is undergoing the transformation. Christ's blood moves through his veins."

"What are you talking about?" I raised my hand as if to hit him again, and Ortega scuttled backward, whimpering.

"I told you," he whined. "I administered Communion. I gave him the flesh to eat and the blood to drink. The flesh and blood of our Lord. The sacrament. He didn't want to partake, of course. They never do. So I had to force him. I clubbed him over the head and then forced it down his throat before he regained consciousness."

I reached down and ripped the collar from around his neck. "Who's blood? Who's flesh? What the hell are you saying?"

"That's where the power comes from—the flesh and the blood of Christ."

Runkle and Mitch came back outside, supporting Tum between them. He looked weak and pale.

"Something's wrong with Tum," Mitch said, sounding worried. "He's really sick."

I flung Ortega to the ground and stood over him, pistol pointed at his face.

"Where did you get *the blood?*"

"What blood?" Runkle asked. "What's he talking about?"

Between them, Tum groaned. Mitch let Runkle take all of the weight and stepped forward.

"Lamar, what's going on?"

"Tell us, Ortega, or I swear to God I'll blow your fucking head off. Where did you get the blood?"

"From the dead," Ortega whined. "I took the body and blood of Christ from those he had already touched. Then I fed it to your friend. Fed it to them all, one by one. I'm doing the Lord's work, just like it says in the book."

"You fuck . . ."

I bit my lip and squeezed my eyes shut. My finger tightened on the trigger. The gun felt heavy in my hand. My breathing seemed very loud. But then my finger eased. I couldn't do it. Even now, after we'd learned exactly what he'd done, I couldn't kill him in cold blood. I didn't have it in me. It pissed me off—this schism inside. When that bitch took a bite out of Alan, I'd had no problem shooting him. I hadn't balked yet when it came to wasting a zombie. Yet Ortega was just as bad, if not worse than them, and I couldn't do it. When that woman had been slaughtered right outside my house, I'd felt no remorse for not helping her. But I felt something now. I felt sorry for this crazy old man who'd butchered people in the name of some insane, murderous God.

"The dead walk," Ortega babbled, clawing at the dirt. "Ye must be born again. The dead are God's children—the chosen ones. They shall inherit the earth. This is not the end. There are many doors. Death is just another doorway that we all must pass through. This is my blood, which has been shed for thee. This is my flesh. Eat of it and have eternal life."

I stepped away from him. "I can't do it. He deserves to fucking die, guys, but I can't do it."

"Ain't no shame in that," Mitch said.

Then he shot him. He didn't flinch; didn't hesitate. He did it mechanically and without emotion, just like he'd done with Hooper. The first round hit Ortega in the neck. The second tore his head apart. Mitch ejected his magazine and loaded a fresh one into the pistol.

Tony whispered, "Fuck . . ."

"When I sold Bibles," Mitch said, "it was fuckers

like him that made my job hard. Nobody wants to buy one if they think everyone who reads it is bat-shit crazy."

"Is he awake?" I asked Runkle, nodding at Tum.

"On and off. He's really sick. You want to tell us what the hell is happening?"

"He's infected," Tony told them. "The preacher fed Tum infected blood and flesh that he got from the zombies."

Runkle looked sick. "Oh, God . . ."

Sighing, Mitch stared into the distance.

Runkle leaned the half-conscious Tum against the chapel's wall and quickly moved away from him. He turned back to us.

"Maybe we could induce vomiting? Get it out of his system."

"That's not going to work," Mitch said softly. "It wouldn't have helped Hooper and it won't help him."

"Guys," Tum whimpered. "I feel like shit. What's wrong with me?"

Mitch stared down at him. "You guys go ahead and get the boat loaded. I'll stay here with Tum. That infection is quick as lightning. It won't be long now."

None of us spoke. If Tum understood what was happening, he gave no indication.

"My guts feel like they're on fire." Sweat poured down Tum's face. His fingers kept clenching up and his legs jittered. "And my muscles and joints hurt. I got a killer headache, too. What the hell is wrong with me? Did that preacher poison me?"

"You'll be okay, buddy," Mitch said. "Just something you ate. I'm gonna stay here with you until you feel better."

Runkle turned to Tony and me. "Come on. Let's get it over with. Our shipmates are counting on us."

Tum sagged lower, his legs and arms sprawled. "I'm just gonna rest for a little bit. Just close my eyes."

Runkle looked away. "You do that, Tum."

"Tell Chief Maxey that I might be late to relieve him on the bridge. Tell him I'm sorry."

"Sshhh." Mitch put his finger to Tum's lips. "No more talking, man. Lay back and try to get some sleep. You'll feel better in a little bit."

"Yeah, man," Tony whispered. "You just rest up. Mitch will take good care of you."

"I can't feel the sun," Tum whispered. "Where did the sun go?"

Runkle walked away. Without looking back, we followed him to the infirmary and began packing boxes of medicine and carrying them down to the lifeboat. On our second trip, a single gunshot rang out. We flinched, paused in our work, and then continued.

"Fuck," Tony said.

"One more trip and then we'll start on the food," Runkle said. "We'll get as much as we can, but I want to be back to the *Spratling* before sundown."

Then there was another gunshot. Then a third. Then a barrage. They echoed across the rescue station, bouncing off the buildings and scattering the birds roosted in the trees.

Runkle looked back at the chapel. "What the hell?"

Four more shots sounded in rapid succession, and then Mitch ran around the corner. His eyes were wide and terrified. His hair fluttered in the wind.

"Zombies," he gasped. "Came out of the woods. Bunch of them."

Runkle dropped the box he was carrying and pulled his weapon. "The ones on the crosses?"

"No." he took a deep breath. "Different ones—from farther inland. They're much more mobile than the ones in the clearing. Hundreds of them. They must have been hunting in the forest and heard all the commotion."

"Well, let's take up positions and—"

"There's no time," Mitch shouted. "And we don't have enough bullets. I'm telling you, there's too many of them. Just fucking run!"

The wind shifted again and brought their scent. I turned around and glanced back at the chapel, and the dead swarmed into view. Mitch hadn't been exaggerating. Their numbers reminded me of the hordes back on the pier at Inner Harbor. They advanced on us, slow but determined. I wondered when they'd last eaten. They looked very hungry.

"Shit." Tony tossed his box aside and fled.

Runkle raised his gun and took aim. The weapon leaped in his hands. With one squeeze of the trigger, he dropped one of the lead zombies. Five more took its place.

"Come on, Runkle." Mitch tugged on his arm. "Don't make us leave you here."

We ran for the dock. Tony reached the boat first. By the time we leapt into it, he'd already started the motor. It choked and sputtered and for one terrifying moment I thought it was going to stall, but it didn't. The zombies lurched after us, outstretched arms waving, dead mouths drooling. Mitch and Runkle laid down cover fire while I cast us off. More and more of the creatures collapsed, minus their heads. I untied the rope. Tony didn't even wait for me to sit back down. He hit the throttle and I almost toppled overboard. Mitch reached out and grabbed my belt loop, pulling me to safety. We rocketed away from the dock and out into the bay, leaving the zombies—and the much needed supplies— behind. We'd only managed to get two crates of oranges and a carton of batteries loaded into the lifeboat. Runkle played with the radio until he figured out how to make it work. Then he called back to the *Spratling* and advised Chief Maxey of what had happened.

Tony released the throttle long enough to pull out his crumpled pack of cigarettes and light one. He inhaled, and then exhaled with a sigh. After he'd stuffed his lighter back in his pocket, he balled up the empty pack and tossed it into the water. It bobbed on top of the waves. We watched it float away.

"Well," Tony said. "That was my last pack of smokes. I guess it's all downhill from here."

"Maybe we'll find some at the next stop," I said.

"No." Tony shook his head. "I don't think there's gonna be any more stops, Lamar."

I didn't respond. Mitch stared out at the ocean. Runkle was still talking to the chief.

"Yep," Tony sighed, "things are going to get a lot worse."

He smoked his last cigarette down to the filter, and after he flicked the butt into the water, he began to cry.

CHAPTER EIGHT

We drifted along the coast for the next two days. The chief said he wanted to look for survivors, but in truth, I think he didn't have a clue what to do next, and was just buying some time while he figured it out. Tum's unexpected death had hit him pretty hard. He'd relied on Tum's expertise more than any of us had realized. Chuck became Tum's replacement, and Chief Maxey trained him further on how to pilot the ship so that Chuck could relieve him for short periods. Chuck filled in when the chief slept, but otherwise, Maxey spent his time on the bridge. Nick and Tran took over the galley, dividing up Hooper's duties, and even though we didn't understand him, Tran seemed happier with the arrangement. I think he liked Nick a hell of a lot more than he had Hooper. We all did.

The rest of us all pulled watch duty. We worked in shifts around the clock, standing fore and aft and watching the shoreline with binoculars. The chief was adamant that we remain vigilant. We stayed alert for lights or vehicular movement on the shore, or even a big HELP sign painted on somebody's roof, but the only things moving on the ground were the dead. It was like spying on hell. Only the sea retained life, as evidenced by the fish we pulled out of it. Mitch hooked a big blue marlin the morning after the disaster at the rescue station, and it was cause for celebration—if only for a moment. The skies were full of birds. They'd grown fat from the easy pickings on land.

We encountered one other vessel drifting on the open water. The chief tried raising them on the radio but there was no answer. Chuck hailed them with a battery-operated bullhorn as we drew closer, but there was still no reply. As the *Spratling* pulled alongside the smaller craft, we saw why. There was nobody left alive onboard. A lone zombie blundered about the deck. Its eyes were missing, probably stolen by birds. Exposure to the elements had sped up its decomposition. Mitch shot it from the signal bridge. Its head didn't so much explode as *implode*. After much debate, the chief vetoed boarding the other craft. Basil and Murphy were adamant that we send a party aboard, even though they didn't volunteer to go themselves. Tony was hopeful that there might be cigarettes somewhere on the ship. But the fact remained that none of us knew what lay below decks, and the boat was small enough that any supplies it may have had wouldn't have lasted us very long anyway. The dangers outweighed the benefits, so we sailed on and left the ghost ship to its fate.

On the third day, Chief Maxey summoned us all to the flight deck again. Chuck remained in the pilothouse, and Carol and Alicia kept the kids occupied. They'd set up a makeshift classroom in one of the berthing areas. Tran stayed behind in the galley, cleaning up from breakfast. Everyone else onboard mustered on the flight deck after we'd finished eating. We moved slowly, the weight of the dead world bearing down on all our shoulders. Gone was the excitement and enthusiasm we'd had after the last meeting. Only Cliff was still optimistic. It seemed like the worse things got, the more he turned to the Lord. Everyone else was lethargic and depressed. Tony and Mitch needed nicotine. Murphy needed alcohol. The rest of us needed hope. None of them were in supply. We stood around without speaking. There wasn't much to say. We'd survived Baltimore, escaped the zombies and the fires, found sanctuary . . . and already, three of our number were dead. It felt like it was just a matter of time for the rest of us. There was no safe harbor.

Like the rest of us, Chief Maxey's mood was sullen. He didn't smile or say good morning. Instead, he got right down to business.

"I've decided to set course for an oil drilling operation farther out to sea. It's approximately a two day trip from our present location. I've tried raising them on the radio, but have received no response. That means one of three things. Either the platform isn't there anymore, which I very much doubt, or the crew is no longer onboard, which is a possibility. They could have been evacuated."

"And the third option?" the professor asked.

"The crew are still onboard but unable to respond because they're dead."

"Wonderful," Basil said. "Just what we fucking need—more of those things."

"Regardless, until we reach their location and know for sure, I'm cutting back further on our rations. If we arrive and find that the rig is gone, I'm not sure where to go next. As you all know, the shore party met with disaster and were unable to replenish our supplies. So I want to double our fishing operations. From now until further notice, we'll subsist mainly on what we can pull from the sea."

Joan raised her hand. "But you said it was only a two day trip. Surely we have enough supplies to last us that long."

"Yes." The chief nodded. "But we don't know if we'll find supplies there or not, and our own stores won't last us forever. We're getting low, regardless. So we're sticking with fish for the time being. All other rations will be used to supplement only one meal per day. No coffee or tea or anything that will diminish our water supplies. Nick, make sure Tran is clear on this as well."

"I'll try," Nick said. "I think he understands more English than he speaks."

The chief nodded again. "I hope that the rest of you will be patient and understanding about this."

There was some grumbling among us, but in truth, we didn't have much choice. He was right. On the mainland, we'd each done whatever we'd needed to stay alive on our own. Now, we did the same thing as a group. If the human race was to survive, we had to work as a team. Even if we no longer saw the point and even if we no longer believed.

I couldn't sleep that night. The sheets stuck to me in the heat. Mitch wasn't in his rack and I hadn't seen him since dinner. Malik and Tasha had fallen asleep while reading their comic books. Despite the temperature, they looked cold. Both were curled into balls. I pulled their blankets up over them and turned off the light.

I stood there in the darkness, debating what to do. I felt wired, nervous. The ship came alive in the silence, groaning and clanging. The engines throbbed and the steam pipes clicked. I decided to take a walk outside. Maybe some fresh air would do me good. I felt guilty about leaving the kids alone, but at the same time, I was restless and didn't want to wake them up if I stayed. I tiptoed out of the berthing compartment and carefully shut the hatch behind me. It banged into place anyway. I cringed, holding my breath, waiting to see if I'd woke the kids. There was no sound from within, so I continued down the passageway.

According to the chief, a storm was due sometime later in the night or early the next morning. It was certainly dark enough outside. A thick layer of clouds covered the sky, blocking out the moon and stars. There were no lights on the mainland, and none onboard ship, either. Chief Maxey insisted on running without them so we wouldn't attract pirates or raiders. I held my hand up in front of my face and wiggled my fingers. I couldn't see them. The night was black as tar. It was easy enough to imagine that the world no longer existed. In a way, I guess it didn't.

I waited for my eyes to adjust to the darkness. It had been warm inside the ship, but outside the wind was chilly and brisk. It felt good on my skin. Once I was able to see the railing and deck, I moved up to the signal bridge. A glowing orange ember bloomed in the darkness. A moment later, I smelled cherry tobacco smoke.

"Is that you, Lamar?" Professor Williams asked.

"It's me. What's up, Professor? You got pretty good night vision."

"It's the only biological function that hasn't failed me yet in my old age. Beautiful evening, isn't it?"

"Yeah," I agreed. "It is."

I carefully felt my way along the handrail until I'd reached him. Even though my eyes had adjusted, I could barely see him until he puffed on his pipe. Then the soft glow illuminated his features. The professor looked tired.

"What brings you out tonight?" he asked. "Bad dreams?"

"No, I don't dream. Just couldn't sleep. Too hot. How about you?"

The professor chuckled. "I've always enjoyed a good pipe before bed. If I don't get one, I can't sleep worth a damn. But Tony's compartment is right across the passageway from mine. If he smells the tobacco, then he'll want to borrow some, and I'm afraid that my reserves are nearly depleted."

"We're running out of everything," I said. "Guess we've got to hoard where we can. You know what I'm saying?"

"Yes," he agreed. "Although it's rather uncivilized, I suppose we do. I love my fellow man, but I love my tobacco more. Smacks of the old world, doesn't it?"

I shrugged, staring out at the dark water. The horizon was just a shadow. The wind picked up speed and I shivered.

"What's troubling you, Lamar? It's not like you to be so laconic."

"I don't know," I said. "Just have a lot on my mind. Ever since . . . what happened to Tum and Hooper, I just can't seem to get my head together."

"How so?"

I paused, gripping the rail tighter. "Well, I mean . . . what's the point, you know? Growing up, I didn't have a real good life, but I fought to make it better. Same thing as an adult. Lost my job a few months back, but still, I fought hard to make things better again. Fought to survive. And then everything went to shit. Everyone I've met since then is doing the same thing. They're all fighting to survive, even when the odds are against them. My neighbor, Alan—he and I used to talk about it at night, while we watched those things outside. Neither one of us had an answer, but we went on fighting anyway. Didn't matter in the end. We went on a supply run and he got bit. I had to . . . I had to shoot him before he turned. When we made it to the ship, I thought maybe that would be the end of it for a while. But then Stephanie went. She knew she was dying. She must have. But she never said a word. She was still anxious to help. Eager to hold on. And Tum—even after he'd been exposed, he was fighting it. I don't think he was even aware, but he was fighting it just the same. You could see it in his eyes. Hear it in his voice. Kept saying that he just wanted to rest a minute. Like he'd be okay again if he could just do that."

The professor nodded. "The human spirit is indeed strong."

"Sure it is. Survival instinct is a motherfucker. But why? I mean, you saw what happened back in Baltimore. What's the point? Don't you think that maybe we're all just biding our time? The zombies have to outnumber us by now."

"If they don't, they soon will."

"So then why don't we give up? Seems like it would be easier. I'm fucking tired, Professor. And so are you. Don't bullshit me. I can see it in your eyes. I feel like I just want to give up. So why can't I?"

"Well, there are a lot of reasons why someone would continue to fight even when there's no chance of success. For some it's an individual choice; an aspect of one's core belief system that says 'I'm going down swinging.' That's especially prevalent in the past few generations, who were exposed to such iconography in cowboy films and Stallone movies. Others may fight because they've been culturally conditioned to never give up, to believe that there is some kind of inherent nobility in raging against an unbeatable foe. I don't know you very well, Lamar, but from what you've told me about yourself and your childhood, and from what I've observed about your character, I'd say that second one applies to you."

"Yeah, maybe. I guess that's fair. My mother always taught me to be proud and never surrender."

"I thought as much. And that is a very fine and noble lesson."

"Doesn't apply to everybody, though."

"No, it doesn't. Others may be motivated to keep fighting because they simply don't know what else to do."

"How about you, Professor? What keeps you going?"

"Me?" He laughed softly. "I think I'm like many others. I think we continue to fight because an element of our collective unconscious demands that we do so. Even at my age."

"What's a collective unconscious?"

"The collective unconscious is a theory—one I happen to agree with. Basically, it says that people all over the world share a set of unconscious memories that have been passed down through the generations ever since mankind learned to walk upright. These aren't regular memories like when you remember your high school prom or your first kiss or where you were on the morning of September Eleventh, but rather, unconscious memories that are hardwired into the brains of everyone who's ever lived. They act as a sort of blueprint, influencing human behavior and making people naturally respond to certain situations in certain ways. For example, you can go to any spot on the

planet and people with whom you don't share a culture or a language will automatically understand that your smile is a sign of happiness, or a frown, displeasure. These are universal signals. If you are crying, they'll know that you are sad or in pain. Ask yourself, why is that? How can people of different cultures all around the world interpret certain things exactly the same way?"

"I don't know."

"Because we've all been hardwired by the collective unconscious to respond to those stimuli that way. Sometimes for good. Sometimes for bad."

"You mean like these gay-bashers who could never explain to me why they felt the way they did?"

"That's certainly a valid example," the professor said. "I'm sure you've dealt with individuals who were against homosexuality but didn't understand why. They probably masked their bigotry with religious or moral beliefs, but deep down inside, their collective unconscious told them that homosexuality threatened mankind's ability to procreate. Thus, they were repelled without truly understanding why."

The professor's pipe went out. Cupping his hand, he tried to relight it, but the breeze was too strong. I placed my hands around it as well. Once he got it going again, he continued.

"It's not just our responses that are influenced, either. It's also our behaviors. You see, the collective unconscious programs a set of figures into our brains, just like you'd program a computer. Psychologists call these figures, or characters, archetypes.

They act as role models for human behavior. Some of the most important of these archetypes are the 'king,' the 'trickster,' and the 'warrior.' "

"You mentioned those before," I said, thinking back to when I'd met him in the ship's galley.

"I did, indeed. This happens to be a favorite topic of mine. I always enjoyed debating it at social gatherings—I even hosted a party once just so we could discuss it over dinner. Sadly, most of my colleagues are dead now."

He was silent for a moment, puffing on his pipe. He seemed lost in thought.

"Its because of these archetypes," he continued, "that everyone shares certain common conceptions about people; for example, in every culture that has ever existed, certain attributes like courage, strength, and fortitude have been attached to the ideal image of the warrior. All human beings, at an unconscious level, know that the figure of the warrior is part of our human makeup, and as such, we recognize the certain attributes that make up the warrior. A soldier on the news. A basketball player in the playoffs. We respond to these. And like it or not, it's our job to either succeed or fail at living up to those attributes. Do you see?"

"When we first met, you said I was an archetype."

"You are, indeed. You're living up to those attributes—embarking on a journey of self-discovery. Even as the world falls into ruin, Lamar, you are being reborn. That's a classic story; one that appeals to all mankind. You are the hero."

"I've got to be honest, Professor. I don't feel like

much of a hero right now. I couldn't even shoot the crazy fucker who killed Tum."

"You may not feel like a hero. And yet, you are. Basically, the hero is a universal archetype that embodies the best and most revered qualities of a culture or society. However, the hero is not simply born. It is never that simple. The hero must be created, forged, if you will, in a fire of turmoil and trials. To do this he must go on a quest, which is what you're doing right now."

"A quest, huh? So, what am I looking for?"

"Well, my favorite authority on this subject, Joseph Campbell, referred to the quest as the hero's journey. Different journeys have different treasures at the end. In your case, you are on a quest for self-discovery. Campbell believed that, regardless of your culture or time frame, the basic structure of this journey is the same, and thus an archetype. He called it a monomyth. In its most basic form, during his or her quest, the hero experiences a call to adventure. They typically refuse or are hesitant about answering the call. They receive supernatural aid and cross the threshold, undergoing trials and tribulations before returning home bearing gifts or boons for their people."

"That doesn't sound like much of a self-discovery, Professor."

"Well, perhaps not. But something that is very important to the formation of the hero is his journeying *away* from home and the ordinary—and entering a world of unfamiliarity, or what Campbell called 'supernatural wonder.' I think you'll certainly agree that is what you're currently experiencing. Wouldn't you say? Think about it. You've left home, abandoned everything you ever knew. You've been thrust into a whole new world, left to care for a new family—"

"They're not my family," I interrupted. "I'm not the best person to be taking care of kids."

"And yet you are, and they want you to be that person. And you haven't shirked that responsibility, even though you could have done so very easily. You are here for them. You continue to exist for them, whether you even realize it or not. That's a very selfless act, Lamar. And that's an important aspect of the monomyth—the hero's selflessness. He may first undergo his journey for his own self, but he returns and brings wisdom and order to his people. Thus the hero is a creation for all the people, not just the individual. Mythic heroes bring back large, worldly benefits. Things that affect everyone, not just the microcosm of a small community."

"But you just said I'm only here for Tasha and Malik. They aren't everyone."

"Perhaps not." He smiled, and then patted my hand. "But perhaps they are. The last two children left on earth? That's a future generation, my friend. The last generation, if we're not careful."

"Last of a dying breed," I muttered.

The wind shifted again, blowing his pipe smoke into my face. I breathed deep, savoring the aroma. I wasn't a smoker, but the smell of the tobacco reminded me of when things had been normal—of a world without Hamelin's Revenge.

"The important thing to remember," Professor Williams continued, "is that the hero is created as an end result of the journey. He is a product of what happens on the quest. The events that shaped him, changed him, made him less concerned with himself and more concerned with those around him, the larger society. These are the important part. Heroes are not simply born, Lamar. They are forged! And how they are forged makes all the difference."

I thought it over and shrugged. "I gotta be honest, Professor. I still don't feel like much of a hero."

"No? Then how do you see yourself?"

"I feel like a failure. A wimp."

"Trust me, my friend, when I tell you that you are neither of those things."

"I kind of see Mitch as the hero."

"Mr. Bollinger is the warrior—another psychological archetype. The warrior is a representation of a pattern of behavior favoring physical confrontation and prowess to achieve one's goals. The warrior can use his physical powers in a positive way to aid others and society. When you were in school, did you ever read the stories of Beowulf, Achilles, or elder Gilgamesh?"

"Professor, where I went to school, our most important concern was getting through the day without getting shot. We didn't have many books. Books were like kryptonite to most of my classmates."

The professor removed his pipe, tossed his head back, and laughed.

"Yes, that's one of the reasons I was so looking forward to retirement. Trust me, Lamar, that particular loathing of literature is not confined to just inner-city schools. It seems to be present across the nation. Very sad."

"Yeah."

"Well, Achilles and the others I mentioned all used their powers to aid their families and loved ones."

"So you're saying Mitch is part of our family? He's the warrior to my hero, and we're both looking out for the kids?"

"Exactly." He put his pipe back in his mouth. "However, some warriors used their prowess for selfish reasons. Grendel and young Gilgamesh are cautionary examples of this. Luckily for you, Mitch doesn't fall into that subarchetype."

I shook my head. "I still think Mitch is the hero. I mean, he saved us all back in Baltimore. If it wasn't for him, Tasha, Malik, and I would all be zombies now."

"Well, I humbly disagree. However, if it eases your mind, the archetypes like warrior, king, and trickster are rather fluid. One can be warriorlike and tricksterlike, a king and a fool. Remember, they represent *aspects* of personality which individuals tap into or manifest in times of trouble. The hero manifests not aspects of personality, but a total person, the summation of all the qualities that have allowed him to successfully complete the hero journey and safeguard his people or bring back gifts. Going even further, I think the archetypes not only provide a guide for our personal behavior, but also role models for us, as humans, to live up to. At an unconscious level, when the time is appropriate, like right now, we strive to live up to the expectations of the warrior that have been instinctively passed down to us since the dawn of man. That's why we fight when all hope is lost; to not fight would be to deny part of the collective memories that define humanity. We fight because that is who we are. We fight because we are human."

"And what are they?" I cast my hand toward land, even though we couldn't see it in the darkness.

"The dead?" Professor Williams frowned. "Roadkill that doesn't have enough decency to lie down and rot in peace. The waste products of our souls. They're walking toilets, Lamar. Nothing more."

A smile crossed his face. After a second, we both began to snicker, and then laugh. I bent over and clutched my stomach. I couldn't remember the last time I'd laughed that hard. It felt good, like a release.

"Walking toilets," I gasped, straightening up again. "That's good, Professor."

"I always end my dissertations with a joke. That way I can tell if I've put people to sleep."

The ladder clanged. We both turned, and saw Murphy walking toward us. He was stumbling in the darkness, his eyes not yet adjusted.

"Good evening, Mr. Murphy," the professor called.

Murphy jumped, his hand flailing for the rail. He peered toward us, blinking.

"Who's there? Professor Williams? Is that you?"

"Yes, it's me. Mr. Reed is here with me. He and I were just discussing mythology."

Murphy crept closer. "Hey, Lamar."

I nodded. "What's up."

Murphy stood beside us, his collar pulled up against the chill. Despite the summer heat, the ocean was cold at night.

"Couldn't sleep," he said. "It's hot and I got the shakes. I'd kill for a drink right now."

The professor nodded. "I think each of us have something we'd kill for at this point."

I thought about the kids. Yeah, maybe I couldn't kill for Tum, but I'd damn sure kill for them.

"A few of us have been talking," Murphy said, his voice low. "We're not so sure about the chief's plan for this oil rig."

"How come?" I asked. "Seems like as safe a spot as any."

"Sure, if there are no zombies onboard. But what if there are? Then what? Do we really want a repeat of what happened the other day?"

The professor tapped his pipe on the handrail. The ashes drifted away. "So where would you suggest we go, Mr. Murphy?"

The big man shrugged. "My plan all along was to head for the wilderness. Go down into Virginia or West Virginia. Get high up into the mountains, where there is snow all year, and live there."

I frowned. "I may be a city boy and all, but I don't think there's mountains in Virginia that have snow all year long."

"And even if there were," the professor added, "the zombies would find you there, too. The mountains are just as dangerous as the cities—perhaps even more. We have no idea how many members of the animal kingdom are now infected."

Murphy rubbed his grizzled cheeks and sighed. He placed his shaking hands on the railing and sighed. I could tell that he was jonesing bad.

"I don't think they would find us," he said. "What are zombies? They're just mobile corpses and nothing more. Cut off an arm or a leg, and they keep coming. They're dead, but they can move and function and take a hell of a lot of damage. My theory is this—if I get to someplace where the temperature is below freezing, the zombies can't move. Think about it for a second. They're dead, so they have no body heat. There's nothing to keep their bodies from freezing. If they tried to attack us there, they'd literally freeze in their tracks before they could ever reach us. That's a lot more convenient than having to shoot them all in the head or setting them on fire."

The professor looked thoughtful. "Well, biology and science aren't my specialty, but I agree that makes sense. In theory, at least. If their blood and tissue freezes, then they would indeed become immobile. But you must consider something. Could we sail to such a location?"

"Basil had an idea," Murphy said. "There are ski resorts in Pennsylvania and Virginia. We could pull into port and make for one of them."

I shook my head. "That's no good. First of all, we'd never make it there."

"Why not?"

"A group this size? Come on, Murphy! Those things would slaughter us before we made it five miles. We'd have to find reliable transport, gas, more weapons, all that shit. But let's say we did make it to a ski resort. What you gonna do then? Get the artificial snow machine running? Maybe. But that ain't gonna chill the air—it's only making snow. Snow won't freeze them. You need to control the temperature for that. Sure, it would make a good winter hideout, but as soon as spring came, we'd be on the run again."

Murphy muttered under his breath.

"What?" I asked.

"I said, I guess we didn't think of that."

"Your idea does have merit," the professor said. "But we'd have to travel to a region where the temperatures remain below freezing all year round— Antarctica, for example. Such an environment would be hostile to the living as well."

Murphy grunted. "Look around next time we go ashore, Prof. The whole world's pretty fucking hostile."

"Yes, it is. That's why I support the chief's decision. If the undead are aboard the oil rig, it would be far easier to exterminate their limited numbers than to do battle with an entire mainland population."

Murphy still didn't seem convinced. "We're on a ship. Don't see why we can't go to the North Pole or Antarctica, like you said."

"We could," the professor agreed. "But a trek of that magnitude would require a lot more fuel than we currently have. Fuel we can possibly find at our current destination."

I stifled a yawn. I'll give the professor one thing—interesting as the old man was, he'd definitely cured my insomnia.

"Guys," I said, "I'm gonna hit the hay. It's been a long day and I'm wiped out. Murphy, make me one promise, okay?"

"What's that, Lamar?"

"That we stick together. All of us. If you guys don't like the chief's plan, let's talk about it as a group. The last thing we need right now is a fucking mutiny."

He half smiled, half nodded. "No worries, man. Get some sleep."

"Good night, Lamar," the professor said. "Give my regards to the warrior."

"I'll do that. Night."

The ship rolled beneath my feet as we crested a swell. Hanging on to the handrail, I made my way through the darkness, back down the ladder, and then through the hatch and down the passageway. I was surprised to find Mitch standing outside our compartment.

"Where have you been?" he whispered. "I came back and the kids were in there by themselves."

"Sorry," I said. "Couldn't sleep. Went topside to get some air. Are they okay?"

"Yeah, they're fine. I was just a little worried, is all. You okay?"

I nodded. "Yeah, man, I'm fine. How about you?"

"Sure. I was playing cards with Cliff, Tony, Chuck, and Tran."

"Tran can play cards?"

"Well of course he can play, Lamar. Just because he doesn't speak English doesn't mean he's an idiot."

"Point taken. So how was the game?"

"I left early. Tony's in a pissy mood—he's having really bad nicotine cravings. I did find out that we may have trouble with Basil and Murphy, though."

"Oh yeah?"

"Yeah. Apparently, they aren't too happy with our current course. Want to second-guess the chief. Even talked about forcing him to change course, head back to land."

"The professor and I ran into Murphy. He mentioned it, too, but I didn't think he was serious. Figured he was just bullshitting, you know?"

Mitch pulled a small square of gum from his pocket and popped it in his mouth.

"Nicotine gum," he said with a wink. "But don't tell Tony. I don't have much left and I need it to last. Anyway, I got the impression that it was more Basil than Murphy. Basil's the ringleader. The question is, how many people has he swung over to his side and how serious are they?"

We walked down the passageway and back out into the night, so that we wouldn't wake the kids up, and so no one else would hear us while we talked.

"Think we should tell someone?" I asked.

He shrugged. "Well, Chuck already knows. He's going to let the chief and Runkle know about it, too. I guess we'll leave it up to them. It's in their hands. I don't think much of Runkle, but I'll side with him on this. If we have to put them in the brig, then so be it. Last thing we need right now is a mutiny."

"Well, I got your back. Just let me know."

He grinned. "Thanks, man. That means a lot."

"Not that I'll do much good, I guess."

Mitch frowned. "What are you talking about? Ain't nobody else on this ship I'd rather have at my side."

"You know what I'm saying, man. If the shit hits the fan, what good am I? I've got nothing to offer. You and Tony are the experts when it comes to guns. Meanwhile, I couldn't hit the broadside of a fucking barn. Runkle is a cop. We know he can handle himself. The chief knows the boat and Chuck's his new apprentice, so that makes him valuable. Hell, even Murphy's good for something. He keeps us moving down there in the boiler room. Everybody's got their place. So far, all I've done is throw up at the rescue station when we saw those crosses and choke when it came to killing that preacher. The professor says I'm the hero, but I think he must be senile."

"The hero?"

I explained to Mitch all about the archetypes and monomyths and the professor's theories on the two of us. When I was finished, Mitch shook his head, laughing softly.

"Well, if that don't beat all. I'm the warrior, huh? I'll take that, I guess. Better than being the trickster. But he's right, Lamar. In those kid's eyes, you're a hero. They look up to you. After all the bad shit that's happened to them, you're the best person they could have come across."

"But I don't know shit about kids. I'm impatient

with them. I curse too much. I'm not a parental figure."

"Too bad, buddy, because you've got the job whether you want it or not. I think you'll be okay. Take it from me. There's no instruction manual that comes with kids. You do your best and try not to fuck up and realize that you probably will anyway. You're their hero. Try to live up to that."

His voice cracked, and I realized that he was crying. Tears dripped down into his beard.

"Mitch?" I was shocked. "What's wrong, man?"

"I . . . Do you remember our first morning onboard? When we were eating breakfast in the galley? You asked me why I'd gone from Towson down into the city, and I told you I didn't want to talk about it."

"Yeah." I nodded, thinking back. "I remember."

"Well, the truth is, I was looking for my son, Mickey. We always called him Mick. Mitch and Mick—our little family joke. My wife and I got divorced when he was fourteen. I was on the road a lot. Had a sales route at the time—copiers and fax machines for businesses. I did something stupid. Had a one night stand with this girl in New York City—a client of mine. Beautiful girl. She made me feel young again. Even so, I felt guilty about it afterward. Swore I wouldn't do it again and figured my wife would never find out. But I gave the girl my e-mail address and we chatted online a lot, and my wife found the e-mails. Some of them referenced that night. Yeah, I know—I'm a dumb ass.

Anyway, we split up and my son blamed me. He had a hard time with it. A few years later, he got into drugs and dropped out of school. I lost all contact with him. When they declared martial law, I called my ex-wife. I hadn't talked to her in about six months, but it was the end of the world, you know? I was worried about him—about them both. My ex-wife answered. She was worried sick. Turned out she hadn't seen or heard from Mick in months. All she knew was that he was dating this girl named Frankie. She was a prostitute and a heroin addict, and she'd gotten Mick addicted, too. One of my ex-wife's coworkers had apparently seen him and his girlfriend. They were sleeping on the streets down in Fells Point."

"So you went looking for him?"

"Yeah, I did." Mitch sighed. "It was a stupid thing to do, but love makes us dumb sometimes. There was no way he could have been alive. I knew that, deep down inside. But I had to do it anyway, because I'm his father and that's part of it. When you become a parent, you have all these dreams. Maybe your kid will be a quarterback for the Ravens someday, or maybe he'll win the Nobel Peace Prize. My dream was a little simpler than that. I just wanted grandkids. Don't guess I'll ever have one now. But you have these dreams and you'll do anything to help your child achieve them, and sometimes, you do this even if your dreams aren't your kid's desires. You help your kids out. That's what you're supposed to do. But I wasn't there to help Mick, so I had to make up for it, even if he was dead. I had to see it through."

"You could have been killed."

"And I almost was—many, many times. Started out okay. Blew away most of my neighbors—they'd all been infected. But then, once I'd taken care of them, I was home free. My car had a full tank of gas and I had plenty of ammo. Fucking Rambo, right? At first, I stuck to York Road, but believe it or not, it was more congested than Interstate Eighty-three, so I switched to the highway. I made it as far as Television Hill before the fucking car overheated. Then I grabbed my guns out of the trunk and went on foot. Understand me, Lamar. I had to see it through to the end, but I expected to die every second of every minute. Those things were everywhere. The deeper I went into the city, the worse it got. I'd been in the city for two days before I ran across you and the kids."

"Jesus . . ." I was stunned. "Two whole days? How did you make it?"

"Determination. I went there looking for my son and I intended to find him."

"Did you?"

"No." He paused, taking a deep breath. "No, I never did. But I found you guys instead and that's enough for me. I tried. In my heart, I know that and I've made peace with it. I tried to find Mick. I made the effort, and Mick would have appreciated that. It would have been important to him. Nothing else matters. And that's why Tasha and Malik look up to you so much—because they see you trying. So the professor is right, Lamar. You're their hero."

"But I'm not a hero," I snapped. "I'm a fraud, man. A fucking poseur. I'm everything people assume that I am when they first see the color of my skin or find out where I'm from."

"What are you talking about? Is this because you couldn't shoot the preacher?"

"I'm not talking about the preacher. I'm talking about before all of this shit. I did a bad thing, Mitch. A real bad thing."

"What? Were you a drug dealer or something?"

"See?" I pointed a finger at him. "That's exactly what I'm talking about. I'm black and from the ghetto, and when I tell you that I did something bad, you fucking automatically assume it must have been drug related. I must have committed some type of crime."

"Hey," Mitch said, "that's got nothing to do with it. You said you did something bad. Of course I'm gonna assume it's a crime."

"Because I'm black."

"Oh, bullshit."

"No, it's not bullshit, Mitch. You just can't see it from where you're sitting."

He sighed. "Then prove me wrong. Go ahead and tell me what it was."

"That's the thing. I have no right to get pissed off at you, because in the end, I contributed to that bullshit. I became what I hated. See, I lived in the city and shit, but I always felt like an outsider. Not just because I'm gay, but because I didn't do drugs, or sell them, or do any of the other crazy shit that so many people were into. The thug life isn't just something you see in rap videos. So many people emulate it, because it's all they know. It's a way out. A way to fight back. I never wanted to be a part of that."

Mitch nodded silently, encouraging me to continue. I was surprised by the sudden swelling of rage inside me.

"I had a good job in White Marsh, working on the assembly line at the Ford plant. Paid my bills on time, wasn't in too much debt. Didn't have much to show for it all, but I figured good things would come, right? And then I got laid off. They closed the plant down. Opened a new one in China, and shipped our jobs over there. I got on unemployment, but that didn't amount to shit. Couldn't find a job anywhere. Either I wasn't qualified enough or I was too qualified. Shit, I couldn't even get a job in fast food. Every month the stack of past-due bills got higher and I got deeper into shit. Then the phone calls started. Bill collectors. Fucking locusts is what they are. They'd call all hours of the day, even on the weekends. Even on Sunday. I was about to lose everything. And all I could think was 'Why me?' I'd done everything right. You used to see these politicians on TV, saying that black folks needed to work harder—needed to better ourselves and our communities. Well, that's exactly what the hell I was trying to do. And you know what I got for it? I got fucked."

"And that's why you feel like a fraud? Shit, Lamar, it wasn't your fault."

"No, maybe it wasn't my fault. But it sure as hell was a few days later when I took what little money I still had and bought a pistol. And it was definitely my fault when I decided to get even with Ford by robbing one of their dealerships."

"Oh, shit . . ."

"Exactly. I woke up one morning and the bill collectors were calling before I'd even got out of bed. I walked into the Ford dealership with the gun stuffed in my waistband and my shirt pulled down over it. A salesman came over to help me and I told him I wanted to take one of the cars for a test drive. We went out. He was sitting beside me, talking about all the different features and shit. When he told me to turn around, instead, I pulled into an old industrial complex."

"And then what?"

"I robbed him at gunpoint. I was so nervous I thought I'd puke. I think the salesman actually took it better than me. I remember at one point, he was having trouble getting his wallet out of his pants and he apologized. And all I kept thinking was that it should be me who was apologizing, not him. I took all his money, and then I drove us to an ATM and made him empty out his account. When we were finished, I bailed. I was sick for the next three days. Oh, I was out of debt—temporarily, at least. I paid my past-due mortgage and made sure the bank wouldn't foreclose. But the guilt was crushing me, man. I couldn't eat. Couldn't sleep. Figured the cops would kick down my front door at any second. But they never did. And in some ways, that was worse, because that meant I still had to live with the guilt in silence. I'd become everything I hated. And then I was broke again. I was still dealing with all that when Hamelin's Revenge came along. I've been focused on staying alive ever since. But I can't forget about what happened. It's right there, in the past. I can't change it and I can't forget about it. The kids and you and the professor—you all think I'm somebody that I'm not. I ain't no hero. I'm a fucking loser."

He shook his head. "You're a damn fool is what you are."

"Excuse me?"

Mitch grinned. "Don't you see, Lamar? None of that matters now. The past is just that—the past. It's as dead as those things in the streets. We've left it behind. Everyone makes mistakes. That's what molds us. But it doesn't matter who we were or what we did before all of this happened. We're still alive! When the rest of the world is fucking *dying,* we're still here. The only thing that matters now is how we respond and who we become. You know, that preacher back at the rescue station may have been insane, but he was right about one thing."

"What's that?"

"We really are born again. I'm not talking about in any religious sense. We've got a second chance to reinvent ourselves, to become someone different. The professor is right. We're on a quest—all of us. So stop worrying about the past and start thinking about the future. The past is dead."

"So are the zombies," I said. "But that doesn't stop them from coming back and biting us in the ass. What kind of future can we possibly look forward to? Living on the run? Hiding out every time we go to the mainland? That's not living. That's existing."

"It's enough for me. And the same goes for you. Otherwise, you'd walk out on the flight deck right now and jump into the ocean. You're a fighter, same as me—you do it because you don't know what else to do. And now you're fighting for those kids, whether you'll admit to it or not. So suck it up and be a hero. Hell, who knows? We live through this and civilization makes a comeback, then maybe they'll have mythology about us in five thousand years. We'll be history."

I shrugged. "Maybe we already are."

"That's not what I meant," Mitch said, smiling, "and you know it."

His smile grew broader. After a moment, I returned it. We crept back into the compartment and, with the lights out, crawled into our racks. Tasha and Malik didn't stir. The ship gently rolled from side to side, creaking and groaning. Steam pipes along the wall ticked. My stomach grumbled.

"Good night," Mitch whispered.

"Night."

I lay back in my rack and stared at nothing. I thought about the past. Maybe Mitch was right. Maybe it didn't exist anymore. Maybe that version of Lamar Reed was as dead as the city he'd left behind when he sailed out to sea. The future waited right over the horizon, and when the sun came up tomorrow morning, it would rise on the first day of the rest of our lives.

I wondered how long those lives would be.

CHAPTER NINE

The chief had been right about the weather. The next morning we woke to cold rain. A storm had blown in overnight. Massive gray and black clouds swallowed the horizon, obscuring the lines between sea and sky. Thunder boomed across the water. Dime-sized drops of rain pelted the decks. The waves grew larger and the ship tilted like a carnival amusement ride. Most of us hadn't developed our sea legs yet and every time the *Spratling* took a particularly hard roll, we ran into the bulkheads. At breakfast, which consisted of fish we'd caught the day before, we had to hold on to our trays tightly, or else they'd slide down the table and crash into each other. Even those of us who hadn't struggled with seasickness before now looked queasy.

The weather suited the crew's mood. But by noon, the clouds had cleared and the rain stopped. The ocean grew calm, flat like glass, the waves barely cresting. The sun shined down and the temperature climbed again. Seagulls circled the ship, hoping for a handout. Old habits died hard, I guess. There were a million meals walking around on shore for them.

According to the chief, we were still on course for the oil drilling platform. Mitch, Basil, Professor Williams, and I had spent the morning performing other duties below deck. I also spent some time with Tasha and Malik. My late-night conversations with Mitch and the professor kept running through my mind, and I decided to try to live up to whatever the kids wanted me to be. Once the storm had passed, we met up on the flight deck, got out our deep-sea rods and tackle gear, and began the day's fishing. Tran and Nick had saved the guts and heads from yesterday's catch in a bucket so that we could use them for bait. We lined up along the railing with the bait bucket between us and cast our lines. The professor had found a floppy-brimmed hat somewhere onboard and he wore it to keep the sun off his head. He looked like a geriatric Gilligan. Basil was quiet and sullen. He didn't say anything about his mutinous thoughts regarding our destination, and the three of us didn't let on that we knew. Instead, Mitch and the professor traded jokes back and forth, and I laughed. Basil pretty much ignored us, standing off by himself farther down the deck.

We pulled in half a dozen groupers and striped sea bass, and Mitch hooked a small shark, which was about four feet long. Then the professor caught a really nice-sized tuna—enough to feed us all for one meal. He wasn't strong enough to haul it up over the rail, so Mitch grabbed the line and did it for him. The tuna had swallowed the hook. Blood dribbled from its mouth and ran across the deck. The fish flopped around, thrashing its tail like a hammer. Its gills flapped uselessly.

"Can you take it off the hook for me, Mr. Bollinger?"

Mitch grinned. "No way, Professor. I hauled him in for you. You can take him off yourself. I ain't baiting your hook again, either."

"Youth," Professor Williams said in mock disdain. "No respect for their elders."

"You know what they say, man—age before beauty."

Nose wrinkling in disgust, the Professor bent down and grabbed the fish with one hand. His other hand forced its mouth open. Slimy fish blood trickled over his fingers and wrists and dripped onto the deck. He tugged on the line, peering down the tuna's gullet. It wriggled in his grasp.

"Oh dear," the professor said. "He really did swallow the hook. This must be what is meant by 'hook, line and sinker.' Poor thing. He's in bad shape. Will one of you gentlemen please hand me the needle-nose pliers out of the tackle box?"

Basil leaned over and picked up the pliers. As he handed them to the professor, he suddenly drew away.

"What the hell's that on its tail?"

We all looked closer. Near the bottom of the fish's tail was a small, ulcerated sore. It was raw and open, leaking pale fluid.

The professor frowned. "It appears the fish is infected with something; perhaps a parasite or fungus of some kind, or a reaction to some pollutant."

Mitch shook his head. "Looks like a bite mark, doesn't it?"

"That's not a bite," Basil argued. "More like a sore. Professor's right. It's probably a parasite, maybe a worm of some kind. We won't know for sure until Tran and Nick clean it."

The professor took the pliers from Basil and forced them down the tuna's throat. It was still bleeding, and his grip kept slipping as a result. The fish continued struggling. I had to give it credit. Like us, it kept on fighting, even if death was inevitable. Suddenly, the tuna jerked in the professor's grasp. He dropped the pliers. The hook ripped free, taking a chunk of fish innards with it. The line went taught and the hook's point speared the professor's hand, right between his thumb and forefinger. It dug deep, the barbs slipping beneath his skin. Professor Williams shouted in pain and the fish flopped away across the deck. The professor stared at his hand—his own blood flowing overtop the fish blood.

"Jesus," Basil gasped. "You okay, Professor?"

The color drained from the older man's face. "No, I am most assuredly not okay. It hurts a great deal. Could one of you please get it out? I'm feeling light-headed."

I held him up from behind while Mitch went to work on the hook. The professor was bathed in sweat, but his skin felt cold. He hadn't been kidding. He was limp in my arms—on the verge of passing out.

"You'll be fine," I assured him. "You're just in mild shock. Take deep breaths and try putting your head between your knees.

"I'm sorry," he apologized. "I'm afraid that I don't deal very well with pain. I feel pretty silly."

"Don't worry about it. I'd freak out too, if I had a fishhook in my hand."

Frowning, Mitch jiggled the hook. The professor groaned.

"It's in there pretty good," Mitch said. "The barbs are underneath your skin. I'm going to have to work it out slowly."

The professor gulped. "Will it hurt?"

"Yeah."

"Then I suggest that Lamar and Basil hold me down. I'd hate to lash out at you in the heat of the moment, Mitch."

Mitch grinned. "I'd hate that, too. Hold still, now."

Basil held the professor's legs while I held his free hand. He gritted his teeth and moaned as Mitch began working the hook free. More blood flowed. I looked away from it, glancing over at the fish. Incredibly, it was still flopping around on the deck. It almost seemed as if it were trying to reach Mitch, heaving itself toward him in a series of flips and leaps. Then I realized it was probably just trying to get back into the water. Basil turned to look at it as well, his grip on the professor momentarily forgotten. The professor's arm jerked and the hook tore free, taking a good chunk of his skin with it. The professor cried out and Mitch cursed Basil.

"What the hell are you doing? I told you to hold him."

"It's the tuna. Look at it. Damn thing's still alive."

"Throw it back over the side," Mitch said. "That fish is more trouble than it's worth. Nobody is going to eat it with that sore on its tail anyway."

Basil made a grab for the tuna with both hands. The fish was so slippery with blood that it slid from his grasp and fell back to the deck. Its mouth worked soundlessly. He picked it up again and dumped it over the side. The tuna splashed into the ocean and then vanished beneath the surface. Basil looked at his hands in disgust and held them up for us to see.

"Gross. I got blood and scales all over me."

"Go wash up," Mitch said. "And take the professor with you. Get him cleaned up. Find out from the chief if we've got any hydrogen peroxide or disinfectant onboard."

"I'm sure we do," Basil said.

I helped Professor Williams to his feet. "You okay to stand?"

He nodded weakly. "Yes, I think so. I'll be fine now. Thank you both, gentlemen. You see, I was right. The two of you are the embodiments of the warrior and the hero."

Mitch flexed his bicep and laughed. "That's us."

The professor leaned on Basil for support and the two of them went below. Mitch and I fished for another hour, but didn't get any more bites. It was weird—as if the tuna had warned away all the other fish in the sea. Finally, we took count of our catch and decided that we had enough to last the crew till tomorrow. Then we dumped the bait bucket over the side. The chum floated atop the waves—a gory treat for any scavengers lurking below the surface. A few of the birds darted down to scoop entrails from the water. We stored the fishing gear and headed below deck to clean up. Both Mitch and I smelled like fish. I remember thinking at least we didn't have the tuna's blood all over our hands.

"Is Mitch gonna be your new boyfriend?"

I was stunned by the question, and I stared at Malik for a moment, trying to figure out if he was serious or just joking around. His expression was earnest.

"No," I said. "I don't think Mitch is gay, Malik."

Dinner had been over for several hours and the three of us were getting ready to turn in for the night. Mitch was off playing cards again with the guys in the engineering compartment. The ship was quiet, except for the occasional tick or groan from the pipes. Most of the crew had gone to bed. Both Basil and the professor had been absent from the galley during dinner. I'd gone to check on them before we ate. The professor said he wasn't feeling good—too much excitement for one day. His voice was tired. His hand was bandaged and doctored. Basil didn't answer when I knocked on the hatch to his berthing compartment. Curiosity got the best of me, and I opened the hatch and peeked inside. He was asleep and did not stir when I whispered his name. After dinner, Joan and Alicia had volunteered to take them each a plate of food and check in on them. We hadn't seen them since, but I assumed both men were okay. Otherwise, the women would have told us.

"Okay," Malik said. "I just wondered. The two of you are friends. I wasn't sure if that meant you were boyfriends, too."

"Gay men can be friends with other guys, Malik. That doesn't necessarily mean they're 'together.' I like Mitch, but not that way. He's a good guy, and he's helped us out quite a bit. We would have never gotten away from the dogs if it hadn't been for him."

"I like him, too," Malik said, closing his *Walking Dead* comic. I'd been right about that. He'd read it several times every night since I'd given it to him. "Both of you."

Tasha looked up from a picture she was drawing with some pens and pencils that Carol had given to her.

"Malik never knew our dad."

"I did too."

"No, you didn't. You said you can't remember him."

"I do . . . a little bit. I think. Sometimes . . ."

I sat down on the rack next to him. "It's okay if you don't. I don't remember my father. He left when I was still a baby."

"Really? Our dad did the same thing. Momma said he was no good."

I chuckled. "My mother used to say the same thing about mine. I used to worry, when I was your age. Thought that maybe I was somehow weaker or dumber than the other guys in my class, because I didn't have a father to teach me stuff the way they did. But you know what? Some of them would have been better off without their fathers around. Some of their dads were drunks or abusive or just ignored them. And you know what else? I was better off without my dad. From everything I've heard he would have been a lousy role model."

"What's a role model?" Malik asked.

"Someone you look up to," Tasha told him. "Like how you look up to Lamar and Mitch."

Malik twitched uncomfortably, clearly embarrassed that his older sister had revealed that. I wasn't sure what to say, and before I could respond, the hatch opened and Mitch walked into the compartment. Apparently, he'd had a good night with the cards. He grinned from ear to ear. He shut the hatch behind him and started to speak, but then looked at the three of us.

"What's going on? What did I miss?"

"Nothing," I said. "Why?"

"Because the way the three of you got quiet, it looks like you were talking about me."

I grinned. "You're paranoid. Malik and I were just talking about what it's like for a boy to grow up without a dad."

"Probably better off sometimes." Mitch sat down on the rack across from us. "My old man was a real jerk. He didn't beat me or abuse me, nothing like that, but he was never there. He was always working, and if he wasn't at work, then he was at the bar with his union buddies. Never had time for us. My folks got divorced when I was ten. I liked my stepfather a lot more than I did my real dad. He was there, at least."

"What happened to them?" I asked.

He shrugged. "My real dad died of prostate cancer about ten years ago. He was one of these guys that never liked going to the doctor. Usually, you can survive prostate cancer if they catch it in time, and it moves so slowly that diagnosing and treating it are pretty easy to do. But he was a real bull-headed son of a bitch. He didn't go to the doctor until it was too late. My stepdad and my mom retired in Arizona. I talked to them about a week before Hamelin's Revenge. Now . . . I don't know."

Malik sighed. "Shit. I'd just be happy to *have* a dad at all."

"Well," Mitch said, "here's something I've learned over time, Malik. A family isn't just a mom, dad, brother, and sister. It can be any combination of those. And sometimes, the people don't even have to be related. Hell, you could say we've got our own little family right here. Me, you, Tasha, and Lamar. We've been through a lot in the last week, but we've stuck together and looked out for each other, right? That's what families do."

Mitch punched him playfully on the shoulder and Malik giggled.

"So if we're a family," Tasha said with a smile, "then which one of you is the mother?"

Mitch and Malik looked at me, both of them grinning. I cut them off with a laugh.

"Don't even say it or I'll kick both your butts."

Mitch stood up. "Hold that thought. I'm gonna go take a leak and brush my teeth."

He opened the hatch and stepped halfway out into the passageway. He stopped suddenly. We heard Mitch say, "Joan, what's wrong?"

And then he screamed and we were a family no more.

Mitch stumbled back into the berthing compartment. His forearm gushed blood from a large, ragged hole. The wound was alarmingly deep. I could see tendons inside the hole. His free hand fumbled with his hip holster, trying to free his pistol. The shock must have prevented him from doing so, because his fingers slid away. Joan lurched through the hatchway, chewing the missing piece of Mitch's arm. She was obviously dead. The left side of her face and neck had been gnawed off. The bites still bled, so she hadn't been dead for long. Her hands and face were smeared scarlet.

With an angry yell, Mitch spun and delivered a kick to Joan's ribcage. More blood jetted from his arm. We heard Joan's ribs snap, yet in death, she was unaffected. The blow knocked her backward. Grunting, she slammed into the passageway's far bulkhead and slumped to the floor. Then her broken form stumbled slowly to her feet again, licking Mitch's blood from her lips.

"Shut the hatch," Mitch shouted. He held his forearm just below the wound and squeezed, trying to stop the flow of blood.

I slammed the hatch shut just as Joan reached for

the doorway. I heard her fingernails screeching on the other side of the steel. Then she started pounding. I turned back to Mitch. He was crouched in the corner, staring at his arm in shock. Tasha grabbed a pillowcase and approached him with it.

"Here, Mitch. Let me stop the bleeding."

"No," he gasped. "Just hand me the pillowcase and then stay back. Don't get my blood on you. And watch out where I've already bled on the floor. Don't go near it."

"But you need help. You need—"

"I need you to *listen,* girl."

Flinching, Tasha took a faltering step backward.

"I'm sorry," Mitch apologized. "I don't mean to be harsh, Tasha, but I'm already infected and I don't want you getting it, too."

From out in the passageway, I heard Carol call out. Her voice was muffled, but alarmed.

"What's going on? Did someone scream?"

"Carol," I shouted through the closed hatch. "Stay in your compartment. Joan's a zombie!"

"What?"

"She's right outside our door. Just keep your hatch closed."

I took a step forward, making a wide berth around the half-dollar sized drops of Mitch's blood.

"Mitch, it might not be too late. We could . . ."

The look he gave me froze the words in my throat.

"You've seen it happen, Lamar. So have I. Too many times. Infection is instantaneous. It doesn't matter if we cut my arm off or burn the wound or pour a gallon of fucking bleach on it. We both know what's going to happen."

Tasha began to cry. A second later, Malik joined her. The muffled pounding continued outside.

"Goddamn it." I punched the locker in frustration. "God fucking damn it."

"Yeah," Mitch said, wrapping the pillowcase around his arm like a tourniquet. "Believe me, I feel the same way. But that ain't gonna help us right now, Lamar. Hold it together for the kids. We need to come up with a plan."

"We're supposed to be safe," Tasha whimpered. "You guys promised. You said we'd be safe on the ship. You said the zombies couldn't get us!"

"Yeah." Malik wiped his runny nose on his shirt sleeve. "How did they get onboard?"

I shook my head. "We don't know guys. We just don't know. It doesn't make any sense."

Moaning with pain, Mitch tightened the pillowcase. It was already soaked through with blood. Brushing away her tears, Tasha stripped the sheet off his bed, grabbed Mitch's pocketknife from his locker, and began cutting the sheet into strips. Joan kept clawing at the door.

"Can Joan work the latch?" Malik asked, glancing at the door.

"I don't think so." I turned back to Mitch. "There has to be a way. Amputation? Fire? You can't just give up."

Teeth clenched, he finished tying off the bite. The linens were stained red, but the bleeding seemed to have stopped.

"I ain't giving up," he said. "Just making better use of my time. Don't know how long I got, so let's not mess around. Get the guns out. All of them."

Malik stopped crying completely. "The grenades, too?"

"Yeah, Malik." Mitch grinned, despite the pain. "The grenades, too."

I lifted up his mattress and pulled out the rifle and the shotgun. Then I grabbed the ammunition and grenades. Mitch propped himself up against the wall and nodded.

"You'll have to load them. And Tasha, you're gonna have to carry a rifle this time. I can fire the pistol, even with this bum arm. But there's no way I'll be able to handle a rifle."

"I can do it," Tasha said, "if you teach me how."

"Won't be much time," Mitch said. "But I'll try."

"Maybe you shouldn't have a gun at all," I suggested. "I mean, no offense, Mitch, but you said it yourself. We're on borrowed time here."

"Yeah, but I ain't dead yet. What—you think I'm going to turn on you guys? I've got to die before I become a zombie, Lamar. So I might as well take out as many of these damn things as I can before that happens. Who knows how many are loose on the ship."

"How did they get onboard?" I asked, echoing the kids.

"Well, let's think about it for a moment. However it happened, they got to Joan first. By the looks of her, she hasn't been dead long. We saw her at dinner, right?"

The three of us nodded.

"Okay," Mitch said. "Then it happened between the time she left the galley and now."

"Was there anybody else in the passageway?"

"I don't think so." Mitch shrugged, clenching his teeth as more pain shot through him. "I really . . . didn't get a chance to see. She attacked me . . . right away. She must have been coming down the corridor."

I frowned. "Do you remember which direction she came from?"

Mitch paused, thinking about it. "Forward."

"Her compartment is aft. So she wouldn't have been coming from there. After dinner, Joan and Alicia were going to check in on the professor and Basil. . . ."

My voice trailed off. The realization jolted me. My stomach lurched and my head swam. I thought I might pass out, so I sat down on the floor.

"Lamar," Tasha cried out. "What's wrong?"

"The professor and Basil. Both of their berthing areas are in the forward section. Joan was coming from their compartments."

"Maybe," Mitch said. "But that still doesn't explain—"

"The fish." I slammed my palm down on the floor. "The tuna—the one that swallowed the hook. Don't you see? It kept thrashing around even after it had been out of the water for so long. It was wounded. Bleeding! And the professor had an open wound on his hand. His hand was covered with *the fish's blood*."

Malik frowned. "What are you talking about?"

I jumped up. "Remember when the dead first started coming back to life? There were cross-species jumps. Well, that's happened again. Hamelin's Revenge has spread to the fish. It's in the fucking ocean now. The tuna was already dead. We just didn't realize it. Remember that sore on its tail? We thought it was some kind of fungus or parasite, but you were right. You said it was a bite, Mitch. We should have listened to you. We should have paid attention, especially after all we've seen. Horses were supposed to be immune, but the other day, the chief said he'd seen a zombie horse. It can jump species. *We should have fucking thought!*"

"Lamar." His voice dropped to a whisper. "Get a . . . grip on yourself, man. You're hysterical, and that's not . . . going to help us . . . right now."

"Lamar," Tasha pleaded. "You're scaring Malik. Please help."

"Sorry." I took a deep breath. "I'm sorry, guys. It's just not fair."

"No," Mitch said. "It's not. But it happened anyway, and we can't . . . change that. Right now, we need to stop it before anyone else gets . . . killed. Please, Lamar—while I can still think and move?"

"Okay." I forced myself to calm down.

Mitch smiled. "You keep . . . asking everyone why we fight to survive when . . . it all seems so hopeless. Why we continue to go on? This is why. Because you're a hero . . . and that's what heroes do. They rise to the . . . occasion."

I nodded, unable to speak around the lump in my throat.

"What are we gonna do now?" Malik asked, running his fingers over the grenades.

Mitch struggled to sit up farther. "Well, the first thing is that . . . you're not to use those grenades. Set it off in the wrong spot and you'll . . . sink this boat. They are a last resort, and I'm going to keep them . . . on me."

"Well then what the hell am I gonna use? I need something, too. I want to blow stuff up again."

"We'll find something for you. For now, reach into my locker and pull out that big bayonet."

"Man, I don't want no stupid knife. Give that to Tasha."

"I've already got his pocketknife," Tasha said.

"Malik," Mitch groaned. "Don't . . . argue with me."

Sulking, Malik did as he was told. His attitude changed when he saw the size of the bayonet— military-issue and nearly twelve inches long. It looked very sharp. Until now, I hadn't even known Mitch had it.

"Now, that's a knife," Malik said, his demeanor changed.

Mitch grinned. "We cool now?"

"Hell, yeah!"

"Good. Now, Lamar, slide me the . . . weapons and the ammo. Tasha, go listen at the door . . . and tell us what you hear."

While he checked and loaded the guns—carefully, so as not to bleed on them—Tasha crept to the hatch and listened. Her upper lip quivered with fear, and her eyes were wide.

"Miss Joan is still out there," she whispered. "I can hear her scratching on the door. Sounds like when our teacher at school, Ms. Price, used to run her fingers down the chalkboard. And there's a banging noise too, but it sounds far away."

Mitch slid bullets into the pistol's magazine. "No screams or gunshots?"

Tasha shook her head.

"How about . . . Carol? Do you hear her?"

"No."

"Good. That means . . . she listened to Lamar and is still inside her compartment. Okay, Joan is infected . . . so we have to assume that Alicia is, as well. That means there are at least . . . four zombies onboard."

"Four?" I was confused. "There's Joan, Professor Williams, and maybe Alicia."

"Right."

"So then who's the fourth?"

"Basil. He had the . . . tuna's blood on him, too."

"Shit. I'd forgotten about that. But if he didn't have an open cut and didn't get it in his mouth, he might be okay."

"Maybe, but we have to . . . assume he's one of them . . . now."

Carol called out and we yelled back, telling her to stay inside.

"The professor and Basil are probably mobile," Mitch continued. "They died from the disease, rather than from . . . an actual attack by an infected corpse. Alicia's the wild card. Maybe they . . . tore her to pieces, or maybe . . . she's still mobile, too."

"Or maybe she got away from them," Malik offered. "Maybe she made it up to the bridge and warned the chief."

I could tell from the expression on his face that Mitch's pain was growing worse, and when he spoke again, we heard it in his voice.

"I hope . . . that you're right. But . . . we've got to assume . . . o-otherwise. So . . . here's the p-plan. We're going to . . . open that d-door, take care of Joan, and then . . . s-search the ship. . . . Let me go into the passageway f-first. . . . I'm already infected, so I s-should be . . . on point. Once we're sure the . . . passageway is clear, we'll . . . w-work our way f-forward. . . . Lamar, if we get separated . . . we'll meet back here. K-kids, once we're g-gone, I want you to . . . s-shut the hatch behind us and don't open it f-for . . . anybody."

"Screw that," Tasha yelled. "We ain't staying behind. We're going with you. Look at you—you can barely talk at this point."

"Yeah," Malik said, moving to her side. "Ya'll are gonna need our help."

Groaning, Mitch stumbled to his feet. "It's n-not . . . open f-for . . . debate. Now Tasha, come . . . here and let me . . . t-teach you how to use this . . . r-rifle. When you f-fire it, it'll . . . knock you . . . over if you're n-not . . . careful."

"No." She stomped her foot. "We're going with you. It ain't open for discussion."

"Tasha," Mitch sighed. "W-we d-don't . . . have time t-to . . . argue. Now d-drop it . . . and p-pay . . .

attention, or I'll have L-Lamar . . . lock you b-both . . . inside this . . . . c-compartment."

Tasha bit her lip to keep from responding. Her hands curled into fists.

Mitch went over the basics of the rifle, quickly taught her how to hold it and how to sight, showed her where the safety was and how to change the magazine. Then he handed me the shotgun.

"Th-think you c-can . . . handle that b-better . . . now?"

I nodded. "I'm the hero, remember? I'm just glad you had extra shells that would fit this, otherwise it'd be pretty fucking useless."

"Me, t-too. . . . Okay, hero . . . let's d-do this. . . . Malik, m-move . . . away f-from the . . . hatch."

"Mitch. Lamar." Tasha picked up the rifle. "Wait a second."

We turned to her. I heard Mitch take a deep breath, prepared to argue more, but Tasha was done arguing. Even as we turned, she swept past us and ran toward the hatch.

"Open the door, Malik!"

He followed his sister's order and flung the hatch open. Then he ducked behind the steel door. Only his feet were visible. Joan half-tumbled through the doorway. Tasha snapped the rifle upward, set it against her shoulder like Mitch had just taught her, and squeezed the trigger. Her aim was perfect. Joan's head exploded, showering the hatch and the bulkheads with blood, hair and bone fragments. The rifle bucked, and the force of the blast knocked her backward. Tasha cried out in pain and surprise but kept her footing.

Outside, Carol screamed. Her voice was still muffled, which meant she had at least stayed inside her berthing area.

Malik slammed the hatch door shut again, carefully avoiding the gore. He and Tasha checked each other, making sure they hadn't gotten hit by the splatter, and then they turned to us.

"You said we were a family," Malik said, his tone serious. "You said we got to stick together."

Tasha nodded, rubbing her shoulder. "Now let's do it. Or Malik and I will lock you both in here."

Mitch and I turned to each other in disbelief, and then back to the kids.

"Okay", I said. "Let's go. But you stay behind me and Mitch. Understand?"

They nodded.

Mitch and I both tried to stifle grins, but failed. The kids smiled back.

I readied the shotgun. Mitch unholstered his pistol with difficulty, but managed to hold it in his uninjured arm. Malik brandished the bayonet and licked his lips. Tasha's arms sagged from the weight of the rifle. Nodding to each other, we stepped over Joan's unmoving corpse, opened the hatch again, and moved as one into the passageway.

Alicia waited for us there—dead.

She was very hungry.

CHAPTER TEN

Alicia stood at the end of the passageway, leaning against the starboard bulkhead. Her head swayed limply in time to the ship's rolling. Whoever had killed her—Basil or the professor—had done it brutally. One of her arms was nearly fleshless from the elbow down to her wrist. It looked like the skin had been chewed off. The only things left were tendons and bone. A few ragged scraps dangled from the bones. One side of her face had been stripped, too—not just of its skin, but the eye, ear, lips, and scalp, as well. Her torn shirt was so soaked with blood that it was impossible to tell what its original color had been. Now it was just a deep red. Beneath the shredded cloth were more gaping bite wounds. Her other hand was stained red. It was impossible for me to tell if it was from her blood or someone else's. She stumbled toward us, leaving a scarlet trail along the bulkhead. Alicia raised her head. Her lipless gums and teeth worked soundlessly. She took a few tentative steps forward, almost tripping over her own feet.

Carol let out a muffled shout. "Lamar? Mitch? Children? Are you there?"

"Mrs. Beck," Tasha called out, "stay inside your room. There's another one out here."

"What's happening?" Carol yelled.

Mitch drew a bead and gunned Alicia down. The pistol jumped in his hand. She toppled over face-first. Her limp form smacked against the floor like a side of beef. Between the bullet and the impact of the fall, her head split open. All four of us jumped back as her blood splattered across the bulkhead and tiles. One of her broken front teeth skidded toward us.

"Oh my God!" Carol screamed from inside her compartment. It was hard to hear her over the echoes of the blast. "Who got shot? What's going on? Somebody talk to me."

I approached her hatch door and rapped on it with my free hand. "It's okay, Carol. Come on out. The coast is clear."

She opened the hatch and peeked outside. "Lamar, what is going on?"

"Hamelin's Revenge jumped species again."

"What?"

"It spread to the fish. The professor got infected this afternoon, but we didn't know it. Now he's loose onboard. Joan and Alicia were both attacked. We believe Basil might be one of them, too."

"Professor Williams—that nice old man? And J-Joan and Alicia?"

She stepped out into the passageway, took one look at Alicia and Joan's bodies and then screamed. Her fingers dug into her cheeks. Her eyes were wide and terrified. Her shriek seemed to have no end.

Mitch grunted. "W-we . . . d-don't have . . . time . . . f-for this."

His arm was bleeding again. It ran down his sleeve in rivulets and dripped onto the floor. Sweat plastered his hair to his head. His beard was matted with saliva.

"Oh no," Carol gasped. "Mitch—you've been bit, too?"

Mitch nodded. "G-go . . . b-back inside your . . . c-compartment . . . and s-stay . . . there until . . . we come back . . . for you. It's not safe . . . out h-here."

Each word seemed to bring pain with it. His face was bathed in perspiration; the tendons in his neck strained.

"You okay?" I asked him, immediately feeling stupid. Of course he wasn't okay. He was fucking dying.

"N-no." Mitch doubled over, clutching his stomach with his wounded arm. "It s-spreads . . . f-faster than you . . . think. I can . . . feel it . . . inside. . . . Like w-worms . . . c-crawling though my veins."

He collapsed, falling across Alicia's unmoving corpse. The gun slipped from his fingers and clattered across the floor. Both were slick with blood.

"Mitch?"

Tasha started forward, reaching for him. I pulled her back.

"Get inside with Mrs. Beck. Both of you. Right now."

"But Mitch is—"

"Now!"

The kids jumped at the exclamation. Carol ushered them inside her compartment and shut the hatch. I took a few hesitant steps toward Mitch, carefully avoiding the gore on the tiles. Mitch's arms and legs twitched, and he groaned.

"Mitch? Hey man, can you hear me."

He slowly raised his head. His eyes were bloodshot and gummy, and his complexion was eggshell white.

"D-do it," he whispered, his voice slurred. "Don't . . . let me . . ."

I shook my head. "I can't. I can't just shoot you. It's not in me."

"P-please," he hissed. "D-do it . . . Lamar. . . . T-time to . . . b-be a . . . h-hero."

His head fell back again and he closed his eyes. His body twitched a few more times and then he was still.

"Oh, Mitch," I whispered. I wanted to cry, but couldn't. "I'm sorry, man. This is so fucked-up."

Then he began to move again. His legs jittered and his arms jerked. He sat up straight, dead eyes looking right at me. There was no hint of intelligence or recognition—just a naked, all-consuming hunger and need. His mouth opened in a toothy grimace. His arms reached for me, fingers flexing. He moaned.

I shot him. I wasn't even aware that I'd aimed the shotgun. Didn't feel my finger on the trigger. I didn't think about it—it just happened.

The blast echoed down the passageway. My ears

rang. My hands went numb for a moment. Even as the spent shell bounced off the bulkhead and gun smoke swirled through the air, I was running down the hall. I headed for the forward section of the ship. My plan was to find the professor first. I owed it to him. Then I'd deal with Basil. I rounded the corner, still unable to hear anything, and almost slammed into Tony and Chuck. All three of us jumped backward, and for a brief second, I thought that Tony was going to shoot me. Then he realized who I was. Chuck shouted out a frightened cry. The former forklift driver was armed with a handgun.

Tony lowered his weapon. "What the fuck is going on, Lamar? We heard shots."

I had to strain to hear him because of the ringing in my ears.

"We've got zombies loose on the ship. Joan and Alicia were both infected. They got Mitch."

"Why are you shouting?"

"Sorry," I apologized. "Can't hear very well. The professor is one of them, too. We've got to find him before he gets anybody else. Basil might be infected, too."

"Zombies," Chuck said. "How the hell did they get onboard?"

"The fish. It's spread to the ocean now. The professor caught an infected tuna this afternoon. We didn't realize it was a zombie then. It looked normal—must have been a fresh kill. It wasn't rotting yet. He and Basil both had its blood on their hands. The professor got a fishhook stuck in his hand and the blood must have mixed. . . ."

Tony and Chuck stared at me as if I'd lost my

mind. Then Tony shouldered his rifle and peeked around the corner, spotting the bodies. He approached them with caution, stared at the damage, and then turned back to me.

"Okay," he said. "I believe you. Alicia is pretty torn up. The bite marks on her are apparent."

"I don't give a fuck if you believe me or not. I'm finding the rest of the fuckers before anybody else gets killed."

"Then I'm coming with you," Tony said.

Chuck nodded. "So am I."

The hinges on Carol's hatch squealed as it opened. Tasha and Malik poked their heads outside.

"We'll all go." Tasha's tone was defiant.

Behind them, we heard Carol urging them back inside.

"You're staying here," I told the kids. "No more bullshit."

Malik stomped his foot. "But Mitch said—"

I interrupted him. "I don't care what Mitch said. If we're family, then you're going to listen to me when I tell you to do something. Get inside now. Don't make me tell you again."

"We should grab Mitch's gun," Chuck said, "or at least the grenades."

I shook my head. "His blood is all over them. Don't risk getting infected. You got enough ammo?"

"I'm good."

"Then let's go."

Tony, Chuck, and I set off down the passageway. They followed my lead. Somehow, I'd ended up in charge. The professor had been right—my journey was changing me. I hadn't even been aware of assuming leadership. Just like shooting Mitch. I hadn't thought about it. I'd just done it. Gone were my fears and my hesitation. I moved with an air of self-assuredness that I'd never possessed. My stride had a grim purpose. The gun felt like an extension of my body. My head was clear. So was my conscience.

We continued working our way forward, staying about five feet apart from each other. I kept the point position, Tony followed me, and Chuck brought up the rear. I clutched the shotgun tightly. My hearing had returned and the ringing in my ears was gone, but there was nothing to hear, anyway. Silence engulfed the ship. The only sound was my heart pounding in my head.

"Did you guys see anyone else?" I asked.

"Chief Maxey and Officer Runkle are on the bridge," Chuck said. "Or at least they were when I went to bed. They were monitoring the radio, trying to raise any other ships in the vicinity."

"Did they find any?"

He shook his head.

"So, let's see." Tony tilted his head from side to side, cracking his neck. "Carol and the kids are back there, safe. The chief and Runkle are topside. That leaves Nick, Cliff, Murphy, and Tran unaccounted for. Nick and Cliff probably went to sleep. They were watching a movie earlier."

The ship had a small TV/VCR combo unit that the chief and various security guards had used when the *Spratling* was tied-up in port. With no broadcast or satellite television signals to pick up, our selections had been limited to repeated viewings of *The Wild Geese*, Clint Eastwood's *Pale Rider*, Tom Skerritt in *Bonneville*, and *Delta Force* with Chuck Norris—all on grainy old videotapes. Nick, Cliff, and Tum (when he'd been alive) had been known to argue about who would win in a fight—Chuck Norris or the zombies. My money was on Chuck.

"No telling where Murphy is," Tony said. "And Tran . . ."

He trailed off. I knew what he was thinking.

"None of us know shit about him," I said. "We don't even know if he's Korean, Japanese, or Chinese. We just think of him as the Asian guy. That's pretty fucked-up. He deserves a lot better. I mean, think what it must be like for him. A stranger among strangers, left alive with a bunch of people who don't speak his language. That sucks."

Tony grimaced. "Yeah, that's some life."

"If he's even still alive," Chuck muttered. "Let's face it, guys. We don't know how many of us are left—who's dead and undead."

The passageway ended at a closed hatch. I opened the hatch and stepped in Nick Kontis.

He'd been shredded. Arms and legs pulled from their sockets, head ripped from the neck, body torn open and his insides scooped out. His clothing was nothing more than rags. His forehead and cheeks had been either slashed or clawed. Long, bloody furrows covered the flesh. Nick's limbs were partially eaten, gnawed on like turkey drumsticks at Thanksgiving. His blood had been splashed all over the walls, and his guts left a trail down the passageway, as if whoever had been eating them had dropped crumbs every few feet. Despite all of this, Nick was lucky. His attacker had succeeded in smashing his skull open and scooping out the insides. His disembodied head would not be coming back. Nick's eyes stared up at us.

I raised my foot and examined my sole. The blood hadn't seeped through. I was okay. No risk of infection—if Nick had even had time to become infected before he was ripped apart. Breathing a heavy sigh of relief, I gingerly picked my way through the slaughter.

"Careful," I warned. "Don't touch the walls. There's blood everywhere. Don't get it on you."

Tony and Chuck waded around the mess. Something squished beneath Chuck's boot heel, and he gagged. He examined the bottom of his foot and turned pale.

"Who do you think got him?" Chuck asked.

"Joan or Alicia," Tony said. "Or maybe both of them."

I frowned. "How do you know?"

"Look at the scratches on Nick's face. Those were made by someone with very long fingernails."

"So that means we may only have to deal with one more zombie; possibly two, if Basil is dead."

We crept on. At the next hatch was a red emergency phone that dialed directly into the pilothouse. I picked it up and listened to it ring. On the third ring, Chief Maxey picked up.

"Bridge." he sounded tired and frustrated.

"Chief, this is Lamar. We've got a problem."

"What's wrong?"

Quickly, I told him what had happened. The chief responded with a string of creative profanity.

"Where are you now?" he asked when he was done cursing. "There should be a stenciled series of numbers next to the hatch. That will give me your exact location."

I found them and read the numbers off to him.

"Okay," he said. "Runkle is on his way down. Continue working your way forward. He'll meet you guys in the middle. I want all of you to check in with me periodically. Use the emergency phones like the one you're on now. And Lamar?"

"Yeah?"

"Be careful."

"Will do."

I hung up and glanced back at Tony and Chuck.

"They okay?" Tony asked.

I nodded. "Runkle's working his way toward us from the other end of the ship."

"By himself?" Chuck snorted. "Dude may be kind of a dick, but super-cop's got balls."

I opened the next hatch. "Let's try to find the rest of the zombies before he does. That way, he won't have to use those balls."

The ship suddenly jolted beneath our feet. All three of us reached for the bulkhead to balance ourselves. It felt like the chief had increased our speed. When we were sure that the ship wasn't going to take a big roll and knock us over, we continued on. As we approached Basil's berthing compartment, we slowed down. The hatch stood open and the light was on inside. Tony and Chuck flattened themselves against the bulkhead. I crept up to the door and jumped through, holding the shotgun at the ready. The compartment was empty. There was no sign of Basil, and no sign of a struggle. The blanket and sheet were rumpled, and the pillow still held the indentation from where he'd slept. His shoes sat on the floor next to the bed.

"No sign of him," I said, stepping back out into the passageway. "Let's try the professor's room."

We went back through the hatch—Tony in the lead this time. Basil was waiting for us. He must have been in one of the other compartments. He'd probably heard us and had been stymied by the closed hatch. Basil's corpse was in good shape—no scratches or bite marks. He'd apparently died in his sleep, even as Hamelin's Revenge coursed through his veins. His mouth was crusted with blood and he clutched a half-eaten heart—probably Nick's.

"Fuck!"

Tony raised his rifle and tried to get off a shot, but the zombie was too close to him. The rifle became wedged against the bulkhead. Chuck and I were stuck on the other side of the hatch, and with the struggle taking place in the doorway we couldn't shoot Basil without hitting Tony. Basil's arm lashed out and he grabbed the rifle barrel. Tony fought to wrench it away but Basil was stronger. He tugged on the weapon and Tony refused to let go. Basil pulled Tony closer. Before he could get away, Basil's teeth snapped shut on Tony's nose. Blood squirted out from between Basil's lips. We heard cartilage crunching, even over Tony's agonized screams. Tony released the rifle and shoved Basil away. The zombie stumbled backward, taking Tony's nose, upper lip, and the soft flesh around his eyes with him. Tony's shrieks became a high-pitched, unending whine. His skin stretched like taffy before finally tearing free. Basil immediately stopped his attack and greedily devoured it, dropping the intestine and using both hands to shove Tony's ripped face into his slavering mouth.

Tony stumbled backward, his arms pinwheeling. He kicked his rifle and it clattered across the floor to Basil. The zombie ignored it. Chuck grabbed Tony before he could collapse, and dragged him past me. Now that I had a clear shot, I opened fire with the shotgun. Flame belched from the barrel. The blast caught Basil in the face. The shot pellets peppered his skin, but he did not fall. Even at close range, the spray pattern was too broad. Instead of falling, Basil swallowed, Tony's flesh bulging in his throat as it slid down his dead esophagus. Still hungry and unperturbed by the damage to himself, Basil lurched forward for more. I pumped the shotgun and fired again. This time, I did more damage. Knocked off his feet, Basil flew backward through the hatch.

Chuck screamed. I whipped around and did the same. Chuck was spinning around and slamming himself against the bulkhead in an effort to dislodge Cliff. I wondered where the hell he'd come from. The passageway had been deserted just moments before. Cliff's corpse must have snuck up behind us. Chuck continued turning. The dead college student clung to his back, his legs wrapped around Chuck's waist, his arms wrapped around his chest, his teeth clamped down on Chuck's right ear. Tony lay sprawled at Chuck's feet, his hands clutching at his ruined face. As Chuck spun around a third time, he tripped over Tony. Both he and Cliff tumbled to the floor.

"Shoot the fucker," he shouted.

Fingers trembling, I reloaded the shotgun and jacked a shell.

Half of his ear had been bitten off. Blood streamed down his face and all over Cliff and Tony as well. Not that it mattered—both of them were covered in gore already. Cliff sat up and ignored us all, content to gnaw on the severed ear.

"Get down," I ordered. "Chuck, you're in the way."

"It doesn't matter," he wailed. "I've been bit. Now squeeze the fucking trigger!"

Before I could, something clawed at my shoulder from behind. Screaming, I whipped around. Basil was back on his feet. Incredibly, the second shot hadn't been enough to put him down for good. The pellets had done a serious amount of damage. The left side of his face looked like it had gone through a cheese grater, but I hadn't penetrated the skull and destroyed the brain.

His cold, bloody fingers pawed across my chest. Recoiling in alarm, I clubbed him in the jaw with the shotgun's stock. Then I shoved the barrel into his gaping mouth. He bit down, shattering his teeth.

"Stay the fuck down, Basil, and go find your wife."

Closing my eyes and turning my face away, I squeezed the trigger. Basil's head exploded. Wetness splattered against my cheek. Frantic, I wiped my face with my sleeve.

"Lamar," Chuck called out from behind me, "take care of Tony!"

A second gunshot exploded in the passageway. When I turned around, Cliff was slumped against the wall, blood pumping from a hole in his head. Before I could act, Chuck stuffed the smoking pistol in his mouth and pulled the trigger again. His body jerked upright, and the back of his head blew apart. He went limp. What remained of his head caved in like a rotten melon that had been left out in the sun for too long. His legs and feet twitched as if electrified. The crotch of his pants turned dark as his bladder failed. And then Chuck lay still.

I prodded Tony with my foot. He didn't respond. I couldn't tell if he was dead or just unconscious. Not that it mattered anyway. Regardless, he was already dead. The poison was pumping through his veins. Soon, he would stand again. I put the shotgun against his forehead and made sure that wouldn't happen.

Silence returned to the smoke-filled passageway—or maybe it was just that I'd gone deaf. Half in shock, I stared down at the four corpses. It had all happened so quickly. There'd been no time to think—just act, let impulse and instinct drive. I patted my pockets and took stock of my shotgun shells. I considered taking

Tony and Chuck's weapons, but both were stained with blood and I didn't want to risk infection. I'd already come too close to exposure when I shot Basil.

Making sure the passageway was still clear, I ducked into Basil's compartment again and searched his footlocker. At the bottom, I found a clean t-shirt with a logo that said, MALCASA POINT IS FOR LOVERS. Inside a small shaving kit, I found a bar of soap, a bottle of aftershave, and a tube of anti-bacterial cream. Using a pair of Basil's socks, I wiped my shotgun clean and disinfected it with the aftershave. Then I poured aftershave over my hands and then scrubbed them with the soap. Next, I wiped them clean on a pair of Basil's underwear. Satisfied that they were spotless, I scrubbed my face with the aftershave. The alcohol burned, but it was a good pain. I checked my complexion in the mirror, looking for pimples or cuts—anything that would have allowed Hamelin's Revenge to get inside me. When I saw that I was safe, I breathed a sigh of relief. Then I removed my gory T-shirt, ripping it down the middle and stripping it off rather than pulling it over my head and further risking infection from Basil's blood. Once it was off, I slipped the clean shirt over my head. It was a little snug around the belly and shoulders, but it would do. Finally, I rubbed my hands and face with the antibacterial cream just for extra protection. I'd seen the effects of Hamelin's Revenge firsthand. When Tum and Mitch were infected, the disease had spread rapidly. They'd both gotten sick within minutes. I wasn't feeling sick yet, so I assumed that I was okay.

And then I closed my eyes and prayed to a God I didn't believe in that I'd stay that way. All my life, I'd been told over and over again that he didn't care for people like me, that he'd sent an angel to nuke the ancient city of Sodom because of men like myself. But I hoped that if he did exist, God would make an exception this time—if not for me, then for the kids. Tasha and Malik hadn't done anything to him. They deserved a better world than this.

"Amen," I said out loud. I could barely hear myself.

I felt no different. There was none of that peace or calm that religious people say comes with prayer. I thought back to the graffiti I'd seen spray painted on the church back in Baltimore: GOD IS DEAD. Maybe it was true. And if so, then maybe he was just another zombie. His son had come back from the dead, right? Maybe he'd come back hungry.

I opened my eyes, picked up the shotgun, and stepped back out into the slaughterhouse. As I walked through the hatch, two things happened simultaneously—an explosion rocked the ship and somebody shot at me.

CHAPTER ELEVEN

At first, I thought the two blasts were actually one big explosion. The first one was muffled, occurring in another part of the ship, but powerful enough to jolt my feet. The *Spratling* rolled hard to starboard and I slammed against the bulkhead, dropping the shotgun. At the same time, there was a second explosion, this one much closer. Something zipped by my head, whining like a mosquito and plowing into the port bulkhead with a loud smack. It was only then that I realized I'd been shot at.

"Hey," I shouted, dropping to my knees, "hold your goddamned fire!"

"Lamar?" The voice belonged to Runkle. A second later, he stepped out from around the corner and leaned through the hatch. "Oh, shit."

"You stupid redneck motherfucker," I spat, climbing to my feet. My legs were wobbly and I had to steady myself against the bulkhead. Then I realized that it wasn't my balance at all. The ship was still leaning to starboard.

"I'm sorry, man." He lowered his pistol and held up his hand in surrender. "I thought you were a zombie. I heard shots and ran down here. Smelled all the gun smoke in the air and just assumed that—"

"Yeah," I interrupted. "Well you know what they say about assuming, Runkle. Makes an ass out of you and me. You nearly fucking blew my head off. If it hadn't been for the ship rolling—"

"What was that, anyway? I felt it vibrate in my feet."

"How the fuck should I know? I was too busy getting shot at, you stupid asshole."

"Look"—he raised his voice—"I said I was sorry. Now we can stand here and argue about it or we can find out what the hell is going on. Do you want to fight?"

Shaking my head, I retrieved the shotgun. "No. I'm cool for now. You're right. We need to focus. I'll take this up with you later."

"Well then, let's just hope there is a later. What the hell happened here?"

I quickly filled him in on everything I knew, ending with Chuck's suicide and me putting Tony out of his misery.

Runkle counted on his fingers. "So that leaves the two of us, the kids, Carol, Tran, Murphy, and Chief Maxey—and there's been no sign of Professor Williams, correct?"

I nodded. "You see anybody other than the chief?"

"No. The passageways were all deserted. I figured everyone was asleep, until I heard the gunshots."

The ship leaned farther to the starboard side, jolting us both again. There was a loud, metallic groan from beneath the hull. An alarm blared, and the chief's voice came over the speakers.

"This is not a drill, this is not a drill. General quarters, general quarters. All hands be advised, we have a hull breach in the aft berthing section. Muster on the flight deck immediately. Again, this is not a drill. Prepare to abandon ship."

Runkle found an emergency phone and called the bridge. I stood there wondering what the hell was happening while he talked to Chief Maxey. Runkle's expression went slack. He stopped talking and just listened. He looked worried.

"Okay." Runkle spoke in a monotone. "I understand. I'll tell him."

He hung up the phone and stared at the floor.

"What's wrong?" I asked. "What the hell's going on? He said to abandon ship?"

"We've got a hull breach."

"What's that mean?"

"It means that we're taking on water. We're sinking."

"Oh, shit . . ."

"Yeah." He wiped sweat from his forehead. "Listen, Lamar, that explosion we heard? The chief says that whatever it was, it blew a hole in the side of the ship. It was . . . well, it was near your berthing area."

I started running before he was even done speaking.

"Lamar!" he shouted. "Wait a second. You can't just go running down there."

"Tasha, Malik, and Carol are down there."

"The compartment is probably flooded—maybe the whole passageway. And what about the professor? We still have to find him before he kills someone else!"

"You find him," I yelled. "I've got to take care of my own."

"Lamar! Goddamn it, get back here. This won't help us."

Ignoring him, I ran on, feet pounding, shoving through hatches, darting down passageways. I held the shotgun at the ready, just in case the professor or anyone else he'd managed to infect jumped me, but I saw no one. I slid through Nick's remains, rounded another corner, and saw Carol, Tasha, and Malik running toward me.

"Lamar!" Tasha screamed. "The ship's flooding!"

"I know, I know." I leaned the shotgun against the bulkhead and hugged the kids tightly. Then I gave Carol a hug, too. She trembled against me, frightened and hyperventilating.

"Is everyone okay?" I asked, checking them over.

"We're all right," Malik said. "But we're in deep shit. Them grenades went off."

I sighed. "I thought I told you to stay inside the compartment. Why were you messing with Mitch's grenades? You could have gotten infected or—"

"I wasn't fooling with them," he interrupted. "Honest."

"Well, then what set them off?"

"Tran did it."

"Tran?"

Malik nodded. "Yeah, he was one of them things."

"Lamar," Carol said. "We need to keep moving. The water is coming."

We ran back the way I'd come. I took the lead, heading for the nearest ladder so we could meet the other survivors topside.

"It wasn't our fault," Tasha explained as we fled. "We stayed in the room, just like you told us to. But then we heard someone out in the hall. Mrs. Beck thought it might be you coming back, so she peeked outside. But it wasn't you. It was Tran. He was . . . all bloody. Some of his fingers were missing."

"I tried to shut the hatch again," Carol said. "But the children insisted on defending us. They ran out into the passageway before I could stop them."

I frowned at the kids. "I told the two of you to listen to Mrs. Beck. You could have been killed."

"On the contrary, Lamar," Carol said. "If anything, it's because of them that we're still alive. If they hadn't run out when they did, I hate to think what would have happened."

"Tran was eating on Mitch," Tasha said, her voice low. "He ignored us. I tried to shoot him, but I couldn't get the rifle to work. Wasn't until later that I remembered the safety was on."

"You should have figured it out," Malik teased.

"That's why Mitch should have given the gun to me, instead of that big ass knife."

"Shut up," Tasha scolded him, before turning back to me. "Anyway, Tran picked up one of the grenades and started licking it. You know—Mitch's blood was all over it. He was licking it like a lollipop and since I couldn't get the rifle to work, we decided to come find you for help. We were scared. He had the grenade in his hand, and we didn't know if he knew how to use it or not."

Each time we entered a new passageway, Carol shut the hatch behind us and made sure they were sealed tight. I led us to a ladder and we started up to the next level. The air smelled charged, like the atmosphere after a lightning storm. Probably an electrical fire somewhere in the ship's wiring. A thin line of smoke floated along the ceiling.

"We started backing away," Malik said, continuing their story, "and got to the end of the hallway when he pulled the pin out. I don't think he knew what he was doing. Just dumb luck."

"So what did you guys do then?"

Malik laughed. "We got the hell out of there. Good thing we did, too."

"It was horrible." Carol shuddered. "Tran—that poor man—he just . . . exploded. It just *smeared* him all over the walls. And the blast set off the other grenades. The berthing area was destroyed. If we hadn't already been through the hatch, we'd be dead. The entire passageway was just . . . gone. The last thing we saw before we closed the hatch was water gushing in. We couldn't see anything else, because of all the smoke. The water came through the first hatch, and the second. It leaked right through the seals. We've been shutting them behind us, hoping to slow it down."

I stopped at another emergency phone and tried calling the bridge. The phone wasn't working. There was no tone or ring—just dead silence. The smoke in the passageway grew thicker.

"Did you guys hear the chief's announcement?"

"No," Carol said. "The speakers weren't working in our section. The explosion must have damaged them."

"He ordered us to abandon ship, so he knows about the hull breach. There must be sensors or something on the bridge that alert him. We're supposed to meet on the flight deck."

"How's he gonna fix the ship?" Malik asked.

"I don't think he can," I said. "That's why he gave the order to abandon it. We'll have to set off in the lifeboat."

Tasha halted. "In the water? But you said the zombies were in the ocean now—that the fish were catching it, too. If we go in the water, what's to stop them from attacking us?"

The three of them stared at me.

"Come on," I said, trying hard to conceal my dread. "Let's keep moving. I don't think the fish can do much to hurt us. Fish are small and most of them don't have teeth."

"Shit," Malik said. "You ain't never seen that movie where Samuel L. Jackson fights the sharks? There's some big ass fish in the sea, and they got teeth."

The smoke grew thicker. It smelled acrid. Bitter. My eyes watered. A shower of sparks rained down from a ventilation shaft. We threw our arms up over our heads to protect ourselves. I led us down the passageway to another ladder, this one leading topside.

"Seriously," Tasha said. "How are we gonna make it out on the water? We'll be sitting ducks."

"We can't worry about that right now," I said. "And besides, we can't stay on the ship. We'll drown."

Malik wasn't convinced. "I'd rather drown than get bit by a zombie shark."

I handed the shotgun to Carol, went up the ladder, and opened the hatch. Cold drops of rain pelted my face and hands.

"Wonderful," I told them. "Besides everything else, there's a storm, too."

"Lamar! Carol. Wait up."

It was Runkle. I climbed back down the ladder and waited for him to reach us. He was out of breath and his hair was slicked to his head with sweat. In the time that I'd left him, he'd found an old peacoat and put it on. It was about two sizes too small for him, and the buttons bulged out.

"Any sign of the professor?" I asked.

"No. But I did find Murphy. He was one of them."

"Did you . . . ?"

He nodded.

"Tran was infected, too," I told him. "He set off Mitch's grenades. That's what the explosion was."

Runkle looked at Carol and the kids. "The rest of you okay?"

"We're fine," Carol said, "but we really should find the chief, don't you think? He'll be waiting for us."

"Good idea," I said. I started back up the ladder again, and then turned and looked at Runkle. "Might want to turn that collar up, Runkle. It's raining outside."

"I know," he said. "That's why I put on the coat when I found it."

I paused. "But how did you know it was raining? Weren't you below decks hunting for the professor?"

He frowned. "Sure. But I talked to the chief on the phone. He told me there was a storm coming in."

"That's funny. The emergency phones weren't working when I tried them. The explosion knocked them out."

"Really?" He shrugged. "Must be a localized thing, then. I didn't have any trouble getting through."

Growing up where I had, I knew when somebody was bullshitting me, and I knew that Runkle was lying now. But I didn't know what about or why. Was it because he'd stolen a peacoat? It seemed like a stupid thing to conceal, but then again, he'd been a cop. Maybe he had conflicting morals about it or something. Or maybe he was just scared in general. I certainly was, so why shouldn't he be, too? I decided to let the matter drop.

Taking the shotgun back from Carol, I crawled up onto the deck. Tasha and Malik came next, followed by Carol, and then Runkle. The rain and wind lashed at us, and the salt spray stung our eyes. The temperature had dropped, and I shivered in the cold air. Basil's thin T-shirt clung to my wet skin. Visibility was limited, but the flight deck appeared deserted. No sign of anyone else, dead or alive. The *Spratling* continued its starboard list, and as we approached the lifeboat it felt like we were walking down a steep hill. Worse, the deck was wet and slippery. Each time the ship crested a wave, we had to struggle to keep our balance.

"What now?" Carol shouted over the roar of the storm.

I glanced around, and caught movement out of the corner of my eye. I raised the shotgun, but it was only Chief Maxey, carefully working his way down from the pilothouse. He held tight to the handrails as the ship twisted again. He was carrying a small radio, and struggled not to drop it.

"GPS," he said, holding the radio up for us to see. "Global Positioning Satellite. Believe it or not, the damn thing is still working. I guess the satellite is still floating around up there, just waiting for somebody to tell it what to do. I've programmed in the coordinates for the drilling platform. We should reach it by morning."

"Morning?" Carol looked startled. "So we have to be on the ocean all night?"

"We have no choice, Mrs. Beck," the chief said. "You can remain onboard if you wish, but I'm certainly not staying here. If you come with me, I promise I'll do my best to see to your safety."

I wiped rain from my eyes. "I thought the captain was supposed to go down with the ship."

"I'm not a captain, Mr. Reed." He smiled. "I'm a signalman chief. And besides, the women and children are getting on first. Now let's ready the lifeboat."

Chief Maxey directed us on what to do. As we prepped the lifeboat, I noticed that Runkle kept wincing, as if in pain. He seemed to be favoring his left side.

"You okay?" I asked.

"Side stitch," he gasped. "Too much excitement for one night. I just need to walk it off."

The chief tapped me on the shoulder. "We'll need a few supplies. Enough water and food to last us for a few days. Want to give me a hand carrying it?"

"Sure."

We left Runkle behind to protect Carol and the kids and made our way to the galley. The ship was listing even worse now. We could hear the hull groaning as the intense pressure split it open wider. Black smoke belched from the open hatches.

Tasha had said that some of Tran's fingers were missing. We found them in the galley, lying on the floor in a pool of blood along with his wedding ring. I'd never even noticed the ring on his finger before, hadn't bothered to learn anything about him—and now I never would. Again, I felt sorry for Tran. Dying was bad enough. Dying and becoming a reanimated corpse was even worse. But somehow, his anonymous death seemed the worst of all. What was Tran's monomyth? What kind of archetype was he—the forgotten one? The sacrificial lamb? The movie extra? The red shirt, like on *Star Trek*—destined only to provide cannon fodder?

I put my fingers to my lips and motioned for the chief to come closer.

"Runkle said he took care of Murphy. The professor must be around here somewhere. Be careful."

He nodded. We moved into the dry goods compartment. I went first, the shotgun ready and loaded. The walk-in locker was deserted. Quickly, we each grabbed a burlap sack that had once held potatoes and stuffed them with as many water jugs and packages of food as we could carry. Then we slung the sacks over our shoulders and made our way back out into the storm.

"Did you find the professor?" Runkle asked when we got back on deck. He sounded out of breath.

"No," I said. "Any sign of him out here?"

"Nothing. And like I said, I took care of Murphy earlier. Didn't see the old man, though."

Another tremor rocked the ship, knocking Malik and Carol to the deck. The waves crashed over the handrail, which was now facing the ocean. Lightning flashed across the sky.

"We're out of time," Chief Maxey said. "You're both absolutely positive that no one else is left alive onboard?"

Runkle and I both nodded.

"Then I suggest we go. Carol and the children first. Then you gentlemen."

We climbed into the lifeboat and Chief Maxey started the winch while I stored our supplies in a dry spot beneath a bench. I noticed the chief taking one last look around. He seemed close to tears. The winch's gears and pulleys squeaked as the boat began descending toward the ocean's choppy surface. As we sank lower, the chief jumped aboard. The ropes swayed from his added weight and the lifeboat crashed against the side of the ship. Carol screamed and the rest of us held on tight. There were six of us and four life vests. Runkle declined his, and the chief insisted I take the spare. The others went to Carol, Tasha, and Malik. Once the lifeboat had splashed into the water, the chief released the ropes and started the motor.

"Thank God we refueled after your trip to the rescue station," he said. "Or else this would be a very short trip."

We pulled away from the *Spratling*, and I got a good look at the hole in her side. It was huge—twisted, blackened steel stuck out like jagged teeth. Wave after wave surged through the gash, flooding the interior. Almost half the vessel was beneath the surface now, and I wondered if there were fish swimming around in the passageways. The stern tilted up into the air. Water cascaded off it in sheets. Thick, black smoke and orange flames erupted from a bilge pipe.

"Jesus Christ," I whispered. "Look at it."

The bow nose-dived for the ocean floor and the stern rose higher. The *Spratling* sat in the water like an arrow. We continued retreating from the sinking ship. Chief Maxey pushed hard on the throttle and increased our speed. Despite the rain, oil fires were beginning to cover the ocean's surface. A whirlpool swirled around the wreckage, sucking in some floating debris that had slid off the flight deck.

"Look!" Malik stood up and pointed. The boat rocked from the sudden movement, startling us all.

"Malik," Carol scolded. "Sit down before you capsize us."

"But it's Professor Williams."

We all looked where he was pointing. Sure enough, the Professor's undead corpse was bobbing up and down in the water, caught up in the churning whirlpool. His arms flailed uselessly, almost as if he were waving good-bye. And then he was gone, sucked beneath the surface. Grief tugged at my heart. I'd liked the old man. I would never be able to smell pipe tobacco again without thinking of him. But even in my sadness, I knew that he was gone long before this. He'd died when the fish infected him.

Soon the *Spratling* slipped beneath the waters as well. Huge bubbles burst on the surface, marking its departure.

Tears welled up in Chief Maxey's eyes as he watched it sink.

"There goes everything I've ever had," he said. "My entire life was tied up in that ship. It gave me a purpose. The best friends I ever had were the guys I served with onboard her. We were so young back then. Good bunch of guys. The absolute best. They were the salt of the earth. I haven't spoken to any of them in years, but I used to think about them all the time. Never knew what happened to any of them after they got out. I guess it's like that for most military personnel. You serve together, live together closer than most folks live. Bonds are formed—unbreakable bonds that are hard for a civilian to understand or appreciate. You rely on those guys for your very life. You trust them in ways you will never trust another person, including your spouse or children. But then, when it's all over, you lose touch with each other. I tried writing to some of them and got a few letters back—the occasional Christmas card or pictures of their children. But over the years we all lost touch with one another. Ran out of things to talk about, I guess. Seemed like all we did was reminisce about the old days. When the maritime museum hired me to serve as the curator and tour guide, I had lots of time to think about them. That ship was haunted. I saw ghosts around every corner."

"Ghosts?" Malik asked, sitting back down.

Chief Maxey wiped his eyes. "Not real ghosts, Malik. Not the scary kind. More like ghosts that existed in my memories. Nobody knew that ship better than me. We were a part of each other. But when they saved her from the scrap yard, I never thought it would end like this. Not after everything she and I have been through together. Never thought she'd die."

"Look at the bright side," I said.

"What's that, Mr. Reed?"

"The *Spratling* may be dead, but at least she gets to stay that way. She doesn't have to come back."

"Good point."

He continued piloting us through the storm. Carol and the kids huddled together beneath a sheet of plastic and tried to stay warm. I rubbed my tired eyes and tried to stay alert. Runkle hunched over on his bench and closed his eyes.

Lightning crashed overhead. Death lurked beneath the waves. We floated into the darkness.

CHAPTER TWELVE

Once we were far enough away from the wreckage, the chief shut off the motor. He said that he wanted to conserve fuel, but I thought the real reason might be that the sound of the engine could attract underwater predators. Occasionally the GPS would beep, letting us know we were still on course.

It was a miserable night. We were cold and wet. Exhausted. Carol and the kids were still underneath the plastic sheet, clinging together and trying to stay warm. I smiled at them, told them that everything would be okay as soon as we reached the oil rig. They didn't respond. I didn't blame them. I knew I was full of shit, and so did they. Sure, maybe things would be cool on the drilling platform. But chances were we'd never reach it, not with an entire ocean full of dead things.

The chief opened up a storage box and took out some plastic oars. He screwed them on to aluminum poles and handed one to me. He and I rowed while Runkle stood guard. The former cop looked worse than any of us. His drooping eyes were bloodshot and he shivered uncontrollably, despite the heavy pea coat. He didn't say much, just sat there staring out at the water.

I noticed that the supplies we'd rescued from the *Spratling*'s galley were getting wet, and I passed them over to the chief so he could stow them in the box. He found some glow sticks at the bottom of the storage compartment. He snapped one in half and a fluorescent green glow filled the air. Its radius was small, but I think it made us all feel better. The light held the darkness at bay, if only for a little while. The chief had taken Mitch's rifle from Tasha and it rested at his side. He laid plastic sheeting over the weapon in an effort to keep it dry, and weighted the plastic down with some emergency flares. I propped the shotgun up next to me. I didn't know if the rain would hurt it or not, but I had no way to shelter it from the elements. The chief had used the last of the plastic on the rifle.

If there were zombie fish stalking us beneath the ocean's surface, we didn't see them. Maybe the sea was too rough. Every few minutes, a wave would crash over us, swamping the boat with several inches of water. Then the kids would have to come out from under their shelter and bail with two buckets the chief had found in the storage compartment. Occasionally, debris from the *Spratling* that hadn't been sucked down with the ship bobbed by, tossed on the waves. There were wooden crates, an aluminum lawn chair, seat cushions, a mattress, a coast guard life preserver, and a push broom. We salvaged whatever useful items we could from the stuff that floated within reach and let the rest of it drift away. After rescuing the push broom, Malik unscrewed the long handle and pulled out Mitch's bayonet. The glow stick's green light reflected off the serrated blade. Glimpsing the knife made me think of Mitch. I fought down a lump in my throat. I could mourn him later, if there was a later.

"My God," Chief Maxey groaned. "It's been a long time since I rowed like this. Quite the workout."

"You okay?" I asked.

He nodded, but I noticed that he was slowing down. My joints were starting to ache, as well. The storm tossed us back and forth, and for every foot we gained, the waves forced us back again.

"How much farther?" Tasha asked the chief.

He chuckled. "Sounds like we're on a family vacation, doesn't it? I increased to our top speed when the trouble started, Tasha. As long as we don't run into any more obstacles or the storm doesn't get worse, we should be there before dawn."

None of us responded. Dawn. That was an eternity.

Malik began sharpening the end of the broom handle, turning it into a makeshift spear. He didn't speak, just focused intently on the job at hand. I watched him in silent admiration. It was no wonder the kid had stayed alive this long. He had heart and then some. I wasn't his father, but I felt an immense swell of pride anyway. I thought back to when I'd first met them—just a few days ago, but it seemed like a lifetime. *I ain't no punk*, Malik had said while sizing me up. *I'm hardcore, G. You try messing with my sister and I'll mess you up instead.* I'd laughed at the time, despite the sincerity and ferocity in his voice. Now, there was no doubt left in my mind that he could have followed through on the threat. Malik was a child of this new world—the perfect inheritor. He had an innate survival instinct. He didn't ask why. He just did.

One of the crates we'd rescued contained oranges—a leftover from our ill-fated supply raid on the rescue station. They'd been fresh then, stored in a walk-in cooler, and hadn't gone bad while on the *Spratling*. Carol handed them out. Runkle declined with a grunt. Another crate contained maritime museum tour brochures for the *Spratling*. Chief Maxey solemnly kept one of the brochures, folding it up and stuffing it into his pocket, and then tossed the rest back over the side. Every few minutes, he'd glance back at the spot where the *Spratling* had been and sigh, but the ship was gone. The ocean's surface was unmarred again, except for the rough surf. There were no bursting bubbles or swirling whirlpools. Even the oil fires were gone, dissipated by the current. With the fires extinguished, the darkness seemed to press closer, as if trying to swallow the lifeboat.

"I'm cold," Tasha complained. Her teeth chattered.

"We all are, sweetie," Carol said, pulling her closer.

Malik jabbed the air with his spear and seemed satisfied with it. He sat it down and peeled his orange.

The wind howled around us as we continued on

into the night. It felt like cold razors on our skin. Waves continued swamping the lifeboat. I focused my attention on rowing. My shoulders and chest began to ache. Chief Maxey was obviously having trouble, too. His breath grew short and I noticed him struggling just to raise the oar. He kept rubbing his chest muscles, wincing with pain.

"Hey Runkle," I said. "How about taking over for the chief for a little while?"

Runkle didn't respond, didn't move. Just sat there, slumped over.

"Yo, Runkle! Wake up, man."

"It's okay," Chief Maxey said. "I'll be fine. Arthritis is just acting up a bit."

"Ain't no reason why you can't act as lookout and let him row for a little while."

I leaned forward and tapped Runkle on the shoulder. He slowly raised his head and turned around, staring at me with empty eyes. His peacoat was soaking wet, and the pistol was still clutched in his fingers. I glanced down at it, and then noticed the dark stain on the coat—a red splotch at his waist, barely visible in the darkness. My eyes widened.

"Hey man, are you hurt?"

"Leave me . . . alone," Runkle slurred, his head drooping down again. "Just . . . row the fucking boat."

"Dude," I said. "You're injured. There's blood on your coat. What the hell happened?"

"Injured?" Chief Maxey pulled in his oar and slid toward us. "Let us see, Runkle. How bad is it?"

"It's not my blood," he said, pulling the coat tighter. "Just some . . . of Murphy. I g-got it on me when I . . . s-shot him."

"Bullshit," I insisted. "I saw you after that and there wasn't any blood on you then. Now let us help you."

Runkle's head snapped up, his eyes suddenly alert. He shoved the gun in my face.

"Sit the fuck d-down and . . . leave me alone. I t-told you . . . it's *nothing*."

Suddenly, I understood. He'd been acting weird ever since I'd encountered him on the ship during our hunt for the professor. He'd lied about the coat. Told me he was wearing it because of the storm. Instead, he'd been wearing it to hide his wound.

"You got bit, didn't you, Runkle? Murphy bit you before you shot him, and you've been hiding it all this time."

He sneered. "You're . . . c-crazy, Lamar. If I'd been . . . b-bitten, wouldn't I be d-dead by now?"

"You ain't looking too healthy. All the signs are there, now that you mention it. You're slurring your words. You're weak. Admit it, Runkle. You were bitten and you've been trying to hide it."

Chief Maxey put his hand on Runkle's shoulder. "Everything will be okay, Mr. Runkle. Just let us help you."

Weakened as he was, Runkle still had strength. He moved fast, swinging his arm out and smacking the chief in the face with the pistol. There was a loud crack and Chief Maxey tumbled backward. His nose and mouth spurted blood. The boat rocked dangerously to one side, and more water flooded in. I lunged for Runkle, intent on getting the gun away from him, but he was too fast for me. He whipped around again and suddenly the barrel of the pistol was pressed against my stomach. Grinning, he shoved me back into my seat.

"D-don't . . . you f-fucking move . . . or I'll . . . w-waste those kids. . . . Just . . . k-keep rowing."

"You son of a bitch. You're a cop. What about your oath—to serve and protect?"

He laughed. "That d-died . . . with . . . the rest of the . . . world."

"You're a real piece of shit, man."

His laughter turned into a cough. "J-just shut up . . . and r-row, f-faggot."

Clenching my teeth in anger, I did as he ordered. Grinning, Runkle waved the gun at me. I picked up the oar and dipped it into the water again. Chief Maxey rolled over onto his back, groaned, and then lay still. Rainwater splashed off his face, washing away the blood streaming from his nose.

"C-Carol," Runkle called, without taking his eyes off me, "you and . . . the k-kids . . . get over here n-next t-to . . . Lamar."

"Officer Runkle," she pleaded. "You're sick. You don't know—"

"Shut up. D-do what I . . . t-tell you, or I'll . . . s-shoot Lamar f-first. N-now get o-over h-here. . . ."

My grip tightened on the oars. Chief Maxey was still unconscious. If I moved, Runkle would shoot me before I made two steps. We were helpless. I decided to try reasoning with him again.

"You're gonna die, Runkle. You know that, right? I mean, if Murphy bit you then Hamelin's Revenge is already in your bloodstream."

He shook his head. "N-not . . . going to . . . die. I'm g-going . . . to l-live."

"The hell you are. It is gonna happen, whether you fight it or not. You can't beat it. So what's the point, man? Why do this to us? What are you hoping to accomplish?"

He didn't answer me. His free hand went to his side, cradling the wound beneath his coat. His skin was slick with rain and sweat. I wondered why it was taking him so long to turn. Mitch had died a lot quicker. Maybe Runkle's constitution was better. Maybe the rate of infection had something to do with how healthy the person had been.

Carol, Tasha, and Malik carefully crossed over to our side of the lifeboat. One by one, they sat down next to me on the bench. Runkle watched them closely. I scooted over so they'd have more room. As Malik turned around to sit, Runkle grabbed his arm.

"Hey," Malik shouted. "What you doing, man? Let me go!"

" "S-shut up . . . you l-little . . . s-shit. . . . When the chief . . . o-opened that s-storage b-box . . . I s-saw some . . . ropes inside. . . . I w-want you t-to . . . take those . . . r-ropes . . . back there and . . . t-tie up C-Chief M-Maxey. . . ."

"I ain't doing shit."

I sat up straight, my body coiled and ready to spring. "Let him go, you son of a bitch."

Runkle twisted his arm and Malik shrieked. I

started to stand up, but Runkle aimed the pistol at me again.

"S-sit d-down . . . faggot, or I'll . . . p-pull his arm out."

"You motherfucker." I obeyed, sitting back down. "You sick, twisted son of a bitch. Let him go!"

He twisted Malik's arm again. "D-do it n-now. . . ."

"Okay, man." Malik tore free from Runkle's grip. "Damn. I can't do shit if you're gonna tear my arm off first. Bitch."

Rubbing his bicep and frowning, Malik made his way across the lifeboat. Runkle didn't turn to watch him; instead, he kept his eyes on me, Carol, and Tasha. I wondered why he didn't simply get up and move to the far end of the boat, where he could watch all of us at the same time. Figured maybe he was farther gone than he appeared; not thinking clearly, dying a death that would not last, already thinking like a zombie rather than a man.

Another large wave tossed the lifeboat to one side. Debris rolled across the bottom of the boat. Icy seawater flooded my boots. Keeping his balance, Malik opened the storage box and rummaged inside until he found the rope. He pulled it out and slammed the lid.

"Y-you got it?" Runkle coughed again.

"Yeah," Malik said. "I found it."

"H-hurry . . . up. . . ."

"Just hold up a second. Don't rush me. You're worse than my sister."

Tasha scowled, but held her tongue. My eyes didn't leave the pistol. Some hero I'd turned out to be. Professor Williams had been way off base, and I wished he was there so I could show him.

Runkle did not turn around. His eyelids drooped lower. The stain on his coat grew broader. A thin line of bright blood dribbled out of his sleeve and ran down his hand, dripping off his index finger. The water in the boat turned pink. Runkle's other hand squeezed the pistol tighter. I watched as I rowed, willing him to die. I licked saltwater from my lips and hoped that the next breath would be his last. But it wasn't.

Instead of tying up the chief, Malik quietly picked up his spear instead. Very slowly, he tiptoed toward Runkle, who still had his back turned. I looked away on purpose, so as not to alert Runkle, and silently willed Carol and Tasha to do the same. Malik lifted the spear over his head and crept closer.

"S-save some . . . rope," Runkle wheezed. "I w-want . . . you . . . to t-tie up . . . the r-rest of . . . them . . . t-too."

"Whatever," Malik said, creeping closer. "You're in charge."

"T-that's right. . . . I am in . . ."

Runkle suddenly doubled over, clenching his side and gasping with pain. He squeezed his eyes shut and his gun hand went limp. The weapon pointed at the deck. With a shout, Malik lunged forward and drove the spear down into Runkle's back. The boy struggled, putting all of his weight behind the shaft. Runkle stiffened, trying to stand. He opened his mouth to scream, but only a strangled sigh came out. The pistol slipped from his fingers, landing in a puddle of bloody seawater. Tasha leapt forward to grab it, but I warned her to stay seated. Runkle's infected blood had mixed with the water in the boat. There was no sense in chancing it.

Malik continued thrusting the spear into Runkle's back. The spear's tip poked through his chest, ripping the peacoat. Runkle tried to scream again. Instead, he gurgled. Dark blood—almost black—bubbled from his gaping mouth.

Jumping out of my seat, I swung the oar like a club, striking Runkle across the face. The shock reverberated up my arms. Runkle grunted. His lips split. Blood and teeth flew through the air. Dropping the oar, I jumped to Malik's side and grabbed the broom handle right above his hands. Together, we spun the impaled man around and pushed him over the side. His blood dribbled down the spear toward us. We needed to hurry. Runkle gripped the edge of the lifeboat, holding on for dear life. Malik and I pushed harder. The tendons stood out on his neck as he struggled with us. The spear sank deeper into his body. The blood ran closer. Tasha ran forward, scooped up the shotgun, and smashed his fingers with the stock. With a final shove, Malik and I managed to topple the crazed cop into the churning waves. We let go of the broom handle, letting Runkle take the bloody weapon with him.

"He shouldn't have messed with us," Malik said, puffing out his chest.

"Are all of you wearing socks beneath your shoes?" I asked.

Nodding their heads slowly, Carol, Malik and Tasha all looked at me as if I'd lost my mind.

"Help me get the chief up," I said. "Runkle bled into the water in the bottom of the boat. I don't want the chief swallowing it."

Tasha looked worried. "How are we going to bail if his blood's in the water?"

"I don't know yet," I admitted. "But first thing's first—help me with the chief. Carol, pick up everything that doesn't have blood on it yet, especially the food and our weapons."

Out on the ocean, Runkle let out a choked scream. I looked up in time to see a huge gray shape rising up beneath him. Runkle waved his arms, frantically beating at the water. His eyes bulged. There was a flash of white, what looked like a fin, and then he was gone in a surge of spray. Whatever the creature was, it had dragged him beneath the surface.

Malik ran to the edge of the lifeboat. "What the hell was that?"

"Don't worry about it now," I panted, sliding my hands under the chief's armpits. "Just help me get him up before he's infected."

Carol collected the weapons and food while Tasha and Malik helped me with Chief Maxey. We got him into a sitting position on the bench. His head lolled back and forth in time with the waves. His nose was swollen and bloody, obviously broken, and he was missing one of his teeth. But he was breathing. I gently patted him on the cheek, and after a few seconds, his eyelids fluttered.

"Are the water bottles okay?" I asked Carol.

"They seem to be," she said. "There's no blood on them that I can see."

"Hand me one."

I unscrewed the cap and put the bottle to the chief's mouth. The rim must have brushed against one of his sore spots, because he winced and then opened his eyes. Spring water ran down his throat, and he choked, spitting it back up.

"Runkle?" he gasped, glancing around. "Where is he?"

He tried to stand, but I gently forced him back down.

"We took care of it, Chief. Relax. You okay?"

"My nose hurts like a son of a bitch. I think it might be broken. But I'll live."

"Good. Might want to pick your feet up and keep them off the bottom of the boat."

He looked down, and then back to me. "Is that my blood or Runkle's?"

I shrugged. "Both, I think."

Tasha grabbed my arm and pointed off the bow.

"Something moved out there."

I squinted into the darkness. "I don't see anything. What was it?"

"I don't know. Something jumped out of the water and then swam underneath again."

"Maybe it was just a big wave," Carol suggested. I could tell by the tone of her voice that she didn't believe it herself.

A blast of thunder ripped the night sky, drowning out the roaring winds.

I turned back to the chief. "Can you row?"

He nodded. "Yes, I think so."

"Okay. I think we should get moving." I sat cross-legged on the bench, keeping my feet out of the tainted water, and grabbed an oar. "Everybody sit back down. Try to stay out of the water. Hopefully, we'll get a few more really big waves and they'll wash that shit out of here. Then we can start bailing. Carol, are you awake enough to act as lookout?"

"Yes. I don't think I could fall asleep right now if I wanted to."

"Okay. You stand watch. Tasha, I want you to use the rifle. Make sure there's no blood on it."

She nodded.

"Hey," Malik hollered. "What about me? How come I never get nothing?"

I smiled. "You get the shotgun. If you have to shoot it though, I want you to be careful."

"Why?"

"Because it's liable to knock you overboard, and we don't need that."

He looked back at where Runkle had been.

"No," Malik said. "We sure don't."

We all took our places. Carol peered out into the sea. The chief and I started rowing. The kids held their weapons at the ready, keeping the barrels beneath some plastic sheeting that had escaped the water and blood. We didn't talk. The GPS beeped mournfully. Chief Maxey glanced at it, checking our coordinates.

"We still on course, Chief?"

"We are," he said, "and please, just call me Wade. I don't have a boat anymore to be chief of."

I nodded. "Okay . . . Wade."

The thunder rumbled again. Then the glow stick went out, plunging us into darkness.

In that darkness, something moved. It splashed just off our starboard side. Whatever it was, it sounded big.

"Chief." I whispered. "Sorry—I mean, Wade. Maybe we should start the motor."

Lightning flashed, and I saw him nodding his head in agreement. Chief Maxey reached behind him and took a deep breath. Another splash echoed across the water, this time to our rear. Something bumped us from underneath the hull. We smelled it—rotten fish. Something dead, but still swimming. Then the motor burst to life. Chief Maxey gave it full throttle and we shot into the night.

The splashing sounds followed us for a long time before they faded.

When I looked back, all I saw was darkness.

CHAPTER THIRTEEN

The storm finally ended several hours later. There were a few last flashes of lightning and some final rumbles of thunder, almost as an afterthought. Then it was gone. During that time, we didn't see anything else in the water, either above or below. Maybe the weather kept the creatures away or maybe there was a war going on beneath the surface, and they were too busy eating each other to worry about us. A replay of what had happened in our cities, a battle between the living and the dead, now being waged under the sea as well as on land.

The sky cleared and we could see again. The sun was still down, but its first few predawn rays were visible as a red glow on the horizon. I wished the sun would hurry its ass up. All five of us were cold and shivering, soaked to the skin from the rain and the waves. The kids had runny noses. The chief—even though he'd asked us to just call him Wade, I still thought of him as Chief Maxey—had picked up a bad cough. Sounded like a goose. His entire body shook each time he coughed. His broken nose had swelled up like a golf ball, and when he talked, it sounded like he had a bad cold.

The storm had battered us about all night long. Luckily, the lifeboat hadn't sunk. I'd been right about the storm surges washing the blood back into the sea. We were able to bail the water out after the first half hour. Carol and I did it while the chief stood guard and the kids held the weapons. We bailed very carefully, mindful of any leftover blood. When we were finished, Carol and I gathered up anything with Runkle's blood on it and then tossed the items over the side, including his handgun. I hated to get rid of it, but we had nothing to clean and disinfect the weapon with. It sank like a stone.

And then we waited, watching each other for the first warning signs of the disease. All of us were sleepy, but there was no nausea, shortness of breath, or decreased circulation. We kept an extra eye on the chief, figuring he'd had the greatest risk of exposure. Hours passed uneventfully. If any of us had contracted Hamelin's Revenge, we showed no indications of it. We all felt and seemed fine. Carol suggested that maybe there was something in the saltwater that killed the disease. But the fact was that none of us knew for sure. I was an unemployed factory worker. Carol was a former quality control manager at an injection molding plant, and more recently, a makeshift teacher for the kids. And the chief was an ex-coast guard chief and museum guide. None of us had the tools to fully understand

and diagnose Hamelin's Revenge, let alone the skills for figuring out how to defeat it.

The sun crept higher and the birds came out, circling over us and screeching at the dawn. I wondered where they'd all come from. According to the chief, there was no land nearby. We'd seen none during the night—no lights on the horizon. They'd obviously taken shelter from the storm. But here they were now, as if materializing out of the clouds.

We shut the motor off again to conserve fuel, and once more began rowing. I looked out across the ocean and sighed. I felt like shit. I was exhausted, grimy, and sore. My ears felt all stuffed up because of all the close-range gunshots without hearing protection. My clothes were soaked. Dried salt caked my lips and the corners of my eyes. The wind scraped against my skin like sandpaper. As I rowed, I blocked out the protests from my arms and back, focusing instead on the sea. It was a big contrast from the night before. The water was so beautiful. The hypnotic rhythm of the foam-topped waves almost lulled me to sleep. I stopped rowing for a second and rubbed my bloodshot eyes. They felt dry and crusty. I kept them closed, and my breathing slowed. I felt relaxed. Peaceful. Then a wave lapped gently against the side of the lifeboat, breaking the spell. I shook my head and began rowing again, forcing myself to wake up. The surface was like the top of a birthday cake—smooth and flat, broken only by small, cresting waves. Farther down in the depths, the deep blue gave way to gray and green, then black. It seemed like it went on forever. Nothing moved down there. I wanted to jump over the side and just sink to the bottom, washing the filth from my body—a baptism.

The chief was also staring into the depths.

"We should be right over the *Ethel C*."

"What's that?" Malik asked.

The chief snorted, clearing dried blood out of his sinuses, and then told us.

"The *Ethel C* was a Lebanese freighter. That's a ship that carries cargo from one place to another. She sank here back in April of 1960. She departed New York on her way to the Mediterranean Sea, hauling a load of scrap iron. Historians believe that the cargo must have shifted, breaching her hull. Some of the survivor's reports indicate that. Others differ. Whatever the cause, the pumps couldn't keep up with the water flooding in, and she sank. They never even managed to get out a distress call. According to reports, she went very quickly."

Malik moved closer to him. "Quicker than the *Spratling* did?"

The chief nodded sadly. "Much quicker, but despite everything, all of the crew made it off alive. There were twenty-three men in the lifeboat. Imagine how crowded they must have been, packed in there like sardines in a can. And you folks thought this little lifeboat was crowded. Of course, theirs was a lot bigger than this one. They drifted for thirteen hours before the coast guard picked them up. That's where their story ends. But that's not the end for the *Ethel C*. She's still there. She's down there right now—sitting upright on the bottom of the ocean."

Malik glanced out at the water. "Just how deep is this, anyway?"

"Where we are?" The chief shrugged. "If I remember correctly, it's right around one hundred and ninety feet deep. The wreck is intact—all three hundred and twenty-nine feet of her—so if you were to dive down there and go scavenging, you'd find her wheelhouse at about one hundred and forty feet and the rest of her below that."

"Intact?" Tasha slid closer, enthralled with the conversation. "You mean like it's still new?"

"Well, not quite. The *Ethel C* has been down there for a long time, so she's in pretty bad shape. The hull is probably corroded. But as I said, she is still upright and divers say that she has a very impressive haul. Over the years, they've brought up the navigation equipment and most of her portholes, along with silverware, mementos, picture frames, pocket watches, jewelry—things like that. People pay big money for treasure like that."

"Dang," Malik breathed. "I'd love to dive down to a shipwreck. Imagine all the stuff down there."

Carol nodded her head in agreement. "It's romantic, in a way."

I tuned them out, thinking about the wreck of the *Ethel C*, sitting on the ocean's floor, dead—and yet, in a way, still alive in the recovery operations conducted by the divers, and alive in the memories of men like the chief. It was sadly poignant. After all, death wasn't the end anymore. Staying in your grave was strictly old school. And if there was such a thing as a soul, what proof did we have that it lived on? What if our souls were trapped inside those rotting corpses—able only to watch in horror and revulsion as our own bodies turned against those we loved? What kind of an afterlife was that? That wasn't heaven. It was hell. Eternal life equaled zombie. Better to achieve immortality another way. Regardless of our religion, regardless of what we believed, the cold, simple truth was that none of us had a fucking clue what lay beyond this life. The only kind of eternal life we could be sure of was the kind enjoyed by this shipwreck—living on in the memories of others. Like a myth. An archetype. The professor had been right. We were monomyths. All of us. Every survivor. If humanity was able to survive, if five hundred years from now Tasha and Malik's descendents sat in a classroom and learned about ancient history, we would take the place of Hercules and Superman. Come hear the tale of Mitch, the warrior, and Runkle, the trickster, and Lamar, the hero.

Bullshit.

A fat seagull darted down to the ocean's surface and then flew back up into the air. Something red dangled from its beak. I noticed more birds doing the same. They were feeding off something floating on the tide. We were too far away for me to tell what it was. I figured it was just seaweed.

Yawning, the chief checked the GPS and nodded with satisfaction.

"We're getting closer," he said, clearing his swollen nose again. "We should be able to see the jack-up in a little while. Not a moment to soon, either, if you ask me. The sun's going to be brutal to-day, out here on this open water. We'd have to deal with sunburn and exposure on top of everything else."

Carol smiled. "Between a bad case of sunburn and an army of zombies, I'll take the sunburn."

He returned her smile and Carol blushed, and then quickly looked away. The chief's ears turned red. I stifled a grin. Maybe there was hope for the human race yet.

"Don't be so sure," the chief told her. "We've been out here all night, exposed to the elements. We're all dehydrated. A few hours with the hot sun beating down on us and we're going to be in even worse shape. First we'll blister. Then we'll—"

"That's okay," Carol said, holding up her hand. "You can spare me the gory details. I believe you."

"Sorry."

"You lost your hat. If we had some sunscreen, I'd rub some on your head so that you don't get burned."

The chief turned beet red.

I hid another grin. He had a lot to learn about talking to women if he was going to be the last player on earth. Taking another break from rowing, I leaned out over the side and trailed my fingers through the water. It was cool, and felt good on my skin. The sun climbed higher into the sky, reflecting off the ocean's surface, shimmering like headlights on a busy city street.

And then something bit my finger.

Screaming, I pulled my hand out of the water.

The others looked at me in alarm. Tasha and Malik jumped up and ran to my side of the lifeboat, rocking it dangerously back and forth.

"What's wrong?" Malik asked. "What'd you see?"

I glanced back down in the water. A dead fish floated just a few inches below the surface. When it turned, I saw that its belly was missing. Its mouth gulped in an O shape. There were no teeth, but that hadn't stopped it from trying to swallow my finger. I held my hand up in front of my face, examining myself for wounds or scratches. There were none. I wiped it on my shirt and shivered.

"Get out of the way," Malik shouted, trying to push past his sister. "Let me kill it."

Tasha shoved him back. "Stop pushing, Malik. You'll tip us over."

"Both of you stop it," I said. It was hard to speak. My heart was still in my throat. My skin tingled. If the fish had been equipped with teeth—well, that would have been it for me. Shuddering, I took a deep breath and tried to calm down. Another dead fish bobbed to the surface, its festering tail flicking slowly back and forth. Even underwater, we could see that its entire length was covered with open sores. Scales and strands of flesh floated from its sides. A third appeared, and then a fourth—then a whole school of fish, varying in size and type. The surface teemed with them. The chief leaned out over the bow and Carol kept watch from her side.

"There's more here," she cried.

"Here, too," Chief Maxey reported. "Dozens of them. Everybody sit back and hang on tight."

He started the motor. There was a grinding sound from underneath the lifeboat's hull. Blood, scales, and a decapitated fish head floated to the surface. The zombie fish had been chopped into bits by the propellers. Chief Maxey gunned the engine and the boat's front end tilted up into the air, knocking us all backward. We held on as he pulled away. The boat leveled out again. I looked back, and in our V-shaped wake, I saw more undead fish—and something else. A sleek, dark shape closed the distance between us and disappeared beneath the boat. Something bumped into us from underneath, scraping along the bottom and jarring the lifeboat. A triangular fin resurfaced on the other side.

Carol gasped, "Oh my God . . ."

"Shark," Malik shrieked, jumping up and down. "It's a shark!"

More fins erupted from the water, appearing on both sides of the lifeboat. They paced us, having no trouble keeping up. The chief pushed the throttle to its maximum and we pulled ahead. The fins fell behind, but the creatures were still determinedly giving chase.

Carol gripped the bench. "Are they alive or dead?"

"It don't matter," Malik shouted at her. "They're sharks. Ain't you ever seen the movies? They'll eat us either way."

Tasha had left the rifle lying on the bench. As the boat shot forward, it slid toward me. Snatching it up, I shouldered the weapon and peered through the scope. Everything was blurry and I had to readjust the magnification. Then, able to see, I moved the crosshairs around, searching desperately for a fin. I found one, and scanned the water, looking for its head. The effort was pointless. The shark's body was submerged, its head hidden. Cursing, I squeezed the trigger, aiming for where I thought the head should be. The rifle bucked against my shoulder and pain tore through my chest. Through the scope, I saw a plume of spray as the bullet sliced the ocean's surface. I must have missed, because the shark didn't slow. Raising my head to get a better look, I noticed more sleek fins dotting the surface. One of the sharks was close enough for me to see that it was missing a chunk of hide. Gray skin gave way to pink and white meat. The open wound confirmed what I'd already suspected. The sharks were dead.

The zombies circled closer. The chief leaned forward, as if willing the lifeboat to go faster. I looked through the scope and fired another shot. The fin changed course, swerving away. I shot at it again, but the bullet still seemed to have no effect. Meanwhile, another of the creatures cut us off from the front and swam head on, as if intent on ramming us. The chief shouted for the shotgun, but before anyone else could act, Malik grabbed the weapon and ran to the bow. He aimed the shotgun, thin arms struggling to keep it aloft. The shark emerged from the waves. Its mouth was open wide, flashing rows of white, razor-sharp teeth. Malik squeezed the trigger. The shark's black eye exploded and some of its snout was sheared away. The blast knocked Malik to the floor. He looked stunned, but he kept the shotgun clutched tight in his hands. As he struggled to stand, I took aim with the rifle. The shark skated along the side of the lifeboat. Its ruined eye leaked blood and pulp, but it didn't cease its attack. Shrieking, Carol scooted out of the way as it raked the hull with its teeth. I lined up the crosshairs right over the gaping hole where its eye had been and took my shot. The shark reared up out of the water and then sank beneath the waves. The frothing surf turned red.

Quickly, I searched for another target, while Malik stumbled to his feet. Gripping the shotgun, he stomped over to the side and aimed, letting the barrel lead the shark by a few feet. Despite the chaos, I was once again amazed at the boy's adaptability. It was like he intuitively knew how to shoot.

Malik and I sank two more zombie sharks before the chief managed to outrace them. Even then, the fins followed along behind us. Again, I thought of the slaughter that must be taking place under the sea. How many different species of fish and crustaceans lived in the Atlantic Ocean? How many of them were dead already, and hunting the others? As Malik and I reloaded, the GPS gave out a series of loud, rapid beeps.

"Look around," the Chief shouted. "We should be able to see the jack-up!"

We glanced expectantly in each direction, but saw nothing except gray water and clear sky. The two merged, indistinguishable from one another.

The horizons were empty except for the circling birds moving across them in great flocks.

A dolphin chattered off the port side. I lined it up in the crosshairs, but held off on taking the shot. It didn't look dead. Then the dolphin leapt from the water, soaring through the air and splashing back down again, sending up a huge plume. When visibility improved again, I saw the water turn red as the dolphin thrashed. Something else was attacking it from below. The dolphin's body turned over again and again. By the third spin, its white underbelly was scarlet. I pointed the scope down and my eyes widened. A school of undead dolphins were ripping their brother to shreds. They spun him with their noses, ramming him and darting in for quick, savage bites. Then one of them noticed us. It swam toward the lifeboat. The scope's magnification made the creature's gaze seem malevolent. Before I could shoot it, the dolphin plunged below the waves.

I moved the scope around, trying to find the dolphin again before it could reach us.

And then Carol screamed.

The zombie dolphin launched itself from the water and soared through the air. I could only stand there gaping as it landed in the lifeboat, knocking my oars into the sea. Carol screamed again, scuttling backward on her hands and feet like a crab. The chief pressed himself against the side, unable to let go of the throttle, because if he did, the boat would stall. Then we'd be dead in the water—in more ways than one. Brave but weaponless, Tasha watched the dolphin warily. I raised the rifle and lined up the crosshairs. But before I could act, Malik pressed the shotgun against the creature's head and pulled the trigger. The dolphin squeaked once and then died. Its tail slapped against the sides of the boat as its brains and blood leaked out onto the bottom.

"Get away from it," I warned them all. "Don't let the blood come in contact with you."

The GPS suddenly rang a shrill alarm, distracting all of us for a second.

"I see it," the chief shouted. "The oil rig. I see it, on our port side!"

We all looked in the direction he was pointing. There was a black dot on the horizon.

"That?" Carol asked, squinting.

"Yes, indeed," the chief said. "That's the jack-up. Ladies and gentlemen, we made it."

We cheered, staring in disbelief. Tasha ran over and hugged me. Carol began to weep with joy. Malik raised the shotgun over his head and laughed.

"Let's go," the chief yelled. "Hold on tight."

Before we could even heed his warning, he turned the lifeboat in a wide arc, flinging us all to one side. We grasped the benches and the sides, trying to avoid slipping or falling into the dolphin gore. The boat whipped forward, racing across the surface, the front end shaking as it bounced up and down on the waves. The zombies fell farther and farther behind. A scarlet cloud spread out in our wake as they turned on the other creatures of the sea.

"We can make it," the chief shouted over the engine's roar.

I wondered who he was trying to reassure—us or himself. I waited breathlessly for something else to go wrong, for the engine to smoke or sputter, for us to run out of fuel or for another school of zombie sharks to suddenly emerge in front of us. But nothing happened. We rocketed across the ocean and the oil rig drew nearer. We could see it easily now—a big black barge with an oil drilling rig and living quarters attached to it. Its size was astonishing. Like a small town. As we drew closer, I noticed there was even a tanker truck and several forklifts parked on the platform. I remembered that either the chief or Tum had told us that a jack-up was actually a small operation. I wondered just how big a full-sized oil rig was.

"Usually," the chief said, "the oil companies bring their personnel in either via helicopter or boat. There's a landing pad on the platform and lower level docks at the water's surface. I'll pull alongside that. Lamar, you stand ready with that rifle while Carol and the kids disembark, just in case any of those things try a last minute attack."

I nodded, and he continued, turning to the others "Once you three are safely on the dock, Lamar and I will hand the supplies to you. Then I'll tie us off and we'll be home free."

Unless there are dead people onboard, I thought.

"How do we get up to the higher levels?" Carol asked. "It seems awfully high. I hope there aren't any stairs. My legs are killing me, and I banged my knee when that dolphin jumped onboard."

The chief gently rubbed his injured nose. "Don't worry. There aren't any stairs, at least not in that section. Not sure what they'll have, though. Some rigs have elevators, and others use cranes to lift all their personnel up to the top in man baskets. But that's not anything to be concerned about. If there are any crew members left onboard, and the rig doesn't have elevators, we'll ask them to haul us up in the basket."

"And what if they refuse?"

"Then Lamar and I will shoot them."

Carol looked shocked, but then the chief grinned. She smiled back at him.

I checked our pursuers, but they were gone from sight. There were signs of battles being fought below the surface all across the open water—splashes and plumes and red-tinted surf. But none of it was close enough to the lifeboat to cause me any immediate concern. I hoped the fish would continue fighting each other and ignore us long enough to get aboard the oil rig.

We drew closer. The massive jack-up loomed over us. We scanned the decks and catwalks, looking for signs of life, but all we saw were seabirds. They covered the rig, perched on every antenna, crane, building, and safety net. There were hundreds of them. At least now we knew where all the ones we'd seen earlier had come from. They must have flown back and forth from the mainland. And with all the offal now floating on the waves, they wouldn't even have to make that trip.

The chief pulled alongside the lower level dock

and shut off the engine. I stood guard with the rifle, watching the sea for signs of trouble while Carol, Malik, and Tasha climbed up onto the platform. The ocean remained clear, but the signs of the terrible battle beneath its surface increased. Huge clouds of blood now floated on the tide like pools of oil. Severed heads, tails, and organs rolled on the waves. A seagull darted down and gripped some fish entrails in its claws, but before it could take flight again, a large blue-and-green fish leaped from the water and seized the bird in its mouth. The bird squawked in alarm. Its wings beat at the water. Then it was pulled below. I turned back to comment to the others, but none of them had seen it happen.

Once Carol and the kids had safely disembarked from the lifeboat, the chief handed the supplies up to them. They set the containers and bags on the deck. Malik started to explore, but Carol warned him to stay close to the rest of us. Sulking, Malik complied. To distract him, the chief handed the shotgun to Malik, stock first, and Malik set that aside as well. Then the chief turned back to me.

"Are we still clear?"

I nodded. "So far, so good."

"Okay. You go on up, and then I'll tie us off."

I eyed the drilling platform. "Is this thing stable? Seems like its just floating out here."

"It is," he said. "Basically, the oil company just floats it out to wherever they want to drill. But there are jacks that extend down to the ocean floor, raising it up and stabilizing it. Kind of like an anchor. So we're not going anywhere."

I passed my rifle to Carol, who took it hesitantly. It was obvious that the weapon made her nervous. Smiling, I clambered up onto the dock and took it back from her. Her posture and expression relaxed again. I stared up into the rigging. If the jack-up was occupied, nobody had come out to greet us. Maybe it was abandoned, or maybe they were dead.

In the lifeboat, the chief began whistling while he gathered up the ropes.

"Hey, Wade," I whispered. "We still don't know if this thing is deserted. Maybe we should try to be quiet."

"You're right," he agreed, lowering his voice. "I'm sorry. Shouldn't be whistling anyway, I guess. It hurts my nose. I'm just excited."

He turned back to the ropes and hauled them over to the side, grunting with the effort. I turned my attention back to the jack-up. Malik and Tasha followed my gaze. Carol watched the chief.

None of us saw it in time.

Our only warning was when the creature surfaced. There was a rushing sound, like a blast of steam from the world's biggest iron. We turned back to the ocean and the chief froze, the ropes hanging from his hands. The ocean's surface rippled with a motion not caused by the pull of the tide. A huge black bulk surfaced from the depths, rocking both the lifeboat and the dock. The motion knocked the chief off his feet.

Water streamed down the creature's sides as it

rose higher. It was a whale—an undead whale. Horrible wounds covered its bulk, and the stench wafting off its hide was worse than anything I'd ever smelled. It was like every corpse in Baltimore had been bottled up and brought here. Gagging, I bent over and wretched. Carol did the same. The kids turned away, coughing. When I turned back, I caught a glimpse of one huge, soulless eye—bigger than a dinner plate and black as night. Then the lifeboat capsized, turning over completely and tipping the chief into the sea. A mouth the size of a car opened up beneath him, swallowing him whole. He didn't even have time to scream. Carol screamed for him. Screamed for us all.

Ignoring the rotting beast's smell, I snapped the rifle up and fired a shot. It was like shooting spitballs at a dinosaur. The whale slammed against the dock, and the entire platform shook. I emptied the magazine into it. Beside me, the shotgun roared as Malik did the same. I don't know if our rounds had any effect. The zombie sank again beneath the waves, taking Chief Maxey with it. The lifeboat drifted away on the tide. The air trapped beneath the hull kept it from sinking. There was no way for us to retrieve it. The lifeboat was already out of our reach.

Carol fell to her knees and sobbed quietly. Tasha and Malik just stared in disbelief. I knew how they felt. It had all happened so quickly. It just didn't seem real somehow. I mean, a zombie fucking whale? If circumstances had been different, I could have almost laughed. You go through life believing only in what you can see. What science can prove. Things like ghosts and monsters are the stuff of fantasy. But then, one morning, you wake up and the dead are out in the streets hunting down the living. Your world comes crashing down when that happens. But even when you get used to the idea that the dead can walk, a zombie whale still seemed incredible. In a way, I think it shook our world view all over again.

The lifeboat drifted farther away. I watched it go, wondering where it would end up and if there'd be anybody left to find it.

"Why him?" Carol sobbed. "Why Wade? He was such a nice man. So gentle. He saved us all. Why did it have to take him?"

I put my hand on her shoulder. "I don't know, Carol. I don't know."

We'd lost yet another member of our group. And now we were stranded. If there were zombies aboard the drilling platform, we'd have no means of escape—except for the weapons we held in our hands.

"We'll grieve for the chief later," I said. "Grieve for them all. But right now, let's check our ammunition and then make sure this place is safe."

Malik shuffled over to me as I dug through a bag and found more bullets.

"If there's dead folks onboard, how we gonna get away?"

I reloaded my magazine and refused to look up at him.

"We'll find a way," I said softly, fingering the rounds. "We'll find a way. . . ."

The floor on the jack-up was about twenty feet off the ocean's surface, but there were levels under the rig as well. We stowed the supplies on the dock, intending to come back for them once we'd determined that the drilling platform was safe. A metal sign affixed to one of the girders said PROPERTY OF BLACK LODGE OIL & GAS—A DIVISION OF THE GLOBE CORPORATION—AUTHORIZED PERSONNEL ONLY. I hadn't heard of Black Lodge, but Globe Corp. was massive. One of those big international corporations that seemed to be everywhere. They had their hands in everything before society collapsed: electronics, defense systems, financing, energy sources, telecommunications. They'd been one of the big darlings on Wall Street. Their shares traded for hundreds of dollars. Now those shares were worthless.

We approached the elevator. I took a deep breath and pressed the arrow button. There was still power. We heard the whine of an electric motor and squeaking cables as the car came down to us. The doors clanked open and we stepped inside. The elevator slowly rose. I tightly gripped the rifle and tried to reassure the rest of them with a smile. My fatigue was gone, replaced with nervous energy.

We explored the jack-up level by level, sticking together as a group. Tasha and Carol were cautious, but Malik was excited. He wanted to run off on his own, and I had to keep hauling him back, warning him over and over not to do it again. We talked in whispers and communicated with hand signals. The silence was eerie. Everywhere we went, the birds watched us warily. We found a skeletal arm on one level, and a disembodied head lying between two drums of oil. The head barely moved, ravaged as it was by the birds. It had no eyes with which to see us. Its lipless mouth moved soundlessly. The zombie's tongue was missing, too. I kicked it over the side and watched it sink. Then I wiped my shoe off with some greasy shop rags that had been stuffed into one of the barrel's openings. Finally, we climbed back into the elevator and took it to the top level.

The elevator doors opened and a dead man was there to greet us.

Carol shrieked. The dead man was dressed in dirty, faded dungarees and a red flannel shirt. A bright yellow hard hat covered his head. Time and the elements had not been kind. The zombie was in an advanced state of decomposition. His flesh and the clothes had melded together. His face was a gleaming skull, stripped clean of all flesh. A few ragged pieces of skin and matted hair hung down from underneath the hard hat. With no eyes left in the sockets, I saw right away that the zombie hunted by sound, just like the corpses back at the rescue station. It had been attracted to us by the sounds of the elevator. Carol's scream had confirmed our location. It reached for us, bones sticking through the split skin of its fingers. Malik raised his shotgun, but I knocked it aside.

"No," I said. "He's too close. The backsplash will hit us."

The zombie lurched into the elevator and we shrank away, hugging the walls. The doors slid shut again, bumped against the corpse, and then opened. The zombie turned toward them in confusion, grasping blindly. I took advantage of the distraction, pushing it out of the elevator with the butt of my rifle. It stumbled back out onto the platform, arms pinwheeling. Before the doors could close again, I darted forward and clubbed it over the head, hoping to knock it down long enough to shoot it. The zombie collapsed to the deck and the hard hat came off its head, spilling soupy liquid. Two grayish-pink lumps—its brains—splashed into the puddle a second later. Gasping, I turned away. Apparently, it had decomposed so badly that the hard hat was the only thing still holding its brains intact. When they splashed out over the deck, the zombie ceased moving. I struggled to keep from throwing up.

Malik fanned his nose. "Oh man, that stinks!"

I nodded. "That's the worst one yet. After all the things we've seen . . ."

I shuddered, unable to finish. Sour bile rose in my throat.

"Let's hope that it's the last one," Carol said. "That would be fine with me."

And it was the last. The rest of the jack-up was deserted. Once we'd finished exploring it, Carol and the kids got settled while I brought our supplies up from the dock. Basically, the jack-up was a giant barge. One end held the actual drilling apparatus. At the other end was a three-story building. On top of the building were a heliport and several big antennas. They even had a satellite television dish and a Sirius satellite radio unit, though I doubted there were any signals still being broadcast. Inside the building were the crew's quarters, a galley, a gym complete with free weights and an exercise bike, a laundry room with three washers and dryers, several restrooms and shower stalls, and finally, a crew's lounge with couches, a television and DVD player, and—much to Malik's delight—an XBox videogame system, a foosball table, and a slate-bottom pool table. On the top floor, there were also several offices. Placards over the doors said things like COMPANY MAN and PUSHER. I wondered what those were. Where I'd lived, company men and pushers had been very different things.

There were also half a dozen storage rooms. One of the supply rooms held janitorial and maintenance supplies. Another held medical supplies and other things we desperately needed, like toiletries and vitamins. But we breathed a sigh of relief when we opened the door to the last storage room. It was filled with food—boxes of dry and canned goods stacked all the way to the ceiling. The chief had said that a jack-up's crew usually numbered between fifteen to twenty people. I figured there was enough food here to last them a month. Since it was just the four of us, it would last us much longer, which was important since we could no longer rely on the sea for food. Not with Hamelin's Revenge infecting the fish.

On the surface of the barge, in between the rig and the building, was a fenced-in area where the drilling pipe and other equipment were kept. It also held a big garbage compactor. There were other pieces of machinery tied down to the rig to keep them from falling into the ocean. The fuel truck that I'd noticed earlier was also strapped down and the wheels were chocked. I peeked inside the cab and found the keys dangling from the ignition. At the end of the maintenance yard was a giant fuel tank filled with thousands of gallons of diesel, and a small trailer housing a generator. Beyond that was another big tank, holding fresh water, according to the sign stenciled on the side of it.

One thing that still bothered me was how the zombies had gotten on the rig in the first place. We'd encountered one, and saw signs of others— the severed body parts and carnage. Had the lone zombie that we'd destroyed been responsible for the other deaths? If not, where were the rest of the creatures? The rig was deserted. And if that single, hard hat–wearing corpse had been responsible, how had he been infected in the first place? I had no answers, and thinking about it made my head hurt. There was a story here, but it wasn't mine. It was somebody else's monomyth, and it had ended badly.

I returned to the building. We set up in the crew's quarters. For a while, we didn't do much of anything. Exhausted, we simply sat there, grateful for the respite. Then we got ourselves cleaned up. I spent twenty minutes in the shower, letting the hot water caress me, feeling my aches and pains subside, washed away with the dirt and grime. It was the most wonderful thing in the world. When I emerged from the stall and toweled myself off, I felt like a new man.

We still had no clean clothes, but we found some spare uniforms in the crew's quarters and we wore those instead. After everyone had cleaned up and relaxed, we ate dinner together—canned green beans and corn, cocktail wieners, crackers, peanut butter, pickles, potato chips, cereal, and bottles of juice and water. It was a feast.

I slept like a rock that night, and when I woke up the next morning, for the first time in my life, I remembered my dreams.

I dreamed I was a hero.

CHAPTER FOURTEEN

That all happened a month ago. The summer is over now and fall is on the way. The days grow shorter. It's getting colder out here at sea, even during the daytime. The winds rip across the water, shaking the drilling platform. When the tide gets rough, it's like being back onboard the *Spratling* again.

After a few days, we settled into our new lives with remarkable ease. It felt weird, at first, not living with the constant danger. Not being on the run or in hiding, constantly glancing over our shoulders and looking for the dead. It was hard to relax, in a way. Felt irresponsible for doing so. But once we'd realized that the zombies couldn't reach us, and that we really were safe for the first time since this whole thing began, we embraced our new home.

Sometimes we talk about what could be happening on the mainland. We have no way of knowing, and it's all speculation on our part, but it helps to take our minds off things. Are the cities and towns full of dead people, or has humanity managed to fight back? If so, is there hope for a rescue someday—a way off this oil rig, and back to the lives we knew before Hamelin's Revenge?

Probably not.

We are surrounded on all sides by a dead sea. Even if the creatures in the water couldn't reach us, their smell still could. With each passing week the stench has grown stronger—rotting fish and brine. The birds have a never ending smorgasbord. But when we're inside the building and running the air filtration system, the smell doesn't bother us too much. It's only when we're outside that it gets to be too bad, and even then it's only unbearable on days with no wind. When it rains, the stench disappears.

Carol and the kids adapted well to our situation. We've each got our own room now. The privacy is nice, after all that time on the ship. She insisted on continuing their education. Both of them grumbled about it at first, but I think they actually enjoy their classes. It gives them something to do during the day—takes their mind off the overall situation. Trapped out here as we are, with no lifeboat or means of escape, monotony and boredom are our two biggest enemies. In the evening, we play video games or foosball, or shoot pool. Malik's gotten really good at the latter. He's a born hustler. One of the oil platform's crew members left behind a kite and a spool of string. When they're not studying or helping me with general maintenance, Tasha and Malik like to fly it outside. They get a really good breeze out here and the kite soars high. Carol reads a lot. We found some paperbacks in the crew's berthing area, along with magazines and even a few old newspapers. The newspapers make me sad; they're full of news that doesn't matter. Current events that once seemed so important—the price of gas, the war in the Middle East, sex on television, celebrity baby photos. Once in a while, when we're feeling hopeful, we turn on the television or radio. There's never a signal, though. The static over the radio is the loneliest sound in the world.

When I'm working outside, I keep an eye out for ships on the horizon or planes in the sky. I've yet to see one. Doubt now that I ever will. Maybe we're the last humans. I don't know. Like I've always said, survival instinct is a motherfucker. It still is. We'll go on living, go on fighting to survive. We have to. If we are the last humans left alive, then God has a pretty fucked-up sense of humor. How are we going to repopulate the planet once the zombies all rot away? Tasha and Malik are brother and sister. I'm a gay man. And even if I wasn't gay, it turns out that Carol has already been through menopause. So much for that idea. The future falls to Tasha and Malik. They are the next generation. They have to survive. I have to be their hero.

We found some bags of marshmallows in the dry goods storage room. Sometimes at night we build a fire in an empty oil drum, using broken up skids for kindling. Then we roast marshmallows. The smoke drifts up into the sky. I like to pretend that somebody up there can see it. Maybe not an airplane, and certainly not God—God is dead. I know that now. God is one of them. But maybe someone else can see it. There are astronauts onboard the international space station, right? They were there when the disease first started, and they're still up there. Like us, they have no way to get home. So I pretend that they can see our smoke, and that they no longer feel so alone. They know that someone else is still alive, that humanity survives, that life prevails.

But it's just pretend.

I found a Bible among the personal belongings the crew left behind. The spine is cracked and the pages marked and worn. Whoever it belonged to read it an awful lot. I've flipped through it a few times, reading passages at random, looking for solace and comfort. I haven't found either. But I did find a verse that spoke to me. Jeremiah, chapter eight, verse twenty: "The summer is over, the harvest is in, and we are not saved."

The summer is over and death's harvest is in. It was a bumper crop this year. And here we are, safe on this oil rig—safe, but not saved.

We've been careful to ration our food supply. The fresh water tank is full. I found an instruction manual that told me how to siphon water up out of the ocean in case of an emergency, but I won't. That's just asking to be infected with Hamelin's Revenge. No sense taking chances. We've cut back on showers, only taking them every few days. We've got plenty of diesel fuel though, so there's no chance of running out of power for a long time, unless the generator dies. On our second day here, we discovered a walk-in freezer filled with meat and frozen vegetables. Twice a week, we get something out of the freezer and defrost it. Otherwise, we stick to the dry stuff and canned goods, and even those are rationed. We've been supplementing our food with the birds. There are certainly enough of them. Rather than wasting ammunition, we hunt them with Alka-Seltzer tablets. We go out onto the platform and scatter a mixture of table scraps and Alka-Seltzer tablets that we found in the medical supplies. The birds gobble it up. But their digestive system is different than a human's. Since they can't burp or fart, the Alka-Seltzer sits in their stomach, fizzing away, until the gas and foam builds up to the point where it has nowhere to go. Then the birds' stomachs pop. Once they're dead, we have to gut and clean them pretty quickly. Otherwise, their burst stomachs leak into the rest of the body, ruining the meat. It's pretty fucking gruesome, but necessary. We've got to save our food supply for as long as we can, and we can't use up the rest of our bullets on seagulls.

Of course, when we run out of Alka-Seltzer, we'll have to come up with another way to hunt them. Maybe nets or nooses or something . . .

Shit. Who the fuck am I kidding, anyway? That doesn't matter now.

Nothing matters.

I told Carol and the kids that we could survive a long time on birds. And we could have. With all of their natural predators either gone or dead—or living dead—there are lots of birds now. Fuck the meek. The birds have inherited the earth.

Yeah, we could have survived by eating them.
But . . .

Tomorrow, when the kids wake up, I'll have to tell them that they can't go outside anymore. I already told Carol. I waited until after Tasha and Malik had gone to sleep, so that they wouldn't hear. When I'd finished, Carol started crying. She retreated to her room and asked to be left alone for a while. I let her go. Nothing I could have done or said would change the situation. I felt like crying, too.

Earlier this evening, when I went out to hunt some birds for tomorrow's breakfast, things changed again for the worse. I was standing on one of the catwalks, tossing Alka-Seltzer coated with hamburger grease out onto the deck, and the birds came in to feast. Their slender gray and white bodies soared through the air and landed on the platform. They began pecking at the bait, but before any of them could eat, another bird swooped down out of the sky and crashed among them. Feathers flew into the air and the other birds squawked in surprise. I wondered what had made it land like that, and then I saw.

The bird was missing its legs and one of its eyes, but it was still moving. It ignored the bait. Instead, it attacked another seagull. Two more of them zipped toward us. The regular birds scattered. I dropped my bucket and ran across the platform, waiting to feel a razorlike beak slashing at my flesh. I didn't, though. I made it inside.

I was damn lucky.

Hamelin's Revenge has jumped species again, just like it did with the fish. The birds had been immune.

And now they aren't.

We can stay inside here for a long time. As long as the generator doesn't break down, we'll be fine. But sooner or later we'll run out of food and water. What happens when there's nothing left to eat? How do we hunt or forage when all of our prey is already dead—and hunting us? If one of us died, could the rest of us eat them? Would that make us any different than those things outside?

The birds are zombies now, and there's a hell of a lot more zombies than there are of us. Humans are a thing of the past. We're the last of them. The last of a dying breed. We are the new dinosaurs. Our civilization ends with us. All of the things we've achieved are meaningless now. All of our advances. All of our stories. Heroes don't matter anymore, and that's okay, because I'm not a hero. I never was. I'm just a fallen archetype, based on a falsehood. What happens to a hero when he dies? He becomes a myth. But what happens to myths when there's no one left to tell about them? Do they just fade away, as we will? I'm sure they do. I bet human history is full of forgotten myths—heroes we've never heard of simply because there was no on left to tell us about their exploits. Their journey—their trials and tribulations—were pointless in the end because they were forgotten. Those myths and archetypes didn't survive.

Forget the meek. The dead have inherited the

earth. They are the new breed—the planet's new dominant species. They rule at the top of the food chain.

Back in the day, there was a rap song I used to like. The lyrics said, "Evolve or die." That line has taken on a new meaning for me. In order to survive, a species has to evolve. We did it when we came out of the ocean, and we did it again when we came down from the trees.

Survival instinct is a motherfucker.

But evolution is even worse.

And if we have to evolve to survive, then maybe I'll just open the door.

Turn the page for an advance look at Brian
Keene's next terrifying novel . . .

DARK HOLLOW

Coming February 2008

CHAPTER ONE

It was on the first day of spring that Big Steve and I saw Shelly Carpenter giving head to the hairy man.

Winter had been a hard one. Two books to write in five month's time. It's not something I recommend doing, if you can help it. There was a lot of pressure involved. The sales of my first novel, *Heart of the Matter*, caught my critics, my publisher, and even myself by surprise. It did very well—something a book of its kind isn't supposed to do, especially a mid-list, mass-market mystery paperback with no promotional campaign behind it other than a quarter-page advertisement in a lone trade magazine. Publishers don't buy a lot of advertising for mid-list authors.

Suffice to say, I beat the odds. Flush with success, I quit my day job—only to learn that I wouldn't be getting a royalty check for at least another year. We'd already blown through the advance—mortgage payments, credit card payments, car and truck payments, new living room furniture for my wife, Tara, and a new laptop for me. Plus, I'd spent quite a bit of my own cash traveling to book signings. Publishers don't pay for mid-list book signing tours, either.

If I'd had an agent, maybe they would have explained the pay schedule to me. Or then again, maybe they wouldn't have. Personally, I'm glad I don't have an agent. They require fifteen percent of your earnings, and I was broke. Fifteen percent of shit is still shit.

I could have gone back to work part-time at the paper mill in Spring Grove, but I figured that if I applied myself to writing, I'd be making about as much money as I would at the mill anyway, so I decided to follow what I love doing. Tara still worked, insisting that she pay the bills while I stayed home and wrote. We needed the health insurance her company provided, but we couldn't survive on just one income. Thus . . . two more books for two different publishers in five month's time, written just for the advance money, which would see us through the winter. Don't get me wrong. It was a nice chunk of change, but when you totaled up the hours I spent writing, the advance for the next two novels came out to about a buck-eighty an hour. And to make matters worse, they weren't really stories that I wanted to write. They didn't speak to me. I wasn't passionate about them, and had lost my sense of wonder.

But we needed the money. Some people call that being a hack.

I call it necessity.

The pressure got to me. I started smoking again—

two packs a day—and drank coffee nonstop. I'd get up at five, make the daily commute from the bed to the coffeepot to the computer, and start writing. I'd work on one novel until noon, take a break for lunch, and then work on the second novel until late evening. After a full day of that, I'd take care of business: reading contracts, responding to fan mail, checking my message board, giving interviews and all the other things that constitute writing but don't actually involve putting words on paper. I'd go to bed around midnight. Then I'd get up the next morning and do it all over again. Seven days a week.

The glamorous life of a writer . . .

During those rough months, I'd have gone insane if not for Big Steve. Tara brought him home from the pound to keep me company during the day. Big Steve was a mixed-breed mutt—part beagle, part rottweiler, part black lab, and one hundred percent pussy. Despite his formidable size and bark, Big Steve was scared of his own shadow. He ran from butterflies and squirrels, fled from birds and wind-tossed leaves, and cowered when the mailwoman came to the door. When Tara first brought him home, he hid in the corner of the kitchen for half a day, shaking, with his tail between his legs.

He warmed up to us fairly quick, but he was still frightened by anything else. Not that he let it show. When something—it didn't matter what, a groundhog or Seth Ferguson, the kid from across the street—stepped onto our property, the rottweiler inside him came out. He was all bark and no bite, but a robber would have had a hard time believing that.

Big Steve became my best friend. He listened while I read manuscript pages out loud to him. He'd lie on the couch and watch television with me when I took a break from writing. We liked the same beer, and the same food (because dog food just didn't do it for Big Steve; he preferred a nice, juicy steak or some cheese-dripping pizza). Most importantly, Big Steve knew when it was time to drag my ass away from the computer. That was how we started our daily walks, and now they were a scheduled routine. Two per day—one at dawn, shortly after Tara left for work, and the second at sundown, before I started making dinner, when she was on her way home. Tara commutes to Baltimore every day, and it was at those times—when she first left and when she was due home—that the house seemed especially lonely. Big Steve had impeccable timing. He'd get me outside and that always cheered me up.

Which brings us back to Shelly Carpenter and the hairy man.

When Tara left for work that Monday, the first day of spring, Big Steve stood at the door and barked; once, short and to the point.

Behold, I stand at the door and bark; therefore I need to pee.

"You ready to go outside?" I asked.

He thumped his tail in affirmation, and his ears perked up. His big brown eyes shone with excitement. It didn't take much to make Big Steve happy.

I clipped his leash to his collar (despite his fear of anything that moves, there is enough beagle in

Big Steve to inspire a love of running off into the woods with his nose to the ground, and not coming home until after dark). We stepped outside. The sun was shining, and it felt good on my face. It was unseasonably warm, almost like summer. Tara and I had planted a lilac bush the year before, and the flowers bloomed, their scent fragrant and sweet. Birds chirped and sang to each other in the big oak tree in our backyard. A squirrel ran along the roof of my garage, chattering at Big Steve. The dog shrank away from it.

The long, cold winter had come and gone, and somehow I'd made it through and finished both manuscripts: *Cold as Ice* and *When the Rain Comes*. Now, I could finally focus on the novel that I *wanted* to write, something other than a mid-list mystery. Something big, with enough crossover potential to really get me noticed, maybe a novel about the Civil War. I felt good. Better than I had in months. The weather probably had something to do with that. Now it was spring, the season of rebirth and renewal and all that jazz. The time when nature lets the animal kingdom know that it's time to make lots of babies. Spring, the season of sex and happiness. The rutting season.

Big Steve celebrated the first day of spring by pissing on the lilac bush, pissing on the garage, pissing on the sidewalk, and pissing twice on the big oak tree, which further infuriated the squirrel. The tree limbs shook as it expressed its displeasure. Big Steve barked at his aggressor, but only after he was safely behind me.

Our house is sandwiched between Main Street and a narrow back alley separating us from the community fire hall. The fire hall borders a grassy vacant lot and a neighborhood park, the kind with swings and monkey bars and deep piles of mulch to keep kids from skinning their knees when they come down the sliding boards.

Beyond the playground lies the forest—roughly thirty square miles of protected Pennsylvanian woodland, zoned to prevent farmers and realtors from cutting it all down and planting crops or building subdivisions. The forest is surrounded on all sides by our town, and the towns of Seven Valleys, New Freedom, Spring Grove, and New Salem. They all have video stores and grocery outlets and pizza shops (and our town even has a Wal-Mart), but you wouldn't know it while standing inside the forest. Stepping through that tree line is like traveling through time to a Pennsylvania where the Susquehanna Indians still roamed free and the Germans, Quakers, and Amish were yet to come. At the center, at the dark heart of the forest, was LeHorn's Hollow, source of central Pennsylvanian ghost stories and legends. Every region has such a place, and LeHorn's Hollow was ours.

An artist friend of mine once visited us from California. Tara and I took him for a walk through those same woods, maybe half a mile inside, and he said something that has always stuck with me. He said that our woods felt different. I'd scoffed at the time, reminding him that his own state had the majestic redwood forests (Tara and I had spent part of our honemoon walking among the coastal redwoods, and I'd wanted to live there ever since). But he'd insisted that our small patch of forest was different.

He said it felt primordial.

After Big Steve finished watering the yard, he tugged me toward the alley, his ears perked up and tongue lolling in hopeful anticipation.

"You want to go for a walk in the woods? You want to sniff for some bunnies?"

He wagged his tail with enthusiastic confirmation and tilted his head to the side.

"Come on, then." I grinned. His mood was infectious. It was impossible to feel anything other than good that morning. He put his nose to the ground and led me forward.

Shelly Carpenter jogged by on her regular morning run just as we reached the edge of the alley. Her red hair jiggled with each step. So did the rest of her. I didn't know Shelly well, but we usually made small talk every morning as we passed by each other.

"Hey, Adam," she panted, running in place. "Hi, Stevie!"

Big Steve wagged the tip of his tail and darted between my legs.

"Oh, come on, Stevie." She turned off her iPod and removed her headphones. "Don't be shy! You know me."

Big Steve's tail thumped harder, confirming that

yes, he did indeed know her, but he shrank away farther.

Shelly laughed. "God, he's such a 'fraidy cat.'"

"Yeah, he is. Runs from his own shadow. We got him from the pound, and we think that his previous owner may have beaten him or something."

Her brow creased. "That's so sad. What's wrong with some people?"

I nodded. "Yeah, people like that should be shot. You out for your morning jog?"

"You know it. Isn't it beautiful today?"

"It sure is. Spring is finally here."

She looked up at the sun and squinted. "Spring is my favorite time of year."

Her thin T-shirt was damp with sweat, and it clung to her bouncing breasts, revealing perfection. Her pert, dime-sized nipples strained against the fabric, hinting at the dark areolas beneath. Before she could catch me leering, I looked down. Big mistake. Her gray sweatpants had ridden up, hugging her crotch like a second skin. They too were wet with perspiration. I quickly glanced back up. Shelly was staring at me with an odd expression.

"You okay, Adam?" She arched her eyebrows.

I cleared my throat. "Yeah. Sure. I was just thinking about my deadline."

"Seems like you're always daydreaming."

"That's the way it is with writers."

"How's the next book coming?"

"Good." I smiled, and bent down to pet Big Steve. Mistake number two. My face was inches from her groin. I imagined that I could smell her sweat—and something else. Something intoxicating.

The scent of a woman.

What the hell was wrong with me? It was like spring fever had turned me into a horn dog or something. My reactions were uncharacteristic, and I felt embarrassed.

Shelly placed a hand on her hip and arched her back. "What's it going to be?"

I jumped. "W-what?"

"The book." Her breasts bounced up and down as she began jogging in place again. "What's it going to be about? Another mystery?"

"I'm not sure yet, actually. Maybe a Civil War novel, but I don't know. Still working it out in my head. Whatever it turns out to be, it's going to be big."

"Big is good." She licked her lips. Her glistening tongue looked so inviting.

I found myself wondering if she was aware that she was doing it. Her eyes seemed to glaze over, and she moved closer to me. Big Steve shifted nervously between my legs. I cleared my throat again, breaking the spell.

"Well," Shelly said, "I'd better let you get back to work, then. See you. Tell Tara that I said hi."

"Okay. Will do. See you later."

Shelly put her headphones back on, raised her hand and waved, and then blew Big Steve a kiss. We stared after her as she jogged down the alley and crossed over into the park. I watched her perfect

ass moving beneath her sweatpants. Then she vanished from sight.

The next time I saw that ass was when she was on
her knees in front of the hairy man.

Big Steve panted heavily, then turned around
and licked his balls. I knew how he felt. My own
erection strained uncomfortably against my jeans.
Shuffling from one foot to another, I made sure nobody was watching. Then I reached down inside my
pants and readjusted.

I took a deep breath, trying to stave off the guilt
that welled up inside me. I'd never cheated on
Tara, but the opportunities were there. The bigger
my career got, the more of them there seemed to
be. Not dozens of them; at least, not yet. But there
were several women who'd brought bourbon and
crotchless panties to my book signings, or asked
me to sign their breasts with magic marker. They
sent me e-mails telling me how much my writing
turned them on. Genre groupies. It was flattering
and tempting and great for selling books. But it
was surprising, too, especially considering my mod-
est success. I often wondered if it would get worse
as I got bigger.

The thing I was most afraid of was myself—my
own libido.

Tara's moratorium on sex affected me more than
I let on. Yes, I loved her, but sex was a huge part of
our lives. I worried sometimes about cheating on
her, was afraid that one day my traitorous libido
would push me into it. But I'd never done anything.
And my erotic overreaction to Shelly's workout at-

tire left me feeling puzzled and guilty, as did her uncharacteristic flirting—if that's what it was. Had she really flirted, or was it my imagination?

I was pretty sure I'd read the situation correctly. At the time, I dismissed it all. Just something in the air. Spring fever, maybe.

But now I know just how right I was. There was something in the air—music and magic—and it affected us both.

Big Steve strained against his leash, urging me forward. We crossed the alley and walked into the field, heading in the same general direction that Shelly had gone. The grass was wet with dew. Steve put his nose to the ground, catching a scent. He started tracking.

In the oak tree's branches, two squirrels began humping away, celebrating the season by making babies.

I wondered if Tara and I would ever have a baby. Then I thought of the last miscarriage. Sadness welled up inside me, and I fought back sudden and surprising tears. Steve tugged at the leash, chasing the bad memories away like the good dog he was.

We walked on. The wet grass soaked my shoes and his paws. I took us around the playground. It wouldn't do to have the neighborhood children come flying down the slide and land in a pile of dog shit. As if reading my mind, Big Steve dutifully dropped a pile in the grass. Wincing at the smell, I turned my nose away. The dog wagged his tail, and it seemed like he was grinning. Then we moved along.

The neighborhood came to life around us. Paul Legerski's black Chevy Suburban roared down the alley, with Flotsam and Jetsam's "Liquid Noose" blasting from the speakers. An oldie, but a goodie. Paul had the bass turned up, just like the high school kids that did the same thing with their hip-hop. He blew the horn and waved, and I waved back. Paul and his wife, Shannon, were good people. One of my next-door neighbors, Merle, tried to start his lawnmower. It sputtered, stalled, and then sputtered again. Merle's curses were loud and clear, and I chuckled. Then I heard the hiss of running water as another of my neighbors, Dale Haubner, a retiree, turned on his garden hose. A flock of geese flew overhead, honking out their springtime return from southern climates. Honeybees buzzed in the clover growing next to the seesaw.

But beneath all of these familiar noises was another sound. At first I thought I'd imagined it. But Big Steve's ears were up and his head cocked. He'd heard it, too.

As we stood there, it came again—a high, melodic piping. It sounded like a flute. Just a few short, random notes, and then they faded away on the breeze and weren't repeated. I looked around to see if Shelly had heard it, but she was gone, as if the woods had swallowed her up.

In a way, I guess that's what had happened.

The musical piping drifted toward us again, faint but clear. I became aroused again, and dimly wondered why. Shelly was gone, and there was nobody else in sight. I hadn't been thinking about sex. It was weird. Big Steve planted his feet, raised his hackles, and growled. I tugged the leash, but he refused to budge. His growl grew louder, more intense. I noticed that he had another hard-on, as well.

"Come on," I said. "It's nothing. Just some kid practicing for the school band."

Big Steve flicked his eyes toward me, and then turned back to the woods and growled again.

The music abruptly stopped. There was no gradual fading away—it was as if someone had flipped a switch.

It occurred to me that it was Monday morning, and all the kids were in school, so it couldn't have been a kid practicing. Then Steve's haunches sagged and he returned to normal, his nose to the ground and his tail wagging with excitement over every new scent.

The narrow trail leading into the woods was hidden between two big maple trees. I don't know who made the path—kids or deer, but Big Steve and I used it every day. Dead leaves crunched under our feet as we slipped into the forest, while new leaves budded on the branches above us. Flowers burst from the dark soil, lining the trail with different colors and fragrances. I stopped to light a cigarette while Big Steve nosed around a mossy stump. I inhaled, stared up into the leafy canopy over our heads, and noticed how much darker it was, even just inside the tree line.

Primordial, I thought.

I shivered. The sun's rays didn't reach here. There was no warmth inside the forest—only shadows.

The woods were quiet at first, but gradually came to life. Birds sang and squirrels played in the boughs above us. A plane passed overhead, invisible beyond the treetops. Probably heading to an airport in Baltimore or Harrisburg. The sun returned, peeking through the limbs. But I couldn't feel its warmth, and the rays seemed sparse.

Big Steve pulled at the leash, and we continued on. The winding path sloped steadily downward. We picked our way through clinging vines and thorns, and I spotted some raspberry bushes, which gave me something to look forward to when summer arrived. If I picked them, Tara would bake me a pie. Blue-tinted moss clung to the squat gray stones that thrust up from the forest floor like half-uncovered dinosaur skeletons. And then there were the trees themselves—tall, stern, and proud.

I shivered again. The air was growing chillier, more like the normal temperature for this time of year. Stepping over a fallen log, I wondered again who'd made the path, and who used it other than Big Steve and me. The most we'd ever gone was a mile into the forest, but the trail continued on well past that. How deep did it run? All the way out to the other side? Did it intersect with other, less used pathways? Did it go all the way to LeHorn's Hollow?

I mentioned the hollow earlier. I'd only been there once, when I was in high school and looking for a secluded spot to get inside Becky Schrum's pants. It was our first date, and I remember it well. Nineteen eighty-seven—my senior year. We saw a

*Friday the 13*th flick (I can't remember which one), and when it was over, we cruised around in my '81 Mustang hatchback, listening to Ratt's *Out of the Cellar* and talking about school and stuff.

Eventually, we found ourselves on the dirt road that led to the LeHorn farm. The farmhouse and buildings had stood vacant for three years. Nelson LeHorn had killed his wife, Patricia, in 1985, and then disappeared. He hadn't been seen since, and his children were scattered across the country. His son, Matty, was doing time for armed robbery in the Cresson State Penitentiary up north. His daughter, Claudia, was married and living in Idaho. And his youngest daughter, Gina, was teaching school in New York. None of them had ever returned home, as far as I knew. Because the old man was legally still alive, the children were unable to sell the property, and Pennsylvania law prevented the county or the state from seizing it. So it sat boarded up and abandoned, providing a haven for rats and groundhogs.

The LeHorn place sat in the middle of miles of woodlands, untouched by the explosive development that had marred other parts of the state, and surrounded by a vast expanse of barren cornfields, the rolling hills not worked since the murder and LeHorn's disappearance. In the center of the fields, like an island, was the hollow.

I'd parked the car near the house, and Becky and I had talked about whether or not it was haunted. And like clockwork, she was snuggled up against me, afraid of the dark. I remember glancing toward the hollow as we made out. Even in the darkness, I could see the bright yellow NO TRESPASSING and POSTED signs hanging from a few of the outer tree trunks. Becky let me slip my hand into her jeans, and her breathing quickened as I delved into her wetness with my fingers and rubbed her hard nipples beneath my palms. But then she cut me off. Not wanting to show my annoyance and disappointment, I'd suggested we walk to the hollow. I hoped that if her level of fright increased, her chastity might crumble.

The hollow was a dark spot, created by four sloping hills, leading down to a place where no chain saw roared and no axe cut. A serpentine creek wound through its center. We heard the trickling water, but never made it far enough inside to see the stream.

Because something moved in the black space between the trees . . .

Something big. It crashed toward us, branches snapping like gunshots beneath its feet. Becky screamed and gripped my hand tight enough to bruise it. We got the hell out of there. We never saw the thing, whatever it was, but we heard it snort—a primal sound, and I can still hear that sound today. A deer, probably, or maybe even a black bear. All I know is it scared the shit out of me, and I've never been back to the hollow since.

Big Steve brought me back to the present by suddenly stopping in the middle of the trail. He stood stiff as a board, legs locked and his tail tucked between them. The growl started as a low rumble deep down inside him, and got louder and louder as it spilled out.

I'd never heard him make a sound like this, and wondered if I'd mistakenly clipped someone else's dog to the leash. He'd never gotten this worked up over something. He sounded vicious. Brave.

Or terrified.

Suddenly, as if summoned from my memories, something crashed through the bushes toward us. Big Steve's hair stood on end, and his growl turned into a rumbling bark.

"Come on, Steve. Let's go!" My heart raced in my chest. I tugged the leash, but he refused to budge. He barked again.

The noise drew closer. Twigs snapped. Leaves rustled.

The branches parted.

I screamed.

CITY

OF THE

DEAD

BRIAN KEENE

Where can you go when the dead are everywhere? Cities have become overrun with legions of the dead, all of them intent on destroying what's left of the living. Trapped inside a fortified skyscraper, a handful of survivors prepare to make their last stand against an unstoppable, undying enemy. With every hour their chances diminish and their numbers dwindle, while the numbers of the dead can only rise. Because sooner or later, everything dies. And then it comes back, ready to kill.

GHOUL

BRIAN KEENE

June 1984. Timmy Graco is looking forward to summer vacation, taking it easy and hanging out with his buddies. Instead his summer will be filled with terror and a life-and-death battle against a nightmarish creature that few will believe even exists. Timmy learns that the person who's been unearthing fresh graves in the cemetery isn't a person at all. It's a thing. And it's after Timmy and his friends. If Timmy hopes to live to see September, he'll have to escape the...

GHOUL
